"What are you doing here?"
Charis stammered. . . .

"It is my house. May I inquire what *you* are doing here?" He strolled into the room, a perfect example of a gentleman of means. If Marcus was annoyed at their appearing in his home, he did not reveal it. He politely shook hands with Harriet, then turned to Charis, clasping her suddenly cold hand in his. He raised her gloveless hand to his lips to place a kiss on her bare skin.

Charis had the most peculiar sensation of little shocks streaking from his touch up her arm and throughout her. It was not an unpleasant feeling but rather one of excitement, a tingling she had never felt before. She could not speak, bewildered by her reaction to one she had known for so many years. Yet, he was not the boy she had once known. Hardly! Marcus fairly oozed masculinity and charm, something that scamp of a boy had not.

Lord
Huntingdon's
Legacy

Emily Hendrickson

A SIGNET BOOK

SIGNET
Published by New American Library, a division of
Penguin Putnam Inc., 375 Hudson Street,
New York, New York 10014, U.S.A.
Penguin Books Ltd, 27 Wrights Lane,
London W8 5TZ, England
Penguin Books Australia Ltd, Ringwood,
Victoria, Australia
Penguin Books Canada Ltd, 10 Alcorn Avenue,
Toronto, Ontario, Canada M4V 3B2
Penguin Books (N.Z.) Ltd, 182–190 Wairau Road,
Auckland 10, New Zealand

Penguin Books Ltd, Registered Offices:
Harmondsworth, Middlesex, England

First published by Signet, an imprint of New American Library,
a division of Penguin Putnam Inc.

First Printing, August 2001
10 9 8 7 6 5 4 3 2 1

Catchpenny:
2: Designed to attract purchasers; got up merely to sell.

—OXFORD ENGLISH DICTIONARY

Prologue

An elegant black curricle approached the austere front of a fine Palladian country mansion at a smart clip, scattering gravel as Sir Marcus Rutledge brought his perfectly matched bays to a halt. He handed the reins to his tiger, then leaped from his carriage, pausing to give a searching look at the house before proceeding up the steps.

His black greatcoat swirled about his tall, lithe figure as he strode to the entrance. An impatient tug on the bellpull brought immediate response.

Once invited inside, he handed his black hat to the butler, then swiftly followed a footman up the fine oak stairs and down a dimly lit hall. No one had to remind him that time was of the essence. He was well aware the hours remaining were few.

He truly had not expected a summons just now. A funeral command, yes. Not a demand that he present himself at once.

The door to his uncle's bedroom was opened for him, and Marcus entered with a cautious step. It didn't look much like the room of a dying man. Jonquil curtains allowed pale sunlight to flood the room. White walls and counterpane added to the illusion of a summer day.

But autumn was here, winter soon to follow, just as his uncle once removed was in the waning moments of his life. His winter's sleep hovered at his bedside, unless Marcus was much mistaken. He rarely was.

Eyes of faded blue surveyed Marcus with still acute vision. "So, you came."

"You knew I would." Marcus stepped closer to the

bed, shedding his coat, then tossing it aside to fall on a bright golden chair. "The message was unexpected. I thought all was settled?"

"Sit down, sit down, my boy. You hover like a hawk about to swoop down on me. My time is near, but not quite, I think." The Earl of Huntingdon managed a weak smile at his jest.

Marcus did as bade. He pushed aside his coat and drew the golden chair close to the bed, lowering his admittedly intimidating height. Silently he studied his father's cousin, who had been like a father to Marcus when his parents died. "There is more?"

"Indeed. I have made changes in the will I wish to discuss with you." The earl's voice might be no more than a strong whisper, but it could be clearly heard in the quiet of the room.

"And?" Marcus leaned forward so that the ill man would not feel the need to force what voice he had left to be heard.

"I have willed everything to you—the property is not entailed, as you know—the house, everything I have. I have made Charis a proper allowance, her sister and mother as well. But you will be my heir in everything but the title."

"And that must go to Charis." Marcus found it difficult to speak; the enormity of what had been revealed over-whelmed. "Why, if I may know?"

"My lawyer made a few notes. Read for yourself." The whisper faded into nothing, and with his eyes closed against the brightness of the day, the earl sought strength in sleep.

The valet who had hovered near the door stepped forward, a few papers in hand. "I believe these are what he wished you to read, sir."

Marcus rapidly scanned the words that covered the pages—legible, but outrageous. He looked to the servant, who stood patiently waiting by the bed. "She will not like this in the least." Marcus considered that was probably the most ridiculous remark he had made in some time. Not *like* this? He would be lucky to escape with his person in one piece. He gave a grim look at the man tucked beneath the covers of the bed; a barely perceptible rise indicating there was yet life in the still form.

What maggoty notion had possessed the earl to this madness? For madness it must be.

Chapter One

Pale winter sun brought little cheer to the young woman staring out of the window at the dreary landscape beyond. On the avenue to the house, a blanket of snow gradually melted, forming muddy slush that was impossible to travel through, no matter how fine the horses or how excellent the equipage.

The February sun picked out copper highlights in her hair and lightly warmed her peach-toned cheeks. She was a pretty young woman blessed with looks and an admirable figure, as well as a fine sense of humor and a spirit of adventure quite lamented by her mama. At present she was garbed in a deplorable black gown, indicating a state of mourning. The dull bombazine rustled when she moved.

"It is the only thing to do, Mama. I must go to London. You know that," Charis insisted, turning from the view to face her parent. "I have little dowry or money, no land—everything has gone to Marcus." She sounded realistic, not bitter as she had every right to be. "But there ought to be a number of decent men who would like a countess for a wife and a title for their eldest son!"

"True," the elder Countess of Huntingdon replied vaguely. She tugged at the cap she wore that was perpetually askew, trying to set it right and only making it worse. If possible, she had become even more absentminded since her husband had died a little over a year ago. She looked at her daughter, now the Countess of Huntingdon in her own right, and smiled. "But you *do* have the title."

Harriet, the younger daughter of the family, studied

her mother and sister, then piped up, "Where could we stay? Cousin Marcus has everything—including the London house." Her blue eyes were alert and auburn curls seemed to quiver with her curiosity—and hope.

With a sigh that acknowledged the truth of her sister's words, Charis looked at Harriet before turning back to her mother. "She is right, of course. We cannot afford the rent of a decent house in the city."

"Huntingdon House will suit us very well, I think," Lady Huntingdon said with a faraway look in her eyes. She gave her daughter a wistful smile, then continued, "We had such lovely parties there."

Charis turned to Harriet. "What do you think?" Even though seventeen, Harriet had ever been a practical girl and was always consulted as to her opinion on matters.

"Well, Marcus liked you when he was young," Harriet said cautiously. "Perhaps he would not mind so much if we stayed in what used to be our home."

"His partiality was hardly evident at the funeral," Charis snapped. She had been stunned when her favorite second cousin had inherited nearly everything that ought to have come to her. But when he gave her an aloof stare, looking for all the world like a hawk surveying its kingdom, she had felt crushed. This cold, enigmatic man, so virile, tall, and terribly handsome was a stranger to her. She had not been resentful as much as forlorn, as though she had lost far more than her inheritance. She chewed at her lower lip before venturing to give her thoughts voice. "Well, we live *here* at his sufferance. I can see little difference if we exchange this house for the London one."

Harriet looked rather dubious. "He might be living there, you know."

"Nonsense. He has a perfectly good house of his own." Charis abandoned the drapery cord she had toyed with while speaking and began pacing before the window while considering the matter at hand.

"So our former home ought to be sitting empty," Harriet said, eyes gleaming with obvious delight.

Charis plumped herself down on a nearby chair. "We

will go." She glanced out at the scene beyond the window and grimaced. "That is, as soon as the roads improve."

"What shall we take with us?" Harriet said, rising from her chair and leaving their dog, Ruff, to his toy. "I have grown out of nearly all my dresses, and yours are so frumpish you would never catch the eye of a smart gentleman," she stated, her voice and manner the frankness of a younger sister.

Charis gave Harriet a vexed look. She had not bothered obtaining fashionable mourning clothes. Buried as they were in the country, she had not deemed it necessary. Besides, none of her beaux called once word got about she had been left almost penniless.

"If we save our allowance and take more care than usual, we ought to have enough for a few new gowns. I shall be a catchpenny countess. I will have little value and be got up to attract a purchaser." Charis did not feel very optimistic and said nothing about how poorly her father had seen to her future. What had possessed him to will it all to Marcus? She had adored Marcus as a child. She had *not* expected to see him win the estate and all the money, leaving her with but a pittance.

"Are you going to write Marcus?" Harriet wondered. She tossed a toy for Ruff, then watched him fetch it.

"No need," Charis replied carelessly. "It is not as though he is my guardian. He is merely the cousin who has it all." Whether she meant the money and land or his handsome looks and polish, she did not say.

Harriet studied her sister a moment before heading to the attics and their trunks.

Charis was hopeful the roads would dry with the next wind and they could be off to London. Pleased at the prospect, she followed Harriet to the attics. They would not need much in the way of baggage. Goodness knows, they had little enough to bring with them.

So it was that as soon as the weather took a turn for the milder and the roads were passable, the Huntingdon traveling coach headed to London with a concerned

Charis, a jubilant Harriet, and a preoccupied dowager countess aboard.

Charis observed that Harriet did not miss a thing on the way. With a travel book in her lap, she peered out of the window to make note of every landmark mentioned. When Charis failed to respond to her eager comments, Harriet fell silent but did not cease her scrutiny.

Even a necessary stay overnight at an inn did not dampen Harriet's enthusiasm. Two Countesses Huntingdon and Lady Harriet Dane brought very nice attention, and Harriet clearly reveled in it. When they at last approached the City, she could scarce contain herself.

Huntingdon House looked precisely as it had the previous and only time Charis had been in London. An elegant brick edifice, it was a trifle larger and more imposing than its neighbors. The steps to the large black door glistened with scrubbing, and the brass knocker gleamed with polish.

The groom dashed smartly up the stairs to give the knocker a firm rap, then returned to the coach.

"How good to know the staff is not lax merely because the ownership has changed," Charis murmured to Harriet while the groom assisted their mother out of the coach.

The door opened, and the butler who had been there since the dowager had come to the house as a bride, stepped forth to greet them. "My lady!" That he was visibly taken aback to see the countess exiting the traveling coach and revealed it said a great deal about his astonishment. Not only that, Charis thought he appeared a little discomfited as well.

"We are come for the Season, Seymour," the dowager said when at last untangled from her various shawls.

"I confess, I am surprised, my lady," the butler replied at his most dignified. "Sir Marcus said nothing to me."

"That is because he does not know," Harriet said with a grin. Her auburn curls danced in the breeze while her bonnet dangled from impatient fingers. "Charis figured he has his own house anyway, so we need not bother."

Suddenly seeming aware it was not the thing to stand

conversing on the steps, the butler ushered the three women into the house. Directing them to the library, he promised tea and sustenance shortly. Frowning heavily, Seymour disappeared in the direction of the kitchen.

Harriet gave him a thoughtful look, then followed Charis and her mother into the well-remembered library.

Charis walked to the center of the room, looking around her. She stripped off her gloves, dropping them on the desk in preparation for their tea. "Little has changed, although I must say that it seems as though someone has been here recently." She paused to peer at the papers on the desk, taking note that the top page had a recent date on it. "This is addressed to Sir Marcus Rutledge." To her mother she added, "Do you suppose he uses this library rather than his own?"

Seymour entered bearing a tray covered with dishes, a teapot, and a plate of delectable-looking biscuits.

Ignoring the tray for the moment, Charis turned to the butler. "Does Sir Marcus use this room?"

"Indeed, he does, my lady." He stood stiffly at attention, looking, Charis thought, as though he would rather be elsewhere. "Will that be all, my lady?"

"Yes, thank you, Seymour," Charis replied, deciding she would find out more later and took note how he hurried from the room as though chased by Ruff. The dog was busy sniffing at all the corners.

"Why are you frowning, Charis?" Harriet queried. "These biscuits are wonderful. Do try one."

"Do you not think Seymour's behavior was a trifle odd?"

"He always was reserved," Lady Huntingdon murmured from the depths of the most comfortable chair in the room.

Putting aside the peculiar attitude of the butler, Charis poured tea for all, then helped herself to a biscuit. There was far too much to do to wonder about a butler.

Their maid directed the disposal of the small trunks and portmanteaus, quite aware of her superior position. She also collected Ruff, taking him along with her to the room set aside for Charis, a fine bedroom to the rear of the house.

Harriet explored the ground floor, then ran up the stairs to see what the rooms on the main floor were like.

"Charis, come see. These rooms are truly splendid. It is like a palace!" she called, leaning over the stair railing to be certain Charis would hear.

Charis responded to Harriet's excited call with amused tolerance. She had felt the same way when first viewing the London house. It was a good thing that Marcus handled the financial aspects—this house must cost a huge sum to run. She hurried up the stairs to join her sister, entering the drawing room in a rush.

"It looks just the same, love," she said when she studied the lovely room.

Indeed, the pale green silk on the walls had faded but slightly, and the elegant gilded trim shone as bright as ever. The numerous chairs and sofas covered in the same delicate green silk looked fresh. A tall flower-filled crystal vase graced a Sheraton mahogany sofa table. The Moorfield carpet in pale green and gold on ivory looked to have been freshly brushed. Indeed, it appeared to Charis that the room was fit to be occupied, even suitable for entertaining. She ran a finger over the smooth finish of one of the dainty side tables. Not a speck of dust in sight.

Charis gave Harriet a puzzled look. "I'd expected to find Holland covers on the furniture and certainly no fresh flowers about. You do not suppose that Marcus uses the entire house, do you? After all, he has his own."

"It is not only possible, it is an actuality, dear cousin Charis," said an amused voice from the doorway.

She whirled about, gasping at the man who filled the doorway. He must tower above other men, and if that was an example of his London attire, he could easily grace the regent's court. He was even more handsome than she remembered with that devilish half smile and those eyes twinkling at her with engaging charm. "What are you doing here?" she stammered.

"It is my home. May I inquire what *you* are doing

here?" He strolled into the room, a perfect example of a gentleman of means. If Marcus was annoyed at their appearing in his home, he did not reveal it. He politely shook hands with Harriet, then turned to Charis, clasping her suddenly cold hand in his. He raised her gloveless hand to his lips to place a kiss on her bare skin.

Charis had the most peculiar sensation of little shocks streaking from his touch up her arm and throughout her. It was not an unpleasant feeling but rather one of excitement, a tingling she had never felt before. She could not speak, bewildered by her reaction to one she had known for so many years. Yet, he was not the boy she had known. Hardly! Marcus fairly oozed masculinity and charm, something that scamp of a boy had not.

"We came for the Season so Charis can find a husband," Harriet blurted when her sister was slow to speak.

"Is that true?" he asked Charis, not releasing her hand but giving her a look that seemed to judge.

After darting a look at Harriet that promised later retribution, Charis nodded, hastily pulling her hand from his clasp and ignoring his look of mockery. "Without a large dowry, no money or land, I must find a husband as soon as possible. We cannot continue to live on your charity." She lifted her chin in challenge. It galled her to admit that all they enjoyed was at his sufferance.

"No trouble at all, my dear Charis. What do you have in mind?" He gestured to a group of chairs, then sat after Charis sank down on the nearest one. Her knees were about to fail her, so his act had been most providential.

"I need to see who is in Town, look about. . . ." Words failed her at his expression. He had tilted his head in an attitude of polite attentiveness, but in his eyes she thought she saw a gleam of amusement.

"I suggest you see the premier mantua-maker in Town before you do anything. Your clothes are hopelessly out of date if that rag you are wearing is any indication." He leaned back in his chair, rubbing his chin pensively as he examined her appearance.

"We have been in mourning, sirrah," she snapped. "And you are as blunt as you ever were."

He nodded before continuing, as though she had not spoken, "If you seek a husband, you must not *look* penniless."

"But I am penniless," she reminded, matching his bluntness with her own. "I shall be a catchpenny countess on display." Now she mocked him.

"However, you have the title," he countered.

"That is just what Mama said," Harriet inserted. "So, may we stay here? Charis said we do not have the money to rent a proper house in the City, and this is a very big place for just one person." Harriet gave him a saucy grin, her blue eyes likely sparkling with the thought that perhaps she had put him on the spot.

"Perhaps we might work something out," he conceded.

"I thought you had a house of your own," Charis said, a puzzled frown creasing her forehead.

"When I inherited Huntingdon House, I decided to rent mine. There is always a dearth of available housing in the better part of Town."

Charis narrowed her green eyes. "I'll wager they fetch a pretty price as well."

He bowed his head in agreement.

"We would stay out of your way," Harriet promised.

"We would indeed try to remain out of your way, and if there is anything we could do on your behalf, you have only to ask," Charis added rashly.

He studied one of his hands before looking up to meet her concerned gaze. A slow smile crossed his face, and Charis uneasily wondered what he was thinking. She did not particularly trust that look. He did not reveal his thoughts, however.

"It will work," Charis persisted.

"Actually, it might do very well. I have wanted to give a few dinners, and your mother will serve well as hostess. I saw her when I entered the house."

"Mother?" Harriet said with a squeak. "You would have to be sure to remind her that there *is* a dinner. You must know how absentminded she is."

Charis found her eyes trapped in the depths of his gaze. His smile had broadened, and she wondered if he recalled a few of the more outrageous incidents from their childhood.

"I am aware of my aunt's weakness."

"So . . . we may remain?" Charis persisted.

"Was it ever in doubt? My dear cousin, I would look like the most hardened of ogres were I to turn you out when you have no place to go. Of course you remain."

He rose, and Charis watched him as he walked to the door. He exuded an aura of masculinity that went far beyond anything she had experienced to date. He was awe inspiring, to say the least.

"I wonder if . . ." she began, then thought better of her remark.

"We shall make out very well, I believe," he said, pausing in the doorway. "In fact, I could not have hoped for better. And it is more than time that you find a husband."

When he disappeared from sight and they no longer heard his steps, Charis turned to Harriet and said, "Surely he does not intend to rely on Mama to that extent."

"I devoutly hope not," Harriet agreed. "But he agrees that it is time for you to marry. I wonder if he has someone in mind?"

Charis walked to the door, ignoring the beauty around her to contemplate what manner of man Marcus would think suitable for her husband. Her mind boggled at the images conjured up at the very thought.

Later, when the baggage had been unpacked and their dearth of fashionable clothing had been made painfully evident, Charis sought paper and pencil in the library. She was in the midst of drawing up a modest list of necessities when Marcus entered the room. At his look of inquiry she explained her task.

"With our budget, I must spend with care. I am trying to create a wardrobe that will be attractive, yet not too expensive." She glanced at the paper and crossed out an item.

He walked around the desk to peer over her shoulder. Ignoring her gasp of indignation, he pulled the paper from her hand. He scanned the unpretentious collection of garments and other things, a frown growing as he perused the list.

Defensive, Charis said, "I have tried hard to put down *only* what we truly need. Harriet has grown so much, she has little to wear, and I've not bought any gowns for over a year. I dyed a few old dresses rather than have new black ones made up," she confessed.

"This will never do," he said dismissively, tossing the paper into the empty fireplace. "I would be declared a villain were you to have such a paltry wardrobe. And, dear cousin, no man wants to marry a woman who wears the same gown forever—as you would of necessity do if you adhered to that list." He gestured to the paper as though it contained something poisonous.

"You know I have little money! Even were Harriet, Mama, and I to combine our total allowances, it would barely cover what we need—and only if we went to a modest mantua-maker!" Charis was outraged and rose from the chair to remove the list from where he had tossed it. Glancing at it again, she had to admit it was not a list a countess would tolerate normally.

Again he took the paper, studying it with care. "Triple everything and send the bills to me." He handed the slip of paper to her and headed toward the door.

Angered at his high-handed behavior and dismissal of her straits, Charis followed him. "You want it known we depend on your charity?"

He paused in the doorway, giving her a remote look that chilled her to her bones. "Not in the least. Recall, the money would have been yours had not your father changed his will."

"I wonder when he did that?" Charis mused as she followed him. She narrowed her eyes and gave Marcus a speculative stare. She recalled that hasty trip made by Marcus a week before her father died.

"If you think I had any influence in his decision, you are far off the mark." He turned to clasp her upper arms, giving her a slight shake. His eyes held a fierce look. "It was not my choice."

Charis trembled, not only at the fierce look, but also at her reaction to his touch. What in the world was the matter with her? She did not adore him anymore. That had been no more than her childish affection. Now she could barely tolerate him. And she did *not* wish to be beholden to the man! Yet she was realistic enough to know he was correct in his estimation of her situation.

"You feel that if I want to capture a husband, I must dress the part of a countess while in Society," she stated flatly.

"Indeed."

"Very well," she said, capitulating. "I suppose you intend to supervise the ordering of gowns as well," she mocked, wanting to get under his skin, taunt that imperious male superiority.

"Curious you should think of that, little cousin. I believe that is one way the expenditure would be highly acceptable. Your mother always had a difficult time making decisions, and Harriet needs a nudge to know what is proper for a girl her age." His eyes teased her, making her realize he was quite aware of her tactics.

Horrified at his words and totally ignoring the expression in those dark blue eyes, Charis sputtered, "But surely I can guide both of them."

"You have been out of Town for some time—you cannot know what is all the crack now. Not that you do not have refined taste, dear cousin."

"Do not call me 'dear cousin' in that odious manner," she grumbled.

"Ah, but you are—my cousin and most dear." With that startling remark, he dropped her arms and left the room at once, leaving Charis in a confused muddle.

"What is the matter with you?" Harriet demanded. She waltzed into the library to pluck the paper from her sister's hand. A quick perusal brought a frown.

"Do not worry, Marcus said to triple the list!" Charis

snapped out of her bemusement. Taking Harriet along with her, she sought out her mother to make plans.

She explained what had happened and all that Marcus proposed for them.

"So much?" the dowager exclaimed. "Such a darling boy to be so concerned for our place in Society. We shall visit Madame Clotilde tomorrow. She is the best. Leave a message for your cousin to that effect. He knows everyone and what is the latest fashion, you may be certain."

Charis wondered what the "darling boy" would have to say to such a presumptive command.

Rather than request that a servant take Ruff for a walk, she persuaded Harriet to go with her. They headed for Hyde Park as the nearest spot of greenery where the dog might have a little run.

About to cross the street, Harriet clutched her sister's arm and whispered, "There's Marcus. And he has a lady with him!"

Charis kept a tight hold of the dog's lead while she took note of her cousin's fine equipage, the high-stepping horses, and the elegance of the woman at his side. Fortunately they did not spot Charis and Harriet in the shadows.

"She is beautiful!" Harriet said, still whispering, although it was doubtful that Marcus might have heard her with the noise from the carriage as it rolled over the cobblestones.

"Indeed, she is very beautiful," Charis agreed, with an odd little pang in her heart. Suddenly she was resolved to purchase a gorgeous wardrobe, one that would enhance her green eyes and mahogany-colored hair that her country beaux declared so unusual.

"I think Marcus may regret telling you that you could have so many clothes. You mean to compete with her?" Harriet wondered in her usual frank manner.

"Compete? Heavens no," Charis replied with a laugh that did not ring quite true. She hurried across the street and let Ruff off his lead to chase a squirrel. When it ran up a tree, he sat at the base and barked until Charis called him away. She attached his lead and walked toward Huntingdon House again.

"Well, whatever you do, be careful," Harriet cautioned. "You do not want to antagonize the man who is making it possible for us to be in London."

Charis looked thoughtful and nodded. "I have no intention of antagonizing him." What she did intend, she failed to say.

Chapter Two

The next morning Charis dawdled over her tea and toast while considering ways and means of ensuring that Marcus did not go along with them to the mantua-maker. Not certain why this was so necessary, she just knew she did not want him inspecting her choices, possibly deriding her selection.

The memory of that elegant woman at his side was quite strong. Charis did not dream of copying her cool stylishness. Rather, she intended to create her own fashion. But this meant that she make her own look, not something foisted on her by Marcus.

"I must say, you are in a blue-devil this morning," Harriet said candidly when she joined Charis at the breakfast table. "I should think you would be in alt to select new dresses." She looked about, specifically at the head of the table, where no one sat. "Marcus gone?"

"I devoutly hope so."

"Why, dear cousin, can it be that you do not wish my esteemed presence this morning?" Marcus asked in a sardonic manner from the doorway, startling Charis. "Let me tell you that any number of women in this fair city would be thrilled to have me assist in selecting their wardrobes." He helped himself to coffee at the sideboard. He indicated a scone, and a footman quickly placed one on a plate, adding marmalade before setting the plate on the table.

Charis glowered at the confident man now seated where her father had once reigned. Then hastily smoothing her expression to one of polite interest, she replied,

"I merely expected you to be occupied in more important matters."

"Like that elegant lady who was with me yesterday whilst you were on your way to the park?" he said, almost sounding as though he might be teasing her.

"I did not think you noticed us. After all, with the carriage and your cattle, plus a companion, you had sufficient to keep your eyes from straying. Besides, we were in the shade."

He smiled—that same smile that she did not trust in the least. "I believe I should always be aware of your presence, dear cousin."

Apprehensive as to his meaning, Charis turned the subject. "I cannot think why you would want to waste your time escorting us to select our gowns."

"Dear Charis, think! I have my reputation to uphold. As a connoisseur of all that is in fashion, it would be disastrous were you to appear in something less than utterly beguiling." His smile broadened. Charis trusted it even less than before. She had once read about the crocodiles in the Nile that were said to seem smiling before they snapped up their victim. She wondered how much like Marcus they were.

"I think we ought to be glad to have him along," Harriet said forthrightly. "I would love to look like that lady."

"You will do no such thing, brat." He gave Harriet an amused look, then turned his attention to Charis again. "Perhaps you now begin to see why an impartial observer is helpful. Harriet, as a young lady making her come-out, requires an entirely different wardrobe than you will. She must present the illusion of innocence and charm. White will become her and add to the impression. Madame will know precisely what she needs."

Transfixed by his assessing stare and that low, rich voice, Charis asked, "And what do I require?"

He tilted his head, studying her with a gaze that began to warm her skin and send her insides to fluttering. "Greens in various shades in sheer muslins and silks that will flatter your slender figure and your vivid coloring.

Your hair will need dressing," he concluded abruptly. "I shall contact Truefitt to come over. He was doing men, but I am reliably informed that now he takes selected ladies as clients as well. Bond Street, you know, is a place you cannot go just anytime, and I would have him here later today."

"I am aware that Bond Street is the province of men in the afternoons, cousin," Charis replied crisply. "But there is no reason why I might not go there in the morning."

His answering look was daunting. "I wish to speak with him first, and no *countess* would dream of going *to* a hairdresser."

It was a wonder she did not turn to ice. "But we go *to* Madame Clotilde's," Charis shot back before recalling she did not wish him along.

"I thought your mother would see sense. She may be absentminded, but she knows what you are due. I wonder if you do?" He drained his coffee, brushed the crumbs off his fingers, then rose. "I shall meet you all in the entryway in one hour."

Charis rose from the table once he had left the room and gave Harriet a fuming look. "To think I once liked him!"

Her sister chewed her scone and for once remained silent.

It took a bit of cleverness to persuade her mother to be ready on time. Charis had no doubt that Marcus was perfectly capable of ordering them about, flustering her mother even more than usual. They gathered in the entryway, with Charis whispering instructions to Harriet as they waited for Marcus to join them. He appeared suddenly, surprising them all.

Hands on his hips, he surveyed them. "Well, well. I am amazed. It says a great deal for your capability that all three of you are here on time," Marcus said, directing his gaze and words at Charis.

Charis glanced back at the library door, now standing ajar. Marcus had been sequestered in there since breakfast. She was reminded of all it took to manage the London property as well as the Huntingdon estate, not to mention his other properties. Yet he looked as though he did not do a thing all day—calm, unruffled, his cravat a wonder of simplicity and his dark blue coat without the slightest wrinkle. If he chose to give the illusion that he was no more than a Corinthian or a dandy, she was not about to say a thing.

He gestured to the door, and Seymour opened it with stately dignity. The dowager sailed forth to the carriage.

"Are you a dandy?" Harriet asked as they filed out of the house.

"Hardly," he responded with hauteur. "I am merely a man of fashion and good taste."

Charis repressed a grin with difficulty. That "merely" hardly applied to him. When she had come to London before, she had observed how the men dressed and heard whom they imitated. She suspected that now Marcus had established himself in London, he would be one who was aped by those men who cared about fashion. Not that she had heard a word, or seen anything in the papers. It was an intuitive feeling.

She regretted they had no maid or footman to carry parcels. The three of them would manage well, but it was to be hoped that no one of importance took note of their deficiency. With Marcus being as generous as he was, she was not about to chastise him for their lack.

Even though the hour was early and many of Society's matrons were still in bed, there was an abundance of elegant carriages in the shopping area of London. Ladies of varying degree of style left their equipages to inspect the offerings to be found in the modish shops.

The smells of the city were impossible to escape, and Charis made a mental note to carry a small posy with her henceforth. Not that the country did not have objectionable odors. They were more concentrated in the city.

The chic shop before which the landau drew to a halt was clearly a cut above the ones Charis remembered. Discreet letters proclaimed the owner's name in fine gold script. Sheer white curtains shielded the customer from rude stares. Upon entering, Charis took note of soft gray walls, gilt chairs, and fitted carpeting in that same shade of gray. The shop oozed quiet refinement, and she prepared herself for an experience to remember.

Madame Clotilde could not conceal her reaction when Marcus introduced Charis, Harriet, and the elder countess, then lastly, himself. She was clearly impressed.

"I believe we shall do the younger countess first," he stated. "She has the greatest need. Then do Lady Harriet and the elder countess. Lady Harriet will be making her come-out to Society." He smiled, then added with a nod to the dowager, "Lady Huntingdon remained at home following her husband's death and returns to London to renew friendships and enjoy a bit of Society."

Charis supposed it was reasonable to explain why they all looked like dowds, although why he bothered to inform the mantua-maker as to the precise circumstances, Charis did not know.

Once seated on the dainty gilt chairs, Charis willingly ignored Marcus to consult with the obviously talented Madame. Anyone who could set up a shop of this style must be highly successful!

It quickly became clear to Charis Madame Clotilde well knew who Sir Marcus was and that he indeed had a high position in Society. Every length of silk and muslin, along with the suggested sketches, was displayed to him and his opinion sought before being shown to Charis.

She thought she held her temper in rein very well. He had suggested shades of green, and she secretly agreed. It was her favorite color along with buttery yellow and peacock blue. But when he suggested a gown of gold tissue, Charis objected.

"I do not wear that color or cloth." She cast him a look that revealed her tightly leashed annoyance. In her mind it was a color and fabric associated with actresses and other women far more worldly than she was.

"You will now, and be delighted in what you see. In fact, I suggest that gown be made up as soon as possible. Oh, and a few day dresses, carriage dresses, at least two pelisses, and a ball gown or two to begin with. Madame well knows the wardrobe required for the Season, and you have just come out of mourning with not a decent stitch to wear."

Before Charis could say a word, he rose, bowed, and declared he would see them later. Madame seemingly knew precisely what he would select for his relatives. Charis thought his smile should have had the mantua-maker on her knees thanking him for the privilege of dressing his relatives, even if they were not to pay for her expensive creations.

While it was a relief to have his intimidating presence gone, Charis found that she missed him. However, the first thing she did was to cancel the gold tissue gown. He would not order her in such a manner, even if he paid the bills.

"Marcus certainly has impeccable taste," her mother murmured to Charis when the mantua-maker showed them a day dress already made to give an idea of how a sketch would look once completed.

"I cannot begin to think of the cost of all this," Charis replied quietly, so that she was not overheard when Madame Clotilde left them for a moment.

"Well," Harriet inserted, quite unwilling to be left out, "think of it as money that ought to have come to you had Papa been in his right mind."

Charis and her mother gave Harriet such a stare that she remained silent until they at last left the shop, a considerable wardrobe having been ordered for each of them.

Once on their way to select dainty slippers and stout shoes, bonnets and hats, plus reticules and other necessities, Charis touched Harriet on her arm.

"I think it best if we say nothing about that infamous will or the circumstances that resulted from it. Let people think we are here as . . ." She frowned and turned to her mother. "What do we say we are? Guests? Visiting relatives?"

"Say nothing," her mother advised. "Let Marcus sort matters out. He has the money and all the obligations of the estate. In a way he has acquired us as well. Where would we be without him?"

Charis had visions of the three of them perched on a roadside, penniless and homeless, without food or clothing. "Well, we do have our allowances so we are not destitute."

"We could afford but a maid and a cook, nothing more, and the most modest of cottages. And what gentleman would pay the slightest attention to a countess in a cottage?"

"I think a good many of them would look at Charis. She is uncommonly pretty," Harriet stoutly maintained.

"Thank you, sister," Charis said in surprise. She never quite knew what her sister was thinking or what she might say next. That she was never deceitful but always honest—as she saw it—made her quite dear, however.

They went about the selection of gloves and reticules, parasols and slippers with the belief that at least these items might be paid for out of their allowances. Charis exulted in the thought she now possessed so many pairs of gloves and not a one of them darned!

They continued along Bond Street, examining the wares on display in the shopwindows, ignoring the dandies that strolled along making rude comments and taking care to avoid those men who thought it clever to snag or tear a gown with their spurs. They were studying the array of bonnets in a millinery shop when the elder Lady Huntingdon dropped the package with their gloves.

Arms moderately full of packages, Charis could only gaze helplessly at the package and hope that Harriet might retrieve it without too much difficulty.

"Allow me, ladies." A gentleman dressed in the height of refined taste stepped forth to pick up the parcel of gloves, offering it to the elder lady with a side-glance at Charis.

"How kind," murmured the countess, looking vaguely at her packages to see if anything else might be missing.

"Portchester, at your service," he said with a winning smile.

"How lovely. I knew your father," her ladyship replied, giving him a sharp look before lapsing into her vague mien once again.

"May I have the pleasure of knowing who you are?" he inquired with a certain audacity. Although he addressed the elder lady, it was obvious he hoped to discover the identity of the newest charmers in Town, even though he undoubtedly well knew that it was more proper for another to introduce them. It seemed he lacked patience.

"I am," she responded dryly, "Anna, Countess of Huntingdon. This is Charis, the new countess, and my other daughter, Lady Harriet Dane. Girls, Lord Portchester's father nearly won my hand many years ago."

"I am heartily glad he did not, for we would be deprived of admirable beauty and charm," Lord Portchester gallantly replied.

While admiring his distinguished appearance, Charis thought it better not to remain in conversation with a stranger while out on the street, particularly Bond Street. "Good day, my lord, and thank you for your assistance. We had best be on our way, for we have much to accomplish today."

He bowed, but did not step away from them before asking if he might call on them.

The elder Lady Huntingdon nodded graciously while Charis merely smiled, hoping she looked demure. It would not do well for her to appear eager to collect a beau.

"Nice lad," her mother said once inside the shop. "His father was a nodcock. An elegant, well-garbed nodcock with enough charm to bring forth birds from a tree. Not much in the brain box, though. My father thought him quite the catch."

"But you chose Papa," Charis said with a chuckle. She never tired of hearing of her parent's courtship and marriage. She hoped she might have a love match like theirs.

Harriet tugged at her sleeve, drawing her attention from the display of bonnets and looking out of the window. "There goes Marcus with that woman again."

Charis doubted if the whisper carried much beyond her but said nothing in reply. She slanted a glance at the landau as it proceeded along the street. Indeed, the proud tilt of her head and the cool elegance of her garb proclaimed her as the Incomparable who had driven out with Marcus the day before.

"I wonder who she is?" Charis whispered, following their mother to where she was studying a chip straw bonnet trimmed in garish purple flowers.

In the process of dissuading the dowager from the one bonnet and directing her to another, Charis forgot about Marcus and the woman, whoever she might be. It took but a little time to convince her mother that a bonnet of finely woven straw trimmed with pale pink roses that complemented her silver hair and delicate skin to perfection was the thing to purchase.

Charis found a dear little bonnet with a neat brim, trimmed with rich green ribbons and a cluster of white silk roses. Harriet opted for a plain chip straw with no more than a blue ribbon to tie beneath the chin.

They were debating the addition of a pink rose when the bell of the shop jangled and Marcus joined them.

"Whatever are you doing?" he demanded, albeit discreetly.

"Shopping," a mystified Charis replied. "How did you know we were here? Mother and I have selected our bonnets, and now we wonder if Harriet ought not have a pink rose on her choice. What do you think?"

Charis, while not truly wanting his opinion, thought perhaps she could direct his mind from whatever had been on it when he entered. He looked utterly furious.

"The pink rose, by all means," he said impatiently. "I saw you on the street, burdened with all manner of parcels. Why are you carrying all those packages? It is most unseemly for a countess and family to be seen toting so many parcels while shopping."

"We do not have a footman to order about, nor do we wish to wait to have them delivered," Charis replied with dignity, while she selected a pink silk rose the perfect size and color to grace Harriet's bonnet.

For once Marcus looked thunderstruck. "I could have sworn that I ordered . . . That is, I feel certain Seymour knew you would need . . ."

"A nice gentleman picked up the parcel Mama dropped out in front of this shop," Harriet helpfully informed him. "His name was Lord Portchester, and he looked almost as fine as you."

"Portchester? Oh, lud, it will be all over Town in no time that you are here, without assistance, and looking countrified." Marcus looked fit to be tied.

"I doubt his lordship would be so unkind. He asked to call on us, you know," Charis said, hoping to sooth her cousin's ire.

"How did you know where we were?" Harriet inquired.

"I saw you whilst taking Lady Alicia Dartry to join her mother." He seemed flustered, and Charis wondered if it was because he had to reveal the identity of his fashionable lady friend or because he had actually failed to provide a footman for them.

"We saw her before, you know," Harriet kindly advised.

"Come, let us stow all those parcels in the carriage. You must be about finished with the shopping for today." He summoned his groom to take all the parcels her mother carried, then edged toward the door. He ignored what Harriet had said, merely nodding to her to go ahead of him.

Charis gave him a cool look, then turned to pay for the bonnets before joining him.

"I believe I am quite tired," their mother said in a wispy voice, suiting her words by looking as though she might disappear in an instant.

Marcus muttered something under his breath before assisting the elder Lady Huntingdon into the carriage. Harriet climbed in to sit beside her mother, settling quite happily on the cushions. Marcus turned again to find right behind him Charis with the shop assistant who held three hatboxes. He set the hatboxes on the floor of the landau, then held out his hand for Charis.

"Thank you, sir," she said, after giving a modest tip to the shop girl, an action that made Marcus seem all the more angry. With a carefully neutral expression Charis joined the others, sitting as far away from Marcus as possible.

"I am not angry with you. Only myself. I cannot imagine how I allowed you to go without a footman."

"Or a maid," Harriet added righteously.

"Harriet," Charis said quietly, thinking discretion was needed at the moment.

"Another thing, a gentleman ought to be the one offering a gratuity to a serving person," he said, sounding aggrieved.

"Rubbish," Charis declared. "She served me, not you. I was happy to have her carry all those hatboxes."

Marcus merely groaned and put his hand over his face.

"I must say," Charis said before she could consider her words, "it is nice to see you being human." She wished the words unspoken at his look.

"Is that how you regard me?"

"Well," Harriet inserted without regard for propriety, "*I* think you are overwhelming."

Marcus shook his head, saying nothing. The remainder of the short drive to Huntingdon House was accomplished in silence.

Once Seymour had settled them all in the drawing room, promising to return with tea and sandwiches, Marcus broke the silence.

"What is this about Portchester?"

It was not what Charis expected to hear. "Little enough, I fancy. He picked up Mama's parcel—our gloves, you know—and restored it to her. I must say that he was a perfect gentleman, Marcus."

"He did not waste any time getting to know who you are and seeking to call upon you." Marcus had all the manner of one who has been thwarted.

"Mama knew his father, and that made it seem acceptable. Did we do something dreadfully improper?" Charis inquired.

"No, I suppose not. But your new clothes have not

been delivered yet. You are scarcely ready to greet a prospective suitor. Truefitt ought to be here before long to style your hair. I would prefer you to be prepared before you gather a court around you."

Charis sat up a trifle straighter. "You consider him to be a prospective husband for me?" Had she not been so curious, she would have distrusted that bland expression he assumed. But she was surprised at his use of the word suitor.

The muscles in his jaw tightened. His chiseled features seemed tense, carved from stone, actually. Did that make him stone-hearted as well? Yet he had not been totally uncaring of their needs. Witness his forgetting the footman this morning and seeming distressed that he had. Charis supposed that if he wanted her to remain under wraps until her hair had been properly styled and her garments fit to be seen, he had a plausible point.

"As to suitors, they will come in time. You are aware that people in general will believe you are being sponsored by me—as your cousin. I will likely be asked for your hand should some gentleman seek to marry you."

"Actually, I believe we are but second cousins. Your father was cousin to mine. We are not all that close, dear Marcus," Charis said, stopping abruptly as Seymour entered the room, followed by a maid.

What amounted to a late luncheon was served, which was good as Charis did not think she could have managed to walk down to the dining room. She had not realized how tired she was.

"I believe I shall retire," the elder lady said once she finished a dainty repast. "I am not accustomed to such activity."

The maid assisted her out of the room, and they could hear them going up to the next floor, talking quietly.

Harriet jumped up, a biscuit in hand. "I found this splendid book I want to read. I'll see you later."

This left Charis facing Marcus alone.

"You have no objection to my vetting your suitors?" he asked.

"Do I have a choice?" she countered.

"No, but I did not want you to become annoyed or worse when it occurs." He leaned back in his chair, rubbing his chin with a casual air and studying her with that disconcerting gaze of his.

"How lovely that you say when and not if," Charis declared. "You must be aware that it is imperative that I find a husband." She experienced a fluttering feeling inside when he nodded, yet wore a peculiar expression. Surely he thought she would be successful!

"Oh, yes, in spite of your penniless state, I have no doubt you will find a husband," Marcus responded.

What else he might have believed was not to be known. To her frustration, Seymour entered precisely at that moment to announce that Truefitt had come to style Lady Huntingdon's hair.

Before she could move, Marcus was out of his chair and the room, running down the stairs to confer with Mr. Truefitt.

Charis followed slowly, wondering what was in store for her, and not just her hair.

She might have known that Truefitt would agree with anything Marcus suggested. His attitude was that Sir Marcus was the epitome of style and his suggestions were as gold.

Charis was not allowed to look while the snipping and combing was going on. She sat silently and worried. When the man completed his performance—for it could be called nothing less the way he had danced around her, waving those long scissors in the air—she awaited her cousin's reaction with breath suspended.

Marcus merely stared at her. Harriet entered.

When Harriet saw the results, she smiled broadly and turned to Marcus. "How right you were. Charis was nice before and now she looks beautiful."

Truefitt bowed as though Charis was entirely his creation.

Still Marcus said nothing. At last he walked around to inspect her and nodded. "It will do quite nicely."

Seymour ushered the gratified hairdresser out of the room, likely paying him as well.

Harriet was not appeased by the modest assessment of her dear sister, however. "Is that all you have to say?"

Marcus's look of disdain should have silenced her forever. "For the moment, yes. She still needs the correct clothing to appear as she should."

"I never thought you would turn out like this," Charis said, hurt at his assessment. "I believe a stone would think of a kinder answer than that." Without waiting for a reply, she flounced out of the room and marched up the stairs to her room.

Once in the privacy of her bedroom, she studied the reflection in her looking glass. How different she seemed! Gone was the provincial nobody. Now she had the look of a sophisticated lady of London, nearly ready to take her place in Society.

Marcus had been right, of course. To go with the charming hairstyle, the curls that so beautifully clung to her head, she needed the proper gowns. Why she hated to admit he was usually right, she could not explain. But he had a powerful effect on her that she would do well to ignore. He was not in the market for a penniless cousin as a wife, and she had better not forget it.

And then Charis sat down with a thud on the nearest chair. What a stupid thought that was! She did not like her officious cousin in the least. They barely tolerated each other. She could not imagine what had prompted the thought. Just because she had adored him once . . .

Harriet came around the door, book in hand. "Well, how do you like the new you? *I* think you look smashing, and I wish our maid could do something wonderful with my hair."

"Of course she will, unless you would also like the ministrations of Mr. Truefitt?"

"He scared me half to death! No, I shall inspire Mary to do something creative for a young miss making her come-out. I almost feel as though I ought to have a sign on me." Harriet sighed and plopped down at the foot of the bed, her finger marking her place in the book.

"Who knows, dearest, you may get a proposal before I do. At least father left you a decent dowry." Charis studied her little sister, and wondered just how prophetic her words might be. She was not sure what sort of man she wanted to marry, but she knew he would not be like Cousin Marcus. Not at all.

Chapter Three

Little by little the garments from Madame Clotilde arrived to augment the meager wardrobes belonging to Charis, Harriet, and their mother.

The weeks had been filled with shopping and accompanying the elder countess when she made calls on old friends, ones who might be expected to entertain. Slowly it resulted in a growing number of callers at Huntingdon House, including Lady Sefton. Lady Huntingdon had met her before and was gratified to renew the connection.

Some may have felt genuine regard for the elder countess and her daughters. Others may have appeared with the hope of meeting Sir Marcus Rutledge, the wealthy and handsome new owner. Others may simply have been curious. And to be sure, the thought that some merely liked to claim acquaintanceship with a countess might have played a part. Charis wryly accepted that.

"At last, I feel as though I may face the thought of afternoon callers with equanimity," the elder countess declared to her daughter as she fingered the delicate deep blue jaconet of the new gown she wore.

"Indeed, I know what you mean. Although, I doubt our attire has the slightest impression on the gentlemen who call," Charis replied, pleased with her green-striped muslin.

"Of the gentlemen who have come to call so far, have any captured your eye or your heart?" her mother wanted to know. " 'Tis so tiring to judge their consequence."

"I fear not," Charis said after a pause to consider the few gentlemen she had met so far. "What a pity I cannot simply hang out a sign that says 'Husband wanted. Apply within.' "

"That would set the cat among the pigeons," Harriet said with a laugh, looking up from the magazine she perused. "Have you asked Marcus for help?"

"Not yet," Charis admitted.

"Well, I think you had best try. He must know everyone who is anyone, if you see what I mean." Harriet gave her sister a meaningful look, then buried her nose in the serial story printed in the latest issue of the *Lady's Magazine*.

"I did think we might see more of Lord Portchester," the elder lady remarked.

"I neglected to tell you that he sent around a note requesting that I go for a drive with him this afternoon. How fortunate I have a new carriage dress to wear!" Charis glanced at the clock to see how much time she had before she needed to change.

"I'd be willing to bet he wouldn't notice if you wore a sack," Harriet said, putting aside the magazine. "That has to be the stupidest story ever written. I'll wager I could do better."

"Ladies of quality do not write novels," her mother admonished. "They are not supposed to know how."

"Oh? Well, a Lady of Quality wrote a book called *Pride and Prejudice* that I think is wonderful." Harriet jumped up from her chair and disappeared in the direction of her room. She was heard greeting Marcus in the hall.

"You do not think she will actually attempt to write a book, do you?" Charis asked, slightly horrified at the thought of Harriet writing anything let alone a book.

"Who will write a book?" Marcus wondered as he entered the room.

Charis turned to face her seldom seen cousin. He had certainly made himself least in sight the past few weeks. Had she not occasionally passed him in the hall, she would have thought him living elsewhere.

"Harriet read a story she thought was stupid and says

she will write one better. I doubt that she would complete it." Charis looked to him for confirmation.

Marcus nodded, seeming to share his cousin's skepticism. "I thought you might enjoy a visit to Vauxhall this evening. The place has just opened. I have tickets."

"How fortunate we do not have other plans," Charis said with a touch of reproof in her manner. In spite of all the people her mother knew, no balls or other parties were in the immediate offing.

"Invitations a bit thin on the ground?" Marcus casually walked to a chair close to where Charis sat. He looked mildly interested but not inclined to help. She wondered what it would take to persuade his assistance.

"I drive out with Lord Portchester this afternoon."

"Charles? Be wary of his driving."

"Then, I gather he does not belong to the Four-in-Hand Club? I believe you are a member." She gave him a speculative look, shifting in her chair at his expression. What in the world went on in his mind that he should look at her so? True, the neckline of her green-striped muslin was lower than she normally wore, but Madame Clotilde claimed it quite proper and praised the manner in which Charis filled out the bodice of the dress. Surely he did not disapprove of that! "Is something wrong?" She sat a trifle straighter.

He cleared his throat and seemed flustered. "No, no, not in the least. We shall depart around seven this evening. I trust you will all be on time? Take a cloak as it might be a trifle chilly on the way home."

"Have you ever known us to be late?" Really, why did he stare at her so? There must be something on his mind. "But thank you for mentioning the cloaks. I might never have thought of it." If he had been at home to notice, he would have observed they always took some sort of cloak with them in the evening to ward off a possible chill—not that they had gone out all that often. The gowns worn nowadays were not intended to offer warmth.

"Do you intend to assist Charis in finding a suitable husband, Marcus?" the elder countess inquired absently, as though it mattered not in the least that her daughter was in need of such a commodity. "It would be a help."

"She has not asked for my assistance."

"Then, I hereby ask," Charis said promptly.

"What are your requirements?" He sounded languid, but his eyes had an alertness she did not miss.

Charis considered the matter again for perhaps the hundredth time. The trouble was that when she thought of the qualities she wished in a husband, the image that popped into her mind all too often resembled Marcus. That would never do because she did not like him.

"Well?"

"I am thinking," she snapped. "I would wish him an agreeable companion, a thoughtful conversationalist. It would be nice if he enjoyed books, evenings by the fire."

"What? Not one to take you to balls, the theater, opera, parties? I thought you were tired of the country and quiet pursuits."

"I do like all those things, but I have observed that a husband and wife rarely attend them together here in London. So"—she swallowed with care before continuing, for actually she would far rather be escorted by her mate than someone else or go alone—"that is not a *necessary* attribute."

"Handsome? Tall? Fair or dark?" he demanded.

She laughed. "Yes to all of those. Although I prefer dark to fair, I think."

He almost smiled, softening his chiseled features into a less stone-like facade. "That makes it easier. But do remember that few men wish to be wed for their wealth alone. A man could wish for love as well."

She did not probe further because she suspected he would not tell her. Marcus was not precisely withdrawn, rather he kept his own counsel, and that was likely a wise thing to do given the propensity for all to gossip. Charis had observed that men were as guilty of tittle-tattle as women. As to his suggesting a possible *parti* for her, she would wait to see what happened next in that regard.

"We seldom see you, Marcus," Lady Huntingdon said,

her gaze straying to him, then focusing on the distant painting across the room. It had been painted many years ago of a previous Lord Huntingdon as a young man. The clothes were of the distant past, but the gentleman had the same dark red hair and green eyes to be found in Charis. There was clearly a family connection.

"Perhaps I can remedy that. At least we will share company this evening." He bowed in her direction, a courtly bow that revealed his respect for the older lady.

"You spend a good deal of time at your club?" Charis probed.

"Some" was his laconic reply.

Charis gave up asking anything more. "You are the most vexing creature alive! I know so little about you," she cried, rising from her chair to head for her room. "I shall change into a suitable carriage dress for my drive with Lord Portchester. And I will be certain to bring a cloak with me this evening."

"I shall see you later." His eyes gleamed, and she wondered if he inwardly laughed at her.

Charis paused by the door. "Do join us for dinner—we are quite civilized, I assure you."

"I have little doubt of that."

"In spite of what someone else has said?" Charis gave him an arrested look. "For that is what your tone implies."

He refused to answer her, merely shook his head.

Charis was thoughtful as she walked up to her room. She had scarcely been about Town enough to cause any gossip. So who could have said something derogatory?

From the pleased expression worn by Lord Portchester, it seemed that he had not made the disparaging remark. He was as affable as anyone might wish—quite genial, and nice-looking to boot. Although of medium height and possessing sandy hair, he could not be rejected for those qualities. His kind expression and words were balm to her heart, still faintly bruised from her cousin's attitude.

Charis, in spite of what she had told her cousin about

particulars, could not afford to be a beggar when it came to a husband. She required a man who was not on the hunt for an heiress with pots of money! She had no desire to remain beholden to Marcus any longer than necessary. One would think—in view of the sum expended upon their clothes—he would have wanted them all gone as soon as possible. Instead he had done nothing to help her. It seemed odd to her, but then he was not the same Marcus she had known some years past.

She put aside the twinge of guilt that she and her family had pushed him out of what was now his home.

While it was cloudy, the breeze was gentle and the park a joy to behold on a spring day. Charis twirled her new pagoda parasol and settled on the seat of the new curricle belonging to his lordship. "Lovely vehicle," she commented, aware every gentleman appreciates a kind word.

"Is it not!" he declared enthusiastically. He went on to offer details on the construction, the difficulty of getting just the proper paint job, and the importance of excellent quality for upholstery.

Charis soon learned more than she ever expected to know about acquiring a carriage. Philosophically, she considered that she might make such a purchase one day, perhaps, if her hoped-for husband did not buy it for her.

"I must say, you are quite astute, Lady Huntingdon. It is not everyone who takes notice of the quality of a carriage, let me tell you." His smile charmed her, and she thought what a pity it was that his intellect did not appear to match it.

"I can imagine," Charis murmured, thinking that if one was prepared and sufficiently clever, one might never learn the details of carriages. She decided then and there that her husband would have to be able to discuss something besides a carriage.

Unfortunately, Lord Portchester did not have that insight. He nattered on about carriages he had previously owned and one or two he would truly like to own. He also digressed to comment on the various carriages they passed and who owned them.

"Your cousin has fine taste in vehicles, my lady. Of course, as a member of the FHC, he would be bound to. I see he approaches with the charming Lady Alicia Dartry. She is quite wealthy as well, being the daughter of the Marquess of Berkshire, not that he has need of another fortune. And he has his bays today. Now, there is breeding for you."

Charis would dearly loved to have inquired whether it was Lady Alicia or the horses whose breeding he admired. Instead she quietly agreed, as it seemed to make little difference what she said.

Lord Portchester bowed to Sir Marcus and Lady Alicia. Charis gave them a polite look, but she did not nod. She had decided she did not particularly like Lady Alicia and certainly did not seek to know her better. That she had never met the woman did not come to mind.

"You should have nodded to Lady Alicia. She is a force to be reckoned with in Society, you know. Or perhaps you do not? I forget you have been out of touch this past year or more." He sounded truly distressed.

Charis sought to soothe him. "No matter. Surely she does not have more influence than one of the patronesses at Almack's?" she inquired mischievously.

"No, no. Of course not." He glanced about him as though to ascertain that no one had overheard his rash assessment.

Charis was delighted when he turned to head toward home. Huntingdon House, that is. She must never forget that it was no longer hers. Sir Marcus Rutledge, Bt. possessed it now, thanks to the idiotic will her father had written. Why? Surely he did not think to promote a marriage between Marcus and her! How laughable! He could barely stand to be in the same room with her. And she . . . well, she could tolerate him, perhaps more than that.

She gasped, torn from her mental wanderings, when Lord Portchester took the next corner at far too fast a pace, plunging his horse into the path of an oncoming carriage. She decided that fate was most unkind when she saw that Marcus drove the other vehicle. Lord Portches-

ter pulled frantically at the reins trying to avoid a colli-
sion, but the wheels of his carriage still nicked those of
her cousin's, a touch far too close for comfort. She closed
her eyes, certain her days were over.

Only Marcus's skill saved them from ruin.

The words muttered by his lordship were unintelligi-
ble, which was probably just as well. He managed to calm
his horse. Marcus drove on, but not before giving Charis
a stare that promised later reckoning.

She said nothing while a red-faced Lord Portchester
continued on to Huntingdon House. She clasped her
trembling hands firmly in her lap. It is not every day that
you wonder if you have drawn your last breath on earth.

"I trust this has not given you an aversion for drives
in the park, Lady Huntingdon," he said when they drew
up before the house. The poor man looked horribly em-
barrassed, and it was impossible not to pity him.

Feeling as though she had aged ten years in the past
minutes, Charis summoned a smile, assuring him, "Not
at all. Why I'm sure things like this must happen every
day." Not to her, however. She did not invite him into
the house, citing the lack of a groom and his horse likely
wanting attention.

She hurried into the house. After one look at her face,
Seymour offered to bring tea. She gratefully accepted,
requesting it to be in the library.

She hunted for a book to soothe her frazzled nerves
when Marcus stormed into the room. At his look, she
froze near the shelf of books on botany.

"Are you thinking to plant yourself in the garden,
cousin? Perhaps you wish to join the daisies?" He looked
utterly furious with her, and why she could not imagine.
She had not been the one who was driving that curricle.
She backed away from his intimidating figure as he
stepped toward her.

"Of course not!" How she wished her voice did not
tremble. Even her body betrayed her fright, she felt as
shaken as a leaf in a strong wind. It helped not that he
appeared to stalk her.

A projecting volume poked her in the back. She

winced at the pain. There was no place she might go, however. Besides, she would stand up to him. The books did not yield an inch. He walked closer, keeping his eyes focused on her, meeting her gaze unflinchingly.

"Perhaps not, but sure as anything you were very close to doing precisely that. Little fool! I told you to beware of Portchester's driving."

By this point he was close to her, so close she could feel the texture of his pantaloons against her legs, for the muslin of her gown was very thin. He grasped her arms as he had done once before, and she gave him a wary look.

"I fail to see what I might have done to . . ."

"Fool!" he whispered and crushed her to him, his mouth descending upon hers to steal a fierce kiss that made others she had received in the past pale in comparison. The trembling she had felt after the episode in the carriage with the near crash was as nothing to her shaken sensibilities now.

Abruptly he set her away from him and turned to walk toward the door, leaving her distraught. She was like a tender flower swept along on a stormy current, likely to plunge over a waterfall to her fate, crushed more surely than any accident.

"I trust you have an explanation for that," she said, her voice sounding choked and uneven to her ears. Tears stung her lids, and she trembled more than before. She hesitantly placed one hand behind her, gaining support and strength from the books at her back.

"I trust I do." He said nothing more, however.

It pleased her to note that his breathing was as ragged as hers and his usually tan skin had paled.

"And you do not intend to share it with me?" She could not believe this had happened, and he was simply going to walk away from her with no explanation—not even an apology!

"I cannot. It would be difficult." He turned away, refusing to meet her eyes.

"You might try me, Marcus." How patient she sounded when she would like to box his ears. All he did was to shake his head as though he could not understand it himself.

"I shall see you at dinner." He disappeared, to be shortly heard marching up the stairs. Then somewhere upstairs a door slammed shut, the sound reverberating through the house.

Charis groped her way to a chair and sank down, her knees still weak and her breathing not yet normal. Why? He did not even like her. He must very much resent her and her family intruding on his life. How could he kiss her and in such a manner! One thing certain, it was a kiss against which she might measure all in the future!

Seymour brought in her tea along with a few crisp lemon biscuits. Her pulse slowly calmed as she sipped her tea and nibbled a biscuit. First, the near accident, then the kiss from Marcus—both unsettling to say the least, and she could not think which had shaken her the most.

When she went down for dinner, Charis discovered Lady Alicia was to be with them—not only for dinner but also the evening at Vauxhall. It was not a particularly pleasant surprise. Fortunately three of her cousin's gentlemen friends had turned up as well.

Suddenly Charis was very thankful she had a new gown to wear, a shimmering spangled gauze of a color called sea-foam green. Madame Clotilde had sent a shawl to wear with it that looked as though it was the actual sea foam, for Charis felt as though she wore a frothy mist over her shoulders when she draped it about her. She wondered what Marcus would think of her shawl when it came time to depart, considering what he had said earlier.

Trying to be unobtrusive, she studied him where he stood chatting with a gentleman by the name of Lord Egerton. He was as tall as Marcus, though a trifle thinner. His dark hair was not as thick nor did he have the tan Marcus had acquired while out driving his coach to Salt Hill and elsewhere.

The procession to Salt Hill that the Four-in-Hand Club

made the first and third Thursdays in May and June were the envy of all men who considered themselves good drivers. The club was terribly exclusive. It was to be expected that keeping in form for this club meant frequent drives—to make certain one did not lose one's skill. Perhaps that was one of the things that kept Marcus away from the house so often?

Sensing a movement at her side, Charis turned her attention from her cousin to a guest. "Lady Alicia, how lovely you could join us this evening."

"Yes, it was, was it not? Are you enjoying your foray into London Society, miss, er, Lady Huntingdon?" She bestowed a patronizing smile on Charis, as though she was a country nobody. This—in spite of Charis having the title of countess. Granted, a title did not inevitably give one the airs and graces of a London lady; nevertheless, it was not to be sneezed at, and Charis outranked the daughter of a marquess.

Charis knew a strong urge to walk away from this beauty. Not only was she aloof, she was outrageously condescending. Charis was quite certain that Marcus had made her name and title clear when they had been introduced. Unless Lady Alicia was deaf, she would have heard the same words Charis did.

"Oh, yes. People are so interesting, you never know what you may discover as you become acquainted with someone. Do you not find that to be true?" Charis gave her a limpid smile and waited.

Obviously not sure how to take her remark, Lady Alicia changed the subject. "Do you plan to remain in London for long? It must be a dreadful strain for Sir Marcus to have to share his home with so many others."

"Actually, there is not the slightest difficulty." Charis ignored the scene in the library that afternoon. She could not put it out of her mind, but she had managed to relegate it to the back somehow. And as to it being a strain, well it had been for her but Marcus looked unscathed by it. "Our families have always been very close over the years. Marcus was like a son to my father." And he had willed Marcus everything he could!

"Ah, so you are more like brother and sister, then?" Lady Alicia said with an expression that seemed relieved. She so rarely altered her face to any but an expression of ennui that it was hard to tell what she actually felt.

"Not quite that of brother and sister," Charis replied, thinking back to the sizzling kiss of a few hours ago. "But at least friends." And if that was not precisely the truth, it was close enough.

"How, er, nice," Lady Alicia said as though commenting on a particularly repulsive piece of artwork she loathed. It was amazing how in spite of the lack of variation in her tone she could manage to convey such feeling.

Charis would wager that Lady Alicia took strong exception to the presence of his relatives in his house. But . . . had she said anything to Marcus about it?

Just how close were these two? The thought of Marcus kissing Lady Alicia as he had kissed Charis was not at all palatable. He could not. Charis thought further and decided that Lady Alicia would freeze his lips had he attempted such a thing.

"You have had a humorous thought, my lady," Lady Alicia observed coolly. "Do share it."

Never had Charis been so grateful as when Seymour appeared to announce that dinner was served. When she entered following her mother and Marcus, she was happy to find that she sat nowhere near Lady Alicia. True, her regal ladyship was across the table, where she could speak exclusively to Marcus and ignore Lord Baylor. He consoled himself by chatting with Harriet on his other side. But—Charis did not have to say a word, since the table was broad, and besides, one did not converse across the table in Society.

As to her feelings regarding Marcus, she dare not examine them until in her room, where she could sort them out properly. There had to be something that had prompted his behavior. She intended to learn what it was.

Nice Lord Egerton leaned toward her and said, "You seem quite pleased about something."

"I am, actually. And you? Do you tolerate life, or do you hunt for things to be pleased about?"

"Never thought about life that way before," he admitted.

There followed a charming conversation about what to expect when you met someone new, and impressions of Society in general. On her other side the smart guardsman made reasonably intelligent conversation when she needed to turn her attention, as one ought to at a dinner party.

She still had not solved the mystery as to how a simple family dinner before going to Vauxhall had turned into a much larger affair with many people present. One might almost think Marcus feared being alone with her.

Of course, it was his home, he could do as he pleased. It made her doubly thankful for the new gown. But Marcus might have warned her!

The dinner over, the group gathered in the drawing room, smilingly agreed it was time to depart for Vauxhall, and straggled after Marcus as he led the way to where several carriages awaited them.

Charis was amazed at his planning. The dinner, now the carriages, and probably everything at Vauxhall proceeding like clockwork. His secretary had truly worked at top speed to produce such results!

Was that perhaps what he had intended to tell her when he had entered the library? And then something provoked him into kissing her? But what? She was quite sure she had said or done nothing to anger him. Except for the near accident, that is, and that was scarcely her fault. What could she have done, pray tell? Marcus had not forbidden her to drive out with Lord Portchester. She could hardly tell the man to mind his driving, could she?

She chatted absently with the lieutenant and Lord Egerton until they reached the entrance to the pleasure gardens. She was anxious to see the various walks and the other celebrated sights of the gardens.

"Do not stray from our sides, Charis," Marcus cautioned, bending to her ear so she would be certain to hear him.

"I feel certain that either that nice lieutenant or Lord Egerton will squire me about. Do not worry about me."

"The lieutenant has agreed to assist your mother. Baylor will keep an eye on Harriet, and Egerton will 'squire' you about. He has the most money."

Charis would have loved to inform her cousin that she favored that gentleman more for his pleasant conversation than his money. Hadn't she insisted that she required that ability in a husband as well as wealth?

They enjoyed the famous shaved ham and arrack punch—although Charis admitted she did not care for it and drank the lemonade also provided instead. Lord Egerton was as nice a companion as one could wish. Charis hoped she might come to like him.

The fireworks were definitely the highlight of the evening as far as she was concerned. Somehow Marcus came to stand next to her while Lady Alicia argued politely about something with Lord Egerton.

"Did you enjoy the evening?"

"Indeed, very much," Charis replied, relishing the soft wrap about her shoulders and the distinguished gentleman at her side.

"You are not cold? You look like Aphrodite arising from the sea in that attire. Most becoming, I must say."

She had observed that his eyes frequently rested on her during dinner, but what his thoughts might have been, she could not imagine.

"Thank you. I am pleased with it. And I am not cold."

"No—I do not suppose you are." His words were accompanied by a look she could not begin to interpret.

Chapter Four

Morning brought common sense to Charis. All foolish thoughts must be banished. She did not like her cousin, she reminded herself. Merely because he had been charming and attentive last evening was no reason to weaken her view of him. Doubtless he was only being polite, perhaps hoping to intrigue Lord Egerton so he would develop an interest in a penniless countess.

Morning also brought the vouchers to attend Almack's. Apparently the call Lady Sefton had paid them met with success. Just because Charis was a countess in her own right and her mother the countess of the late earl did not necessarily mean the vouchers would be forthcoming. One had to be proposed for such by a patroness, then approved by the rest of them in one of their weekly meetings. Charis was well aware that she could just as easily have been rejected on a whim by such as Lady Jersey.

"You look pleased, cousin," Marcus said, joining her in the hall, where Seymour had placed the morning mail on a silver tray. He picked up a delicately scented letter with his name inscribed in violet ink, ignoring the rest of his mail.

A whiff of violet teased her nose. Charis concealed a smile, for Marcus looked at the thing as though it might bite him. Now, who could write such an epistle? She would wager it was not Lady Alicia! But who else would dare send such a letter!

"Indeed. I believe the vouchers to Almack's came, brought by Lady Sefton's groom. Here is a missive from her," she replied, looking down at it. The last thing she desired was to appear inquisitive about that violet letter.

"Will this require a new gown?" Marcus tapped his intriguing correspondence against his hand, looking annoyed even if he sounded pleased.

"Harriet ought to have her new white muslin by then, and I have a cream satin gown that ought to meet with approval." She turned away from him, conscious of the oddest longing within her to touch him.

"It is fortunate that the patronesses allow three ladies from one family to attend, although only two ladies of a family are to be on the lists. You have three tickets? Otherwise Harriet will have to stay home."

"If I knew of the rule, I had forgotten it. I hope Harriet will not be too downcast," Charis replied, thinking it was a vastly silly rule. Of course her mother would have to serve as chaperone—Charis could scarcely do that duty for Harriet.

"Tell me, did you ever receive that gown of gold tissue?" He leaned against the wall, now looking relaxed and politely curious. His face was as chiseled as ever, but there was a slight softening about his eyes.

"No, I canceled the order, for I thought it a needless extravagance. You must know it would be wildly expensive." She firmed her lips, refusing to again point out that she was beholden to him for most of her wardrobe and she had no desire to order more than she needed. Should she find the wealthy husband she required, he could foot her bills.

"Hm," he murmured, but did not add a comment regarding the gown. "You know your dances?" He studied her face with a disconcerting thoroughness. "I'd not have it said I did not provide you with a dancing master."

Charis drew up to her full height, staring him in the eyes. "We may be provincials, but we have learned most of the dance patterns. I do well at the cotillion, I am told. And country-dances are usually quite simple."

"You waltz? The approval of a patroness will be required first, but you ought to be prepared." He gave her a searching look, one that also doubted she knew the first thing about waltzing.

"I have practiced the steps in Thomas Wilson's book, but alas, there is no gentleman living close to us that has learned to waltz. Besides, it was not considered proper for me to learn such a scandalous dance while we were in mourning." She tilted up her chin to give him a cool look. Did he think her so lost to all propriety?

"You deem it scandalous?" He glanced behind Charis toward the light footsteps that heralded Harriet's arrival. "Harriet, come play us a waltz. I would see if your sister has studied the waltz enough to dance it."

Sputter as she might, Charis was no match for Marcus when he was determined.

Harriet chuckled, hurrying into the music room where she rummaged through a stack of music atop the pianoforte until she found what she sought. Within minutes she was playing a lovely piece with a lilting tune.

Marcus replaced the scented letter on the tray, and then escorted Charis into the music room as well, his hand firmly cupped about her elbow.

She wondered if she could persuade her feet to move as they ought. If only she did not have such a reaction to his touch! Her insides insisted on turning to mush, and that could not be allowed. Quelling all seditious feelings, she turned to face him, resolute in her will to remain firm.

And then he put his right arm about her, gently cradled her right hand in his left, and moved so close she could see black flecks in the dark blue of his eyes. His skin had tiny lines radiating from the outside corners of his eyes, witness to time spent in the sun. His mouth seemed firm, but she well remembered the tender feel of it against hers. Never in her life had she been so aware of another. *This* was why women swooned when waltzing!

Her mouth went dry. The warm touch of his hand wrapped about hers, not to mention the feel of his other hand pressed against her back, was like to send her into a collapse—had she been the silly sort of girl who did such things. Charis was made of sterner stuff.

"Proceed, cousin." It would have helped had her voice not sounded husky and breathless when she spoke.

He had been staring at her mouth, and she had to repeat her command before he seemed to shake himself from his trance. "You know the steps? One, two, three, always revolving, facing your partner with a smile on your face, I should hope."

Charis did smile at this nonsense. Harriet began the tune once more, and Charis, the pattern of the steps in her mind, followed his lead to revolve slowly about the room. The little black squares and dots on the white pages of the dancing book, indicating how one should move, gave not the slightest hint of how one *felt* floating about the room in the arms of an extremely handsome gentleman. She had practiced the steps in her room, trying to imagine how it would be to actually waltz. How glad she was that Marcus was her first partner for this shocking dance. Somehow it made it quite special in a way she preferred not to examine too closely.

A trifle stiff at first, at his prompting she relaxed, allowing herself to follow his steps and the music. She did not pull away from him in spite of his closeness. Perhaps it was done that way, and she hated to appear provincial.

She had read the waltz proclaimed as wicked, and whoever declared it such had a fair notion what thoughts it put into impressionable minds. And bodies. Her tension was not brought about solely by her desire to dance correctly.

When Harriet brought the music to an end, Marcus led a shaken Charis to the pianoforte. "She did extremely well for someone who has practiced without a partner, and I must praise you for your very nice playing. Two talented sisters, I vow." His firm features relaxed into a pleasant expression, reminding Charis that someday she intended to make him smile.

"Thank you, Marcus," Charis replied, quite able to

speak sensibly now that they no longer were in each
other's arms in *such* proximity.

"If a gentleman asks you to waltz, you may feel comfortable in accepting, once permission is granted. The
dance has been around for a few years, but not that long
at Almack's, I believe, nor in more remote areas of the
country. Once you have been observed dancing at that
select assembly, invitations to balls and parties ought to
flood Seymour's tray."

"Harriet, ought you to practice as well?" Charis tore
her gaze from her cousin to look at her sister.

"She may be as pretty as can be, but perhaps she
would do well to wait a time before attempting a waltz.
If she likes, later I can hire a dancing master to teach
her when it comes time for her to make her splash at
Almack's." With that, he bowed and left the girls on
their own.

"How odd he is," Charis said quietly.

"I believe he does not resent us quite so much anymore. Although I heard him tell that nice lieutenant that
we do cut up his peace somewhat," Harriet said once
Marcus had taken his mail and retreated to the library,
closing the door with a thud.

Charis exchanged a thoughtful look with her sister,
then went off to find her mother, so she might see the
coveted vouchers and make plans for the coming
Wednesday evening.

As to the woman who sent Marcus that letter drenched
with violet scent, Charis resolved to discover her identity.
Who might be inclined to write using violet ink? Normally a lady never wrote a gentleman. Yes, she ought to
find out the woman's identity if only to perhaps protect
him against some importuning female, she told herself
righteously.

Marcus seated himself at the library desk, wondering
if he had lost his mind—waltzing with Charis as he had.
He had resolved to remain aloof from his cousin. The
last thing he needed was any involvement with her at

the moment. Anyway, he was too old for a beautiful girl her age.

Breaking the seal of the scented missive, he scanned the contents before tossing the letter into the small fire that smoldered in the grate. He wanted no record of those words around to haunt him someday. It was time to end his relationship with the Divine Delilah, as some called her. He'd pick up a suitable gift for her congé, and that would be it. She pursued him, and he did not tolerate that in anyone. He knew of at least three gentlemen who had the wherewithal to support a liaison with such a creation.

He leaned back on his chair to contemplate what Lady Alicia had said when he took her home last evening. She insisted that Charis, Harriet, and their mother be removed. "They could live in a nice little town house somewhere in London," she claimed. Never mind that there was not a decent town house to be found in the best part of London this late in the Season at any price. A few chaps rented out their houses for the Season and lived on the proceeds the rest of the year!

He thought her demand unreasonable. After all, this house had belonged to the Huntingdon family. Was it not logical they reside here for their short stay in London? Even Seymour, the starchiest of butlers, seemed to sanction their presence. That ought to set a seal of approval for the most strict of matrons.

Marcus did not like having a woman dictate to him in such a manner—imperious and seeming not to care for the welfare of those involved. But then, she had been pampered all her life and never known a day of hardship. What could she know of the difficulties Charis faced? Alicia had only to decide which peer she might wish to escort her and he would be at her side. The same might apply to selecting a husband—although that might take a bit more maneuvering on her part. Perhaps Alicia might be forgiven for her lack of sensitivity. Yet, he admitted, he could not imagine Charis speaking in such a way.

Charis disturbed him. He should not have offered to

see how well she waltzed. How much better it would have been merely to send for a dancing master for both of the girls. The feel of Charis in his arms had proven to be more than he had bargained for, to say the least. He had to confess that Lady Alicia had never affected him in that way. How complicated his life had become of late.

In a restless manner quite unlike his normally contained self, he rose from the desk, leaving the other mail ignored. Within minutes he had donned his gloves and hat and was out of the house. He informed Seymour, "I am off to White's." He seemed to spend an inordinate amount of time there of late.

"Mama, look what has come. Are you not pleased? Lady Sefton did as promised." Charis waved the missive at her mother, giving her a happy smile.

At a nod from her mother, Charis broke open the seal to find affixed within two vouchers that were to be exchanged for tickets. She gave Mama a guarded smile. "Only two tickets."

Ruff trotted over to inspect his mistress. Charis kept him confined to her room and the little sitting room they had appropriated for their own use. When possible she walked him, but otherwise the youngest footman willingly took him out. The last thing she wanted was to have her little dog annoy Marcus or a guest.

Charis knelt to fondle Ruff's sleek head, her eyes on her mother. "We shall attend come Wednesday evening?"

"If you like." Lady Huntingdon inspected the much-coveted vouchers, then relaxed against the cushions of the chaise lounge. "It might be rather interesting to see how my friends have aged," she said in a dry tone.

"We are in London that I might find a husband, so we can achieve a measure of independence . . . from Marcus," Charis reminded. Surely it must bother Mama to be so dependent on her late husband's first cousin, once removed. Marcus was but a second cousin to Charis, and she felt him too distant to allow them to be a burden on him for long. Never mind they had always been close or that her father had considered Marcus the son he had never had. Recollection of the will brought a tightening to her lips. Why had Papa done this? She would never know.

"Do as you wish," her mother said. "But please ring for tea, will you? I believe I should like a cup. Biscuits, as well." She waved a languid hand.

Charis rang, gave orders, then turned to her mother. "I hope Harriet will not be too disappointed that we received but two tickets. It is necessary for me to go at present. If I marry well, she will go later on."

"Discuss it with her. Harriet is such a practical girl, I believe she will understand. I cannot think where she gets it. Goodness knows your father was not."

Charis knew that her mother was not in the least practical, either. She scooped up her little dog in her arms and went searching for Harriet. When she located her in her room, Charis sank down on a comfortable chair to complain while encouraging Ruff to curl up in her lap.

"Well," Harriet replied in her sensible way when Charis had finished with her litany of woes, "I believe you will simply have to take matters into your own hands."

"Dare I? You must know that all proper young ladies have a mother or sponsor to oversee their introduction to Society. Can you imagine what Lady Alicia Dartry would say to such behavior? But Mama will come with me, then I shall do what I can. It is a worrisome matter without having an indifferent mother, I can tell you. She needs a project."

Harriet agreed.

"I am sorry that only two of us can attend. I hate to leave you home alone, but the tickets . . ."

"I shall be fine." Harriet looked more relieved than upset, not that Charis in her worried state took much notice. "And I will have Ruff to keep me company."

Ruff wagged his tail and ruffed as he did when he wanted to go out.

"I'd best take him for a walk. Would you like to join us?" Charis put the dog down, then rose.

Harriet avoided meeting her sister's eyes. "I've been writing. A letter," she added hastily.

"As you please. It is a pleasant day, and I shall enjoy a bit of fresh air." Her mind occupied with the problem of making her entrance to Society and finding an acceptable husband, Charis paid no attention to what her sister had been doing. Quite satisfied with her explanation, Charis went to her room, dressed for her outing, then went downstairs.

Ruff in her arms, she paused before the library door, peeking in to see if Marcus was still there. A fire smoldered in the fireplace, the room was empty. Noting a scrap of paper on the very edge of the fire, she shifted Ruff to one side and walked over to it. Beset with curiosity when she observed the violet paper, Charis plucked it from additional damage. Alas, all she could make out was a signature below a syrupy closing. The scrawl was scarcely the sort a *lady* might write and signed "Your Divine Delilah"! Well, the woman—whoever she might be—possessed an alluring name—most likely selected for that effect. No one was given such a name nowadays. Most likely her true name was Rose or Daisy.

Hastily dropping the scrap of paper back into the fire, Charis let herself from the house, informing Seymour she would return before long. He sent a footman after her so that she would be properly accompanied.

"Divine Delilah," Charis murmured to her dog. "That sounds like the name belonging to a woman who is no better than she should be. That is," she added for Ruff's benefit, "a woman who is not the least respectable. So my cousin has a—well, dare I say it? A demirep? And he courts the proper Lady Alicia as well? My, my. I should think he would want our departure at the earliest date possible. Therefore, I shall tax him with the *urgency* of finding me a husband the next time I see him."

"Ruff," the dog replied, seeing an enticing squirrel ahead. Seeming quite accustomed to the chats his mistress had with him as they marched along the path in the park, he paid her words no heed.

"Indeed," Charis continued, tugging on the lead so Ruff could not harass the squirrel, "I will inform Marcus that unless he assists me in finding a husband, all three of us will likely stay on with him forever. At least, Mama and I will. I suspect there is a gentleman who will like Harriet."

Ruff merely glanced at her and continued pulling her along, intent upon the squirrel. The footman followed.

When Charis had reached her conclusion, she turned with Ruff toward Huntingdon House once again, relieved to have settled her plan in her mind. Marcus had better pay attention to her. Or else.

It was not until just before dinner that Charis had an opportunity to approach her cousin.

"Marcus, could I speak with you a moment?" she said, spying him as he was about to leave the house—as usual off to his evening pursuits without saying a word to them. Not that she truly expected him to give an account in his own house.

He paused in the act of drawing on his gloves. "Well?"

She persuasively tugged him into the library away from Seymour's hearing. "I know how anxious you must be to have us gone from your house. I decided that to speed the process, it would be best were you to assist me more actively. Otherwise, you may end up with Mama and me under your roof forever." She bestowed what she hoped was a wistful smile on him.

His sardonic look indicated what he thought of her ploy. "What is it you want of me?"

"Almack's. Perhaps a few drives in the park. I wish you to introduce me to gentlemen you believe to be acceptable *partis*. Remember, the sooner I have a husband, the sooner we will be out from under your feet."

"A husband for Harriet as well?" he asked, one brow winging upward.

"Oh, no, I shall help find her a husband once I am

settled. If she has such a need. Harriet is very fetching, you know," Charis informed him earnestly.

"As are you. I doubt you will require so much assistance, but if you truly feel it necessary, I will come with you this Wednesday."

"Good." She guided him from the library, wondering what Delilah looked like and how she pleased him. It would have been interesting to know, but she also knew that she dare not ask. "Have a pleasant evening, cousin."

"I intend to, my dear." He placed his hat on at a precise angle, then left the house.

Charis felt unexpectedly lonely when he was gone. How odd that she should miss him so when they usually managed to disagree on something. She considered the manner in which he intimidated her and decided she was a peagoose to worry about it. Quashing any other thoughts about him, she went in search of Ruff and spent some time playing with him until they were both tired and ready to rest. With her little dog curled up at the foot of her bed, she went to sleep dreaming of Marcus pursuing a damsel in exotic silks.

Wednesday evening found the dowager and Charis dressed in proper apparel and quite prepared to face Almack's with Marcus at their side.

He was garbed in a dark blue coat and black silk breeches of breathtaking splendor with a cravat tied in his usual exquisite simplicity. Charis suspected there would not be a gentleman who could touch him for elegance.

She fingered the delicate cream satin of her gown and hoped it would not be too simple or girlish. True, the wine-colored ribbon, tied in a simple bow at the front where the skirt joined the bodice, added a touch of style. And the clever tucks at the back of the skirt swept into a graceful fullness that gave the gown a certain modishness. Puffed sleeves made the gown, the satin elaborately tucked into the band with lavish lace at the edge.

Her mother had merely nodded her approval, and Marcus had not said a word.

Once the carriage halted before the assembly rooms on King Street, Charis felt frightened. This was the matrimonial bazaar, some said. It was where every eligible lady and gentleman might appear and search for a proper partner. She hoped she did not disgrace herself.

Marcus first assisted the elder countess, then Charis from the carriage, retaining her hand in his.

"Will I do?" she asked just before they entered the building.

"If you do not cause a mad dash of every gentleman in the room, I shall be very much surprised. You must know you look very lovely this evening. That wine-colored ribbon catches light from your hair. And that silk rose tucked into your curls is just the right touch for a young woman."

Gratified, Charis replied, "I am not so very young, Marcus. After a year of mourning, I shall likely be older than most of the young women seeking a husband."

"Not an old lady as yet, I vow!" Marcus said.

He assisted the countess up the stairs with Charis immediately behind them. Once in the rooms, she carefully searched the throng of people already assembled to see if perchance there might be someone that she knew.

"Lady Huntingdon, how pleased I am to see you!" Lord Portchester exclaimed as he rushed to her side, totally ignoring her escort. He looked very fine this evening. His corbeau coat was well cut, but his cravat was done in an overly elaborate attempt at a waterfall style. "May I beg a dance, fair lady?"

Charis agreed, quite thankful she would not have to rely solely on Marcus as a partner.

Lord Portchester introduced her to several other gentlemen, who also requested a dance.

"I had best ask for my dances before you have none left," Marcus said quietly when the others had receded. "A waltz, I think. I will ask Lady Jersey. She will delight in allowing it, wondering what an old fellow like me is doing with a chit like you."

"You are not old, Marcus. Why, you are in the very prime of life," Charis countered.

"How gratifying you think so," he said, giving her a sharp look. "I shall tax Lady Jersey with my request shortly before the first waltz." He bowed and sauntered away.

Charis watched him go, then turned to her mother. "I shall not be sitting on the side with you, Mama. I have a respectable number of requests."

"Well, of course, my dear," her mother replied with a fluttery wave of a hand. "And why ever not? I was always in demand as a girl, as I recall." She gave the occupants of the room a shrewd look, as though deciding who might offer the most interesting gossip.

Lord Portchester was her first partner and performed his dancing far better than he managed a carriage. Charis could not deny he was a trifle dull. What was it Harriet had said? He is the drum for his own fife? As she listened to his lordship natter on about his carriage once again, Charis could not help but agree.

The next gentleman to partner her was far less dull. In fact, he was a fountain of information as to where she ought to shop. She listened with amazement as he dispensed advice.

"One must go to Baldock's to find the best boulle and *marqueterie*. And if you desire Dresden, Sevres, and enamels, there is only Jarman's, don't you know. I'd not think of buying my ormolu and bronzes anywhere but Fogg's, and a chap would be a fool to think of purchasing pictures anywhere but Christie's." He gave her a superior smile before parting in the pattern of the dance.

"Books?" Charis queried as they met again. Where she might find any money to buy such precious things she could not imagine. But the information might prove useful someday.

"I bid for my rare books at Evan's. None of the other dealers can match him for quality," he replied with a nod.

"You like to shop?" she asked.

"Only the other day I snabbled up a lovely console inlaid with lapis lazuli, porphyry, and various other colored stones. Good price, I'll wager. Looks nice in my entry."

Well, the man did not dress like a dandy, and he was a serious sort of fellow. She wondered where he came by his fortune.

"You must have a charming home with so many lovely things in it." Not to mention a great sum of money at his disposal.

"Oh, I do, you may be certain."

What else he might have suggested was lost as the dance most thankfully ended. Charis found herself by her mother again, awaiting her next partner. A glance at the paper with the dances listed indicated it was a waltz. When she looked up, she saw Marcus walking toward her with Lady Jersey at his side.

Charis curtsied properly, glancing at Marcus.

"This wag of a gentleman insists he be presented as an acceptable partner for the waltz. I know he will not disappoint you," the lady concluded with a fleeting look at Marcus that seemed sly to Charis.

It was heaven to be in his arms once again. It seemed as though her feet scarcely touched the floor as they skimmed around the perimeter of the room. It did not quite match their first waltz, for now she steeled herself against his charm. But she could not deny his appeal or his skill.

And then she spotted Lady Alicia Dartry. The woman looked like she could skewer Charis on a spit and toss her into a fire.

"Is something wrong?" he queried.

"I think not," Charis said. After all, what could Lady Alicia do to her? But she was glad when Marcus deposited her with her mother again.

She watched as he joined Lady Alicia, who gave him the most fatuous smile Charis had ever seen.

She longed to do something to thwart Lady Alicia's ambitions with Marcus. There was a hint of something about her that Charis could not like. She'd watch and wait. It would come to her sooner or later. Marcus deserved better.

Chapter Five

"She danced every dance and two with Marcus," her mother proclaimed to Harriet the following morning when they met for breakfast.

"How nice!" Harriet said with a grin. "And? Did you meet any particular gentleman? Someone who captivated your heart?"

Charis glanced up to see Marcus watching her with an intent gaze. His dark hair fell across his brow as though he had been running his hand through it . . . in annoyance, most likely. Those blue eyes seemed darker than usual, and he looked positively grim. He certainly must be unhappy with her, wanting her out of his house and his life. Charis felt a shred of guilt gnaw at her, for she had pushed her way into his house, most likely causing no end of trouble for Marcus. Perhaps that was why he had kissed her in such a way—he was frustrated to distraction, unable to do as he pleased!

It was more imperative than ever before that she find an acceptable man to wed. She might not love Marcus but she did not want to make his life miserable. He had been spending a great deal of time at his club. She and her family had driven him from his home. Never mind that it had not long before been her home. She raised her brows in supplication.

"Actually, there were several I thought promising. Tell me, cousin, does Lord Vane have a fortune, or is he up to his neck in debt? He spoke of shopping for *marqueterie*, and Sevres, and pictures until my head whirled. Please do not tell me he needs an heiress."

"Very well, I will not. Actually, he is well to grass. His

grandfather left him a fortune, and he stands to inherit even more from his father. He believes in buying only the finest but otherwise is very careful with his money." Marcus turned his attention to his morning coffee.

"A stingy spender, how odd," Harriet said, chortling with delight.

"That does not make him less eligible," Charis objected.

"Of course not, dear," her mother inserted. "I seem to recall his father. He was also close with his money." At her daughter's questioning look, her mother added, "His wife often wore the same gown more than a few times, you see. Not that the present Lord Vane would be the same."

Feeling a trifle beleaguered, Charis went on. "Sir Henry Frogmorton was quite pleasant."

"Charis," Harriet exclaimed, "I forbid you to even think of becoming Lady Frogmorton. Think of your children. Imagine little Peregrine Frogmorton going to Eton! He would be teased unmercifully."

"No more so than Crakenthorpe. And his lordship was very amiable. You place too much on a name. The man is far more important," she declared with a defiant look at her cousin.

"Charis is right. Those men and others with names quite as unusual are not unacceptable merely because of a name. You first note the fortune, then the man. I have the right of it, do I not, Charis?" His gaze challenged hers. Was there a hint of scorn in those dark eyes?

She longed to toss something at that arrogant head. Of course he was correct in what he said, but it sounded terribly callous, as though money was her only concern.

"I do not think that is quite what Charis had in mind," her mother said. "I should dislike it very much." At their blank faces, she added, "If she marries only for money and a name. She needs more than that."

"True," Harriet added. "I think she ought to be madly in love with the gentleman. I shall never marry unless I am wildly in love."

"Well, at the moment I am mildly interested in several

of those I met last night. I must thank Marcus for introducing me to some of his friends." She dared him to sneer at her pursuit.

"Only two," he admitted. "Most of my friends are either married, engaged, or hunting for an heiress. They would not do for you, dear cousin."

"What do you plan to do?" her mother inquired of Charis after carefully putting her cup in its saucer, adding, "For today, dear?"

"We have been invited to take tea with Lady Penston and her two daughters. I fancy there will be several others there as well. Mama, you *do* plan to go?" Charis looked expectantly at her mother.

"Go? Oh, yes, the tea. I believe I should. Like to, that is. What time?" Her ladyship rose from her chair, leaving a scone on her plate and her tea half consumed.

"Three of the clock. I'll tell Mary so she can remind you to be ready." Charis took note of her mother's absentminded reaction with amusement.

"Do that, dear." Her ladyship wandered from the room, murmuring something about a dress.

"That is quite normal for her, I assure you," Charis told Marcus when he had raised a brow.

"I am aware that your mother is somewhat distracted at times. More to the point I am curious that you should accept the invitation to take tea with the Penston ladies."

Charis studied his face, trying to figure out what he thought. Then she blithely replied, "One must become acquainted with as many ladies as possible. One never knows when an eligible gentleman may be mentioned over the tea table. One can learn a great deal in that manner." She folded and refolded her linen napkin into different shapes, trying to avoid looking at him. In the end she forced herself to return his gaze.

He frowned. "You might do better to see your man of business to request a list of possible gentlemen who do not require an heiress."

The biting satire in his words cut Charis to her heart. "Do not think I particularly enjoy this search. I would far prefer to have a gentleman seek me out because he has fallen in love with my green eyes!"

"And they are a spectacular green at this point," he retorted.

Charis rose from the table, attempting to retain a semblance of dignity. "It is plain you do not admire green eyes. I wonder . . . what color eyes does Delilah have?" The moment the words were out, she wished them unsaid. If Marcus had looked cool before, he now wore an icily furious expression. Charis would be fortunate to escape with her head intact.

"Harriet, you will please leave us," he instructed, never taking his eyes from Charis.

Harriet took a fearful look at both and hurried from the room, carefully closing the door behind her.

Marcus had managed to come around the table with surprising speed. Charis had but taken two steps toward the door, and he was in front of her. This time he did not take her arms as before. He merely stood there, staring at her.

"What do you know of Delilah?" he demanded.

"Not a thing," Charis replied, thankful her voice was light and steady.

"But you know a name. What else?"

Charis gave up without a fight. She knew her cousin well enough to be aware he would be ruthless in his quest for an answer. She did not wish too much importance to be placed on her words. "All I know is that a person named Delilah wrote to you on lavender paper using violet ink and excessive violet scent." Charis wrinkled her nose at the very memory of it.

She wondered if that was a sigh of relief that he gave or possibly one of exasperation.

"There was a scrap of paper in the fireplace," Charis explained carefully.

"And you just had to read it?"

It seemed to her that his face lightened, although with Marcus it was often hard to tell.

"I thought you might need protection from some opportuning female. After all, you are handsome and wealthy and usually very nice. There are many women who might see this as a means to gaining a fortune, one way or another." She studied her hands, wondering what manner of scold he would read over her head. Marcus struck her as the sort of man who would not welcome interference in his life.

"And you do not?"

"Gracious me, no. I could never harm you, cousin. Besides . . ."

"Go on," he commanded gently.

"I would prefer that the man I marry be . . ." She looked up at him and took a swift breath at what she saw, or thought she saw, for it disappeared at once. She clamped her mouth shut. Nothing would persuade her to complete that sentence.

"Delilah is a person you need not concern yourself about. She is out of my life, most likely forever. Does that reassure your lovely active mind? I need no help, Charis."

"Well," she said thoughtfully, "you might have done so. Needed help, that is." She gave him a dismayed look. "Now you have me sounding like Mama!"

He laughed at her.

Charis was captivated by the rich sound. The wrinkles fanning out in his eyes were a bit deeper. The expression in his eyes—well—had it been possible, she would have thought it a tender look. That was nonsense, of course. Marcus had no reason to feel any tenderness toward her. She upset his life, heaven knows what else. But she had made him laugh.

"I promise you that if I find someone agreeable I shall marry him out of hand. I'll not be a burden on you any longer than I must." She placed her small hand over his, where it now rested on the top of a dining chair. His was a strong, capable hand, well formed and admirable.

He sobered at once. "You are not a burden in the way you may think you are. Promise me that you will not wed unless you are strongly enamored of the gentleman. In my mind that is the only reason to marry. I'd not see you tied to a man you cannot love just to achieve security."

His words whirled around in her mind. If she was not a financial burden, what manner of burden might she be?

"I do so promise," she said fervently. "But, Marcus, I do not understand you. I doubt I ever shall."

He gave her a wry look, then walked to the door. Upon opening it, they discovered an anxious Harriet in the hall outside. She clasped her hands, looking from one to the other as though searching for visible wounds.

"Well, how was I to know if Charis needed help when you finished with her," she said in her defense.

"Oh, I doubt I am finished with her, but you may console her for the moment."

He left them then, striding along the hall before he disappeared into the library.

"As I believe I said once before, what an odd man." Charis took Harriet in hand, and they went up to their mother's room.

They paused outside the sitting room.

"Did Cousin Marcus give you a scold over that name? And who is Delilah, anyway?" Harriet asked.

"He asked a few questions about what I knew of her, which is nothing. And that is true, I know nothing other than a name on a scrap of paper." It did not mean she would not try to find out, however. Charis had decided that anyone with a name like Delilah was suspect.

Even if Harriet was not able to attend Almack's with them because of the ticket problem, she could go everywhere else with them. And she did. Her care in dressing for the tea at the Penstons' proved a fine example of her concern.

"That pale periwinkle dress is truly lovely, Harriet," Charis said with a touch of surprise when they met in the sitting room later. "I'd not thought it a good color for you, but it is."

"It is soft enough so I ought to pass with all those who demand white. I do not look my best in white."

"Nor do I," Charis said with sympathy.

"Isobel and Barbara," her ladyship said suddenly.

Charis and Harriet exchanged looks. "Who?"

"The Penston chits. Know their mother."

"That likely explains our invitation," Charis said. "It will be nice to know a few more girls. You really have little time to become acquainted at a ball."

"Lady Penston was nice as a young lady. Ought to be the same. The girls, that is," their mother explained.

Accustomed to the way their mother's mind worked, the girls nodded, then made their way down to the entry, where Seymour saw them into a lovely landau.

When her ladyship demanded to know where it came from, the butler calmly replied, "Ordered by Sir Marcus for you. With this fine weather, the town carriage is a trifle warm. As well, I believe there is some repair work to be done on that," he added as an afterthought.

Surprised at his loquacity, Charis followed her mother and sister into the carriage. "How like Marcus to be so thoughtful for our comfort."

"Well," Harriet said, "it was our money only a little over a year ago."

Charis gave a warning shake of her head. There was no point in bringing up that matter, particularly when it might upset their mother.

The Penston town house was smaller than Huntingdon House, but very fine nonetheless.

It gratified Charis to see how graciously Lady Penston received her mother. You would never know by her reception that the Huntingdons were now penniless peeresses. Miss Isobel Penston and Miss Barbara were introduced and looked to be delightful young ladies.

The elegant room decorated in a Grecian style had surprisingly comfortable saber-legged chairs. A fashionable scroll-ended sofa covered in a brilliant peacock-blue stripe reminded Charis of one she had seen in a Sheraton catalog.

Sinking onto a chair covered in a startling shade of green, Charis studied the two young women, who chose the sofa.

"Please call me Isobel," said the elder. "We are so pleased that you could join us."

Barbara added, "And I am glad you came now, before the others arrive." She gave her sister a conspiratorial look. "There are others coming before long."

Charis glanced at Harriet. "We have been looking forward to meeting other young ladies who are also making their come-out in Society."

"I saw you at Almack's Wednesday last," Isobel said quietly with a guarded look at her mother. "Do you know Lady Alicia Dartry?"

"She came to dinner at Huntingdon House not long ago. Why?" Charis was surprised that Lady Alicia's name was brought up. She also wondered if Isobel had noted that narrowed stare Lady Alicia bestowed on Charis.

"Perhaps that might explain it. You are very lovely and, well, you do reside in the same house as Sir Marcus Rutledge." Isobel gave Charis an earnest look.

"I fail to see why that explains anything," Charis replied, deciding it was best to pretend total ignorance.

Isobel took a hasty glance at her mother, then rose. "Mama, may I show Lady Huntingdon and Lady Harriet the painting Papa commissioned?"

Seeming pleased, Lady Penston nodded permission then returned to her conversation with her old acquaintance.

Once the four girls were in the adjacent room, ostensibly admiring the fine portrait of Lady Penston, Isobel returned to the matter at hand. "I saw the way she looked at you, and that does not bode well. It is not good to incur her wrath."

"What can she do? I cannot think why she is angry with me. Sir Marcus is my cousin," Charis said, conveniently forgetting how distant.

"As I said, you are quite lovely. Perhaps she simply views you as a dangerous competitor." Isobel frowned, then continued, "Since you live in the same house, it gives you a decided advantage over her."

"I did not come to London with the thought I would

try to capture my cousin's attentions. My interest is much the same as any other girl—to make an advantageous marriage," Charis declared.

"There is naught else for us but that, is there?" Barbara agreed.

Harriet said nothing, but looked down at her neatly gloved hands.

"Forgive me if I seem forward, but at least you have a wonderful title. That must be an advantage," Isobel said with a lovely smile.

Charis almost explained about her lack of fortune, then thought better of it. It seemed best that few knew of her penniless state. Besides, she had just met Barbara and Isobel Penston. How did she know she might trust them? Even if they cautioned her against Lady Alicia— who seemed to have some antipathy toward Charis for some unknown reason.

"Well," she said at last, "there are those who object to red hair, so perhaps it is good to have some sort of advantage." She smiled broadly at them and was relieved when they smiled in return, setting aside the matter of Lady Alicia.

"We better go back, or Mama may wonder why we are here so long. But if Lady Alicia comes, do be cautious," Isobel warned.

"Have no fear. I have no intention of making any enemies."

"But you are a countess in your own right, and she is but the daughter of the Marquess of Berkshire. That gives you precedence over her. I suspect she might be jealous of that. This is her third Season, you know," Barbara said with a gleam in her eyes.

"Third Season," Charis repeated faintly. "I did not know that." It might explain why Lady Alicia wanted to claim Marcus. Well, good luck to her. Charis hoped it would take a great deal of conniving for Lady Alicia to become Lady Rutledge.

"She has given up on the other, higher peers," Isobel confided as they reentered the drawing room. "None of them came up to scratch."

As little as Charis knew of Lady Alicia, she vowed that Marcus would not "come up to scratch," either. "I confess that did surprise me—that the daughter of a marquess would settle for a mere baronet."

Isobel and Barbara smiled in return.

They had just resumed their places when a stir at the door brought two more guests, Lady Frogmorton and her young daughter, Jemima.

Harriet met her sister's eyes with a look of glee, then placed her hand over her mouth lest she giggle.

There was little chance to do more than be introduced to them before Lady Alicia entered with a harassed-looking lady who was announced as Lady Berkshire, her mother.

"Miss Penston and Miss Barbara, how lovely to see you again. Lady Huntingdon, charmed, indeed," Lady Alicia gushed in an insincere manner. She utterly ignored Jemima Frogmorton and Harriet.

Well, thought Charis, she might be charmed, but it failed to show in her eyes or her conduct.

Poor Lady Berkshire minced her way to where the elder Lady Huntingdon reigned along with Lady Penston. The three were immediately in conversation with Lady Frogmorton, adding a bit from time to time, all the while keeping an eye on her daughter.

"I must say I am surprised to see you here, Lady Huntingdon," Lady Alicia said in her patronizing way. "I trust your cousin is well today?"

"I must assume he is, Lady Alicia. I see very little of him." Which in a way was true. Except when he joined them for meals or she sought to visit with him for one reason or another, he was often gone. "I believe he spends much time at his club. And then of course he enjoys driving."

"Did you know he also sings? He is a member of a glee club, the Noblemen's and Gentlemen's Catch Club. Did you not know this? They meet every week, I believe. Women are not allowed to attend." She gave Charis a superior smile that she had known something which Charis obviously did not.

"He has a fine voice," Charis replied, for indeed his speaking voice had a pleasant quality to it.

Not knowing if Charis referred to his singing voice, Lady Alicia subsided, giving Charis a dubious look.

Tea was brought in with Miss Penston pouring, while Miss Barbara offered dainty biscuits and cakes. A maid stood in the background, ready to render assistance should it be required. Young ladies were expected to pour at tea, it being considered an admired ability in a wife.

Lady Alicia continued to dominate the conversation among the younger women, something the others seemed willing to allow. She talked about the balls she had attended, the people she knew, the parties she expected to attend.

At last Charis ventured to speak. "Lady Alicia, are you acquainted with Lord Portchester?"

"Slightly. Why do you ask?" the clearly vexed lady asked, likely annoyed at being interrupted in full spate.

"I should think you would make an admirable pair. He certainly thinks highly of you."

"And what makes you believe we would suit?" Lady Alicia demanded, preening a trifle at the unexpected compliment.

"You think alike," Charis replied sweetly.

Her remark left Lady Alicia speechless for several minutes, giving the others a chance to talk.

Charis chanced to glance at Isobel and was amused to note the look of approval in her eyes.

At last it was time to depart. Isobel nudged Charis to the rear of the group, not saying a word but indicating she hoped they would be last to leave.

The Frogmortons and Lady Huntingdon, with Harriet at her side, headed toward the stairs first, followed by the meek-looking Lady Berkshire. Lady Alicia gave Charis a cold stare, then came close to her, leaning forward to speak.

"I trust I do not have to tell you to continue to keep your distance from Sir Marcus. He needs a wife who can take a proper interest in his place in Society, not some

provincial miss who happens to have acquired a title."
She looked as though she would cheerfully throttle
Charis—with her gloves off, naturally.

"I will have you know that my title is an old and most
honorable one. And as to Marcus, I would wager he
holds a fine position in Society that needs no help from
anyone, least of all from the mere daughter of a marquess." Charis bestowed a sugary smile on Lady Alicia,
the sort one gave to a little child who is misbehaving in
public and promised reckoning later.

Lady Alicia was not about to take this lightly. "Oh,
you . . . You have been warned, my dear Lady Huntingdon."

"How interesting," Charis answered, trying to look as
puzzled as she felt. Warned? What could Lady Alicia do
to her? Nothing physical. She would not dare. But Lady
Alicia could certainly put a spoke in the wheel regarding
Charis's search for a husband among the *ton*.

With a haughty sniff, Lady Alicia followed the others
from the room and down the stairs.

"Good for you," Isobel whispered. "When we attend
the same parties, we must stand together. My Mama is
everywhere accepted, and she dotes on your mother. I
feel almost certain that we can counter anything Lady
Alicia attempts against you. But she could be an insidi-
ous enemy."

"Sir Marcus has agreed to take us to Almack's next
Wednesday," Charis said softly so that no one else
might hear.

"And she will be there!" Barbara said, sounding
quite horrified.

"If your mother could chaperone Harriet and me, the
three of us could present a united front," Charis said
thoughtfully.

"But it would look strange if your mother is not there
to lend support and countenance," Isobel suggested.

"Well, I will deal with matters as they develop. There
is little else to be done. But I thank you very much for
your help. You scarce know me."

"But we *do* know Lady Alicia," Barbara countered.

"Any woman whom she considers a rival must win our instant approval."

With the kind wishes of the Penston girls in her ears, Charis hastened down the stairs to join her mother and sister. Fortunately the landau had just arrived, so they were not anxious.

"You two girls appeared to enjoy the afternoon very much," the elder Lady Huntingdon declared, leaning back against the cushions with a sigh.

"Miss Penston and Miss Barbara are delightful. Was their mother that as well?" Harriet wondered.

"Indeed, yes. My, when I think back. We were close," Lady Huntingdon murmured, then lapsed into silence.

Charis exchanged a meaningful look with Harriet, then sat quietly until they reached Huntingdon House.

Once there, they urged their mother to take a rest before dinner. When she was settled, with the good Mary in attendance, the two girls found comfortable chairs in the sitting room.

With Ruff curled in her lap, Charis turned to Harriet. "Lady Alicia would dearly love to get her claws into Marcus. The sad thing is that I dare not say a word to him."

"Why not? He ought to be warned what manner of woman she is," Harriet insisted.

"Not after the go-round we had this morning," Charis said sadly. "He says he needs no help of any kind, from me or anyone else. Poor man. I do not see how she can be stopped. She is a very determined and probably desperate woman. If this is her third Season, that would stand to reason. Had she an enormous fortune, her finicky behavior would be explained. But she's all sweetness to him."

"I thought her family was wealthy," Harriet said.

"All the money—save for her dowry—goes with the title to her brother, who is much favored by his father."

"Perhaps you ought to cultivate him?" Harriet suggested with a gleam in her eyes.

"Good grief, no. I would not want anything to do with that family!" Charis exclaimed.

"What family do you so despise, cousin?" Marcus inquired, leaning against the open door they had forgotten to close.

Charis sought Harriet's eyes, silently cautioning her to say nothing. "You seem to pop up when least expected, cousin. And I do not despise them, precisely. But there are families which I would not wish to join," Charis explained, choosing her words with care.

"I agree on that score, and I will not ask you to reveal which family has incurred your displeasure. At least—not at present. You like music, do you not? There is a charming opera to be performed this evening. Would you consider joining me in my box?"

"All of us?" Charis asked politely.

He gave her a puzzled look, as though wondering what prompted that particular reply. "Of course. It would be improper for you to go with me alone—even if we are cousins." He proceeded to give them the time they were to leave, mentioned the work to be performed, then left.

"I do hope that Lady Alicia is not fond of the opera or that she intends to be elsewhere this evening," Charis said, giving Ruff a fond brushing.

"You should be so fortunate," Harriet said, looking worried.

Chapter Six

Garbed in a pale green gown of deceptive simplicity that beautifully draped her slender figure, Charis joined her mother and sister in the dining room.

Marcus followed her, remarking, "It is quite amazing how prompt you three are. I was under the impression that women were never on time for anything."

"Obviously you have been seeing the wrong sort of women, cousin. You ought to give more thought to your companions." Charis smiled demurely, took her seat at the table, and consumed her dinner with the air of one who looks forward to an evening of pleasure.

Marcus studied her from time to time, looking puzzled, but he made no remark about her comment. Clearly he did not expect her to know of his interest in any particular woman, in spite of the fact she did know Delilah's name and that she was likely the wrong sort.

As for Charis, she had dismissed Lady Alicia, assuming that most of the interest was on her side. She could not imagine that a man as dashing as Marcus would settle for a cold fish like Lady Alicia. The Divine Delilah was evidently something else entirely. It would take daring or stupidity to write a letter to a gentleman in the first place, then to use lavender paper and violet ink was almost scandalous.

Charis considered her ladyship and the unknown Delilah. Cousin Marcus must have terrible taste in women. It might be difficult to accomplish, but she intended to help in some manner. First, she would learn more about this Delilah creature. She needed to find some man who would let her identity slip out, for it was clear she was not a proper lady—not with a name like Divine Delilah, signed in violet ink after a gushing sentiment.

Then perhaps she would find some way to expose Lady Alicia. He needed to see for himself what a mean-spirited creature she was. He probably thought her the pink of perfection she showed when he was present.

Once dinner was over, they immediately left for the Opera House. The streets leading to the Haymarket were crowded with carriages.

"I have not seen this production by Mozart," the elder countess declared. "I trust it is amusing? I dislike those distressing operas where everyone seems to die."

Marcus nodded his head, although whether in agreement it could not be said. "*Le Nozze di Figaro* is a comedy that ought to please you, for there is not the slightest hint of tragedy in it. I vow you will find it entertaining."

"I fail to see how a marriage could be a comedy," Charis said in objection.

"It is the series of mix-ups and confusions that are amusing." His eyes held a hint of mirth, and Charis decided it would be fun to tease him a little.

"More like a farce, then. That is, so many marriages seem to be based on pretense nowadays, from what I see and hear. The husband goes to his clubs and ah, interests—hunting, the races, and the like. The wife calls on her friends and arranges parties. I can see where there might be mix-ups and confusions were things to alter even a trifle."

"You see marriage as a farce?"

"I would not want my marriage to be such, but I fancy there are more than a few of them. That is why it is wise to take care when choosing a spouse. It is good to catch your intended off guard so that you might know his or her true temperament." Charis thought of Lady Alicia.

"You are correct," her mother inserted, surprising Charis, who thought she was not paying attention.

The discussion ended when they arrived at the Opera House.

The box Marcus held offered an excellent view of the

stage. It also presented a very good view of the audience. Charis could not see who else might be on their side of the theater, but she could see who sat across from them. She casually scanned the various tiers to see if she could recognize anyone.

Marcus settled her mother on a comfortable chair. Harriet plumped herself next to her mother, craning her neck to see everything at once, if possible.

"Here," Marcus said with a gesture to a chair close to the front of the box, "you will see better from this vantage point."

Charis contentedly accepted her seat, catching sight of Lady Alicia on the other side as she did. Her ladyship did not appear the slightest bit pleased at the sight of Charis with Sir Marcus.

Refusing to be intimidated by that icicle, Charis thought it might be fun to flirt with Marcus a bit. It was not as though they were brother and sister, or even close cousins. He was but a distant relative and as such, fair game.

"I should like to know what is going on behind those green eyes this evening. They positively glitter with mischief, I'd say." Marcus leaned forward to better see her face, drawing his chair closer to hers.

"It is merely that I have not had the chance to see a production like this before. There is no theater in the country, you know." Seizing the moment, Charis curved her lips into what she hoped was a seductively alluring smile and fluttered her lashes a bit. She did not want to overdo her flirtation. Tempt, that was her intent.

Marcus looked thoughtful but did not say anything. However, he shifted his chair a trifle closer, pointing out some of the more socially prominent people as he did.

"I must get about more," Charis said. "If I am to find a husband, I cannot remain quietly at home. Who knows, the man I should marry may be seated right out there." She grinned at her cousin, tilting her head in what she hoped was a provocative manner.

Marcus glanced over the patrons and shook his head. "Perhaps."

Following a rap on the door to the box, a gentleman entered, spoke quietly with Marcus, then bowed to Charis.

"The Countess Huntingdon, Anna, Countess Huntingdon, and Lady Harriet Dane, may I present Lord Pilkington." Marcus introduced his friend, then stood aside.

Charis did not know what Harriet thought, but in her opinion Lord Pilkington was definitely a dandy. Were his shirt points any higher, they would stab his cheek. His cravat was a masterful concoction but overpowered his attire. And as for his waistcoat, well, Marcus would never wear such an outrageous pattern or color. He was certainly colorful, combining puce, lime green, and blue in his attire. But he did look kind and had nice eyes.

"Won't you ask Lord Pilkington to join us, cousin? There are more than enough chairs." She gave Marcus a limpid smile. Even dandies had friends, and she could ill afford to overlook any potential.

Put on the spot, Marcus did as requested but gave Charis an inquiring look that told her he was at sea as to why she would want the company of this chap.

She was disappointed when she had no chance to inquire about Lord Pilkington and his interests. The curtain went up and the performance began.

A delightful woman had the role of Susanna, and Charis thought her fetching in her pretty costume. She found it sometimes confusing as the various characters sashayed forth and then disappeared. In time she figured out the plot, and by the end of Act One, she thought that although it was clear that Susanna and Figaro would eventually marry, there certainly were plenty of obstacles in their path, not the least of which was Count Almaviva.

"Now, there is an example of a marriage gone wrong. See how the count flirts with every woman who comes near him? Utterly disgraceful. And his wife obviously adores him. What a fool he is," Charis whispered.

Marcus pursed his lips, looking down at her with amusement. "A man can flirt, particularly with a pretty woman, and if that is all there is to it, no harm is done."

"Would you be given to flirting were you married?"

Charis demanded to know, but keeping her voice soft enough so her mother could not hear. Considering the noise in the theater, it was not all that difficult. She gave her cousin a wide-eyed look she hoped would seem a bit coy.

"It depends on my wife. Should she keep me, ah, occupied at home, there is no need to look elsewhere."

His low voice sent a thrill of disquiet through Charis. She was not certain what he meant by keeping him occupied, but judging from the gleam in his eyes, she did not want to ask.

She digested that for a bit, then turned to where Lord Pilkington leaned over to speak to Harriet. "What is your view of flirting among wedded people, my lord?"

"I did not do it, 'pon my word." His lordship anxiously glanced about as though expecting to be accused of such.

"Just in general, Perry," Marcus added kindly.

The gentleman gave Charis a wary look. "One needs to be very careful about these things, you know." What else he might have said was not to be known, for the curtain rose once more to reveal the apartment of the Countess Almaviva.

The lament of the countess regarding her wayward husband, sure he no longer loved her, was touching, and Charis leaned over to tap Marcus on the arm. "How sad she is. How can this be a comedy?"

"It ends happily, is that not the criteria for a comedy?" He picked up her hand closest to him, toying with her fingers while he gazed into her eyes.

Of a sudden Charis found it impossible to reply. Even though she wore the obligatory gloves, she could feel the warmth of his hand. When she peered up at him, she could not even recall what had been said. Her mind was in a whirl. Maybe she should forget about teasing him. She hadn't expected him to react like this!

"There is a happy ending, cousin." He actually smiled at her, and Charis completely forgot the performance going on below. It was a good thing her cousin smiled but seldom. He would have half the women in London

trailing after him if he treated more of them to that
smile.

"See how Figaro plans to secure his bride?" Marcus
whispered, nudging Charis back to the performance.

"Well, I think that silly young page ought to keep his
nose out of the affairs of others," she countered shortly.

"That is frequently the case. It seems so often that
there are people who are not content unless they are
putting their noses into someone else's concerns."

Charis wondered if Marcus had developed the ability
to read minds. Ridiculous! Of course he could not. It
was merely an ordinary remark. Perhaps he had seen
something of that in Society. Considering all the gossips
and troublemakers, it would not be surprising. She was
not in the least like that, however. She meant this for
her cousin's own good. She just wanted to protect him.

Turning her attention back to the stage, she concentrated on the convoluted plot. Her Italian was rudimen-
tary, but she caught the gist of what was going on. She
laughed when Susanna attempted to give the page, Cherubino, lessons on how to act like a woman.

"Amusing, is it not?" Marcus whispered in her ear.

Charis glanced up at him to discover he was far closer
than he had been before. Did she not know better, she
would believe him to be flirting with her! He slid his arm
across the back of her chair, ostensibly so he could lean
over to point out something in her program. But his arm
remained there, and she found it difficult to concentrate
on the problems of Susanna and Countess Almaviva. She
was quite relieved when the second act ended and they
could resume talking. This flirtation thing could easily
get out of hand.

Marcus allowed his arm to stay where it was.

Charis shifted uneasily on her chair.

Harriet turned a wide-eyed gaze on them both.

Lord Pilkington fidgeted with his cravat.

The elder countess spent her time with her glasses,
searching the spectators, presumably for old friends.

The third act commenced none too soon for Charis.
The wedding festivities were underway. The count's ne-

farious plans were definitely shaken when it turned out that Figaro was the son of a noble family and proved it. Rejoicing followed, but that did not end the plotting. Charis chuckled as the count lamented that all seemed to go wrong for him.

"Serves the old lecher right," she confided to Marcus. "Anyone who behaves as *he* does ought to have his plans thwarted."

He merely gave her a benign look and did not remove his arm from the back of her chair.

She was relieved when Act Three concluded. That meant there was but one act remaining and she could escape.

Someone entered the rear of the box. Charis twisted in her seat to see an elderly gentleman approach her mother.

"Lady Huntingdon, you are a sight for sore eyes. How many years has it been since we last met? I was amazed to see you up here, but then, Sir Marcus is your nephew."

The elder countess greeted her old friend with pleasure, introducing General Sir William Kingsley to the rest.

"Sir William now. Left the army. Getting too old for all those hardships. Thought it time to settle down and find me a nice estate." He beamed a smile on the lady he admired, and Charis wondered if perhaps he might be looking for a wife with whom to share that estate. She would be glad for her mother, for she needed a strong man to lean upon, and the ex-general looked all of that. And Mama was but rising fifty.

Marcus began to lazily trace a pattern on Charis's shoulder, just above the line of her gown, and she stiffened. It was one thing for her to flirt with him, quite another for him to trifle with her.

"Cousin . . ." she began in a warning voice.

"Hmm?" He sounded as innocent as a lamb.

Then the curtain went up. There was no chance to say more with her mother hushing everyone so she could hear better.

"See, decorations are set for the wedding. Be assured that all will end as it should." Marcus continued with his teasing assault on her bare shoulder. Never mind the stage wedding. He was distracting her. How could she be calm?

"That lecherous old count will still try to compromise Susanna, poor girl." Charis could not help but feel indignant. She had heard tales of such, and this confirmed it. Men were not entirely to be trusted.

"There are times when a woman is so tempting and tantalizing to a man that he forgets all else," Marcus murmured in her ear, disturbing not only her senses but also the little curl that hung there.

"How interesting," Charis stammered. Tempting and tantalizing sounded quite delightful, but she was not certain she could sustain it under such a sensual counterattack from her cousin. He was not supposed to do that!

At that point sanity returned. On the stage Cherubino tried to make love to Susanna, who was actually the countess wearing Susanna's dress. The count walked in and attempted to kiss the woman he believed to be Susanna and wound up kissing Cherubino instead. Rather than hit Cherubino, the count punched Figaro, who had wandered into the room.

Charis thought it rather funny when the count made love to the woman he believed to be Susanna and was his wife instead. She laughed at all the tomfoolery that followed, almost, but not quite, forgetting that touch on her shoulder. In fact, she unconsciously leaned into that touch, quite disregarding how outrageously he was behaving.

At the conclusion of the opera, Marcus removed his hand from her chair, commenting, "You see, the count begs his countess for forgiveness and all is well. Susanna and Figaro are wed, and the villagers are happy."

"I suspect the countess never quite trusts him again. How could she?" Charis turned to stare up into her cousin's dark eyes.

"If you love someone enough, you can forgive almost anything," Marcus replied simply.

Charis wondered what it might be like to know his love. Which had to be a silly thought, for she needed to find a husband and Marcus was not likely to look her way. Even if she wanted him, and she assured herself that she did not, he could have anyone he desired. She doubted he would desire her!

Her mother said, "Sir William has invited us all to join him in a later supper. Would that be agreeable to you?" she asked Marcus.

"Why not? We shall be a jolly group after this comedy." He rose, assisted Charis from her chair, then waited while the others left the box first, detaining Charis by the simple means of tucking her arm against him.

"Be careful how you flirt, little cousin. I'd not like those delectable fingers or lips to be burned."

Charis gave him a highly indignant look. She'd just flirted with him, no other. She walked silently at his side as they left the box, continuing along the hall and down the stairs to join the others near the doors.

Also waiting for them was Lady Alicia Dartry with her parents. She was wearing the white usually seen on girls in the first year of their come-out. The gown did not become her, nor did the irritated expression on her face.

"Sir Marcus, I had no idea you planned to attend the opera this evening." She pointedly ignored Charis and the others, concentrating on Marcus.

"He is a dear to take us all to hear such a delightful performance," Charis said with unfeigned enthusiasm. She beamed a bright smile at her cousin, thankful she could praise him, for he deserved it—at least for his thoughtfulness. She disregarded his teasing, for the moment.

"Lady Alicia, you well know how fond of music I am. I wished to share the evening with my relatives." Marcus gave her a bland look that said utterly nothing.

She tittered. "Of course, I fancy they have seen nothing like it living so retired in the country."

"Yes, indeed," Charis replied gently, trying not to grit her teeth. "We country folk do enjoy a bit of high living when we get the opportunity."

"Time for us to be gone." Marcus glanced at Charis, the clock, then urged his party and Sir William to the doors.

"Marcus," Lady Huntingdon said in a surprisingly firm voice for her, "I do not care for that young lady. I trust she is but a distant acquaintance." Apparently her ladyship had totally forgotten that Lady Alicia had attended a dinner with them not long ago. Perhaps Mama considered her eminently forgettable?

"One meets all manner of people in London, Lady Huntingdon. At times it requires tact and diplomacy to deal with them." Marcus held Charis tightly to his side, not allowing her to sidle away from him.

"Hmpf," the elder Lady Huntingdon replied.

"How thoughtful of you to see that I do not trip, cousin," Charis said as they were about to enter one of the carriages drawn up to take them to the hotel where Sir William wished to entertain them with a late supper. She had hoped to speak with Lord Pilkington, and Marcus had thwarted her efforts.

"Oh, I have no doubt you will trip sooner or later. I did not wish it to be here and now."

She gave him an affronted look before entering the carriage. It helped not the slightest that he followed her into the vehicle and sat closely at her side.

"Beware, little cousin."

"You cannot do a thing to me. You are no more than a distant cousin, after all."

"Yes, I know." Marcus spoke close to her ear, softly, almost ominously.

It was not his words—it was the way he said them that sent tremors down her spine. Charis looked out of the carriage window with unseeing eyes, wondering how on earth she was going to find a husband when it was clear to her that she found Marcus too interesting by half.

The carriage drew to a halt, and they were escorted into the Clarendon hotel, then to a private dining room. Apparently the general had sent word ahead to have everything in readiness for his group. It spoke well of him and his ability to organize. He certainly was the sort of man her mother would like. From what Charis could tell, he seemed very nice.

Marcus made no effort to tease her once they were in the hotel. Indeed, one might think he had not the slightest awareness of her. None at all!

Indignant at his inconsistency, Charis turned to poor Lord Pilkington. He might not turn her upside down, but on the other hand he was comfortable, nice.

Sir William had ordered a splendid repast, and Charis found she was far more hungry than she realized. At her side Marcus also ate well. As for Lord Pilkington, Charis wondered how he ate at all, considering his tight garments. They did not look the sort that offered comfort, but he inhaled lobster patties with amazing appetite.

The evening drew to a predictable close. Sir William asked to call on the elder Lady Huntingdon the following day. Lord Pilkington did as well. Marcus remained silent, but then he lived with them and Charis doubted he would have called on them regardless. She did not think she was the sort of woman to appeal to him. Not when she considered Lady Alicia and that Delilah creature. Perhaps Charis was somewhere in between the two.

Marcus listened to the steps of the women as they went up to their rooms while he entered his library. He poured a generous glass of fine old brandy, then settled on his favorite chair by the fire.

He must have been out of his mind this evening to tease Charis as he had. But . . . Charis had been so tempting. Little fool, playing with fire as she did. Fluttering her lashes and offering that seductive smile that lit up those gorgeous green eyes. Did she have the slightest notion of how appealing she was? Or the effect that smile could have on a man?

Marcus glanced at the stack of mail that he had ignored this afternoon. Idly he flipped through the letters, then stiffened when he found one written on lavender paper and addressed with violet ink. He did not have to wonder who wrote this missive, but why had she done so?

Considering how badly she wrote it took a little time to make out her scribble. Not satisfied with the congé gift, she thought she deserved more. Grasping, greedy creature! She'd not get another farthing from him. He was well rid of the chit. He had heard a rumor that one of the men he'd expected to take her under his protection had done just that. One day she would find her greediness would get her into trouble.

He was about to toss the letter into the fire when Charis entered the room, first pausing hesitantly at the doorway. "May I find a book? I need something dull that is likely to put me to sleep."

"Help yourself," he replied, not bothering to rise from his chair. "I'm catching up on my correspondence. That is dull enough."

She glanced at him, but seemed to pay no attention to what he had in hand or his stack of letters. Without a doubt she wanted a book and had not the slightest interest in his mail—not even the violet missive that had drawn her curiosity before. Marcus waited for her to speak.

"Ah, a book on plants. It is interesting, yet may serve admirably to put me to sleep. Good night, Marcus. I thank you again for the lovely evening and hope you enjoyed it a little. It was a lovely opera and my first."

"You like music?" For some illogical reason he wanted to detain her, even if he knew it might be inviting trouble.

"Very much. Mama has told me how they used to have concerts at the Pantheon. What a pity that is no more. It seems a shame for an elegant building to stand empty. Is there not a way it can be used?"

"The other theaters did not care for the competition. Did she tell you there was a fire? If I learn of another musical evening that I believe you might enjoy, I promise to take you to it." He wondered if he could manage another evening of being so close to her entrancing shoulders. All that bare skin ought to be forbidden in a young woman. That he had seen as much bare skin displayed on Lady Alicia and not had the slightest reaction, he did not consider.

"How very kind you are. I hope your mail is good." She gave him a misty smile, then hurried from the room, book in arms."

"Now," Marcus addressed the flames, "what prompted that hasty adieu?" He tossed the scented letter into the flames, this time making sure that it burned completely.

He was sorry that Charis had not ordered that gown of gold tissue. It would have become her admirably. There was a faint dusting of gold freckles on the bridge of her nose. That was what had made him think of gold tissue in the first place. Madame had his cousin's measurements. It would be but the work of a few minutes to stop by her elegant little shop and place the order himself. He might as well order something he would enjoy looking at if he were to pay for his cousin's wardrobe.

Indeed, he could well imagine what that gold tissue gown would look like on his attractive cousin. What a pity his uncle had written that wretched will. It had totally thwarted his plans for Charis. She had all the reason in the world to dislike him, certainly not any warmer feeling.

Charis placed the book on botany on her night table. Deep in thought, she absently began to undo her gown. He had another of those letters written in violet ink on lavender paper. What did that woman want now? While she did not know for certain, she suspected that women of that ilk were demanding creatures.

Poor Marcus, to be so imposed upon. It was imperative that she learn who this woman was. That Charis had not the slightest notion what she would do if she found out was beside the point.

"He truly needs someone to look after him," she informed Ruff, who had jumped up on her bed. The dog sat looking at her with his head tilted as though in question.

Charis smoothed that soft coat, gazing fondly into

those beautiful brown eyes. Ruff had a brown patch that surrounded one eye, both ears were brown as was the back of his head. The rest of his body was white, which meant he needed a bath often if he thought he would snuggle up to Charis on her bed.

"You would help me if you could, would you not?" she asked her pet in a quiet voice.

The dog gave her a solemn look and tilted his head in the other direction. He gave a short bark, then wagged his tail as though he was in total sympathy with her.

"Tomorrow we shall take a walk in the park at the fashionable hour and see what happens. I have noticed that most men like dogs. I cannot imagine anyone not liking you."

With Ruff curled up at her side, Charis read a bit, then blew out her candle. Tomorrow looked promising. With any luck at all she would perhaps meet a gentleman in the park. She'd take Harriet along as well as Mary.

They really needed a maid of their own, but hesitated to request one, for she was not quite certain how Marcus would react. It seemed to Charis that they were enough of a burden now.

She slid into sleep and dreamed of a tall and handsome gentleman who looked far too much like her cousin.

Chapter Seven

Wednesday brought the longed for and worried about evening at Almack's once again. Charis had a new gown from Madame Clotilde, a fragile-looking pale jonquil dress of sheer jaconet trimmed with the prettiest wisps of fine lace that she had ever seen.

Her mother nodded approval while smoothing down her gown of a delightful violet, reminding Charis all too clearly of that dreadful letter that had so angered Marcus.

He said nothing when he joined them, however. If he even noticed the lavender gown, it was more than Charis could see. He had kept his word and escorted them to the boring confines of the assembly rooms, where the *haut ton* elected to meet once a week in their matrimonial bazaar.

Charis spotted Miss Penston right away and joined her as soon as possible. The girl was garbed in a delicious gown of lavender-blue that nicely complimented her fine blue eyes.

"Isobel, how glad I am to see you," Charis said.

"I am happy to see you as well," Isobel replied. "There is an interesting collection of people here this evening. I cannot believe you persuaded your cousin to bring you again! He usually never attends."

Charis saw her mother settled with Lady Penston, then turned her attention once more to her new friend.

"Lady Alicia is present and is fixing her gaze on your cousin," Isobel said. "It is a wonder he isn't drawn to her side by the mere force of her stare. I am surprised no one else notices."

Charis nodded. No one paid the slightest attention to Lady Alicia. Or so it seemed. "Perhaps they do and are too polite to indicate so." Charis glanced around to see Lord Portchester approaching with Lord Baylor in tow. "I believe we have partners for the next dance at any rate."

"How very nice," Isobel whispered as the gentlemen neared.

Not far away Charis could see Marcus chatting with several gentlemen. She was delighted when he noted her partner and frowned. Well, he could introduce her to more of his own particular friends who would be eligible if he found Lord Portchester objectionable.

He was in fine form. He danced no better but had a tidy collection of tales to impart to do with his new carriage and driving in the park. It seemed as though his life revolved around his drives about town. Charis wondered rather uncharitably if his driving had improved.

Isobel performed her part of the dance with exceptional grace, and it was nice to see how impressed Lord Baylor appeared to be with her.

"Your friend seems a pleasant girl. Does she like to drive out?" Lord Portchester inquired when he met Charis in the pattern of the dance.

"I suppose so. Lord Baylor seems taken with her, I must say." Charis wondered if she had spoken too soon, considering that the pair had just met. Yet the smiles shared and the looks exchanged certainly pointed to an instant rapport or more. Well, Isobel had a tidy portion, according to what Mama said. Lord Baylor, while not seeming to need the money, was doubtlessly willing to welcome an infusion of funds into his coffers should his chosen be so gifted.

"Hm," Lord Portchester murmured, then went on to explain the latest design in whips he had managed to locate.

One thing she had to say on his behalf was that it took little mental ability to follow his conversation. She was free to inspect the other dancers if she chose.

Isobel and Charis had been properly returned to their

mothers when Marcus approached with two gentlemen. He introduced them at once.

"Lady Huntingdon and Miss Penston, may I present Lord Crackenthorpe and Sir Henry Frogmorton."

Charis gave Marcus a limpid smile. "I believe I have met Sir Henry before if I make no mistake. How pleasant to see you again, sir."

Isobel smiled and said all that was polite. Her glance strayed to where Lord Baylor stood at the far end of the room. He stood alone and watched them while smiling slightly.

The introduction to the next dance struck up, and the two gentlemen led Isobel and Charis to join the others.

The ensuing dance was unremarkable. The conversation was extremely proper, what little there was during a country-dance. Charis was not unhappy to return to her mother. How she would select one of these gentlemen, she didn't know. Was the world full of insipid men?

Isobel had somehow ended up at the opposite end of the room. Lord Baylor looked delighted to escort her back to where her mother sat.

"Sits the wind in that direction, does it?" Marcus murmured to Charis as they watched the happy pair approach chatting eagerly and ignoring the rest of the room.

"I suspect it may. He seems a nice man. Is he?"

"Member of my glee club, and a finer chap you couldn't want. There is a waltz next, and I claim it by right of being your cousin," Marcus said, a smile lighting his eyes.

With more than a little trepidation, Charis agreed and accepted his hand. She had not forgotten a single moment of that last waltz with him. It seemed that this waltz was to be equally memorable.

She glimpsed Isobel standing at the edge of the room with Lord Baylor in attendance. After that, the room might have been empty for all she knew.

"I think you are improving, little cousin," Marcus said after a number of whirls.

"Well, since you are more or less my teacher, I should hope so," Charis retorted.

Marcus did not reply to that silly statement.

Charis was surprised that they completed the waltz in silence. She had expected a quiz regarding the other gentlemen, perhaps a query on her prospects. He said nothing more and even looked faintly grim. She had thought him stone-hearted once, and certainly he looked all of that at the moment. While she still felt a certain trembling of being in his arms, none of the other emotions she had known before recurred. It was as though he waltzed with her against his will, which had to be mad. He had asked and seemed to want this dance. So why did he look *such* a way?

When the dance concluded, he returned her to her mother. Once he had bowed, he disappeared into the side room where cards were played for what Charis had been told was mere chicken-stakes. She did not see him again until they left.

Proper dances followed with equally proper partners. Apparently her waltz with Marcus had placed the seal on her acceptance as it had the last time they danced. She glanced around to see if Lady Alicia had found a partner, but she was not to be seen. Perhaps she left early once Marcus retired to the card room? It was pleasant not to have to sense that beastly gaze piercing her back.

At last the dowager collected Charis, declaring they must leave. Marcus was found at once by an alert servant. Within a brief time farewells were made, and they were outside of the building awaiting the carriage.

"Thank you, cousin, for escorting us this evening," Charis managed to say in a subdued voice once the carriage was underway. "I fear it was rather tame stuff for you."

"Nonsense," her mother inserted. "Marcus has always been the one to do it." When the others looked at her, she added, "His duty, of course. As is only right and proper."

Charis thought that being considered nothing more

than a duty was just about the most depressing thought in the world.

Seymour opened the door, ushering the elderly Lady Huntingdon to the stairs with kind courtesy.

Charis entered but paused to stare at her cousin. "I am sorry this so imposes on your time, cousin. I shall release you from the promise to escort us to Almack's again. If I could, I would leave here now and restore your peace and quiet that we have disrupted."

"Rubbish. If I were not seen with you, it would be all over Town that you were in my black books. Another Wednesday will not harm me. You will remain here." The look he gave her was utterly unfathomable.

Charis curtsied, then hurried up the stairs to her room, where for some silly reason she dissolved into tears.

The following morning Marcus entered the breakfast room looking his usual chiseled self. Charis thought he could have posed for a marble statue without any effort at all, particularly when he looked at her.

"All is well, cousin?" she inquired. She folded her napkin on her plate and prepared to escape.

"You enjoyed last evening, I trust?" he said before sampling his just-poured coffee.

"Indeed, you have been more than generous in taking us about—to Almack's, Vauxhall, and the opera. I do think you best introduce me to a few more gentlemen, however. Or is there something terribly wrong with me that so few gentlemen come to call?" Charis shot him a worried look, wondering if she had stumbled into trouble and not been aware of it. She had done that at home often enough. Mama blamed it on her red hair. Perhaps that was why none of the men who lived nearby the estate were interested in her. Or else it was merely the financial aspect that turned them away. Whatever it was, she had not seen hide nor hair of all her country swains since her father's death.

"There is not a thing wrong with you that I can see. While it is true you have no fortune, you do posses a title. That is something a number of men would like to obtain for a son—or a daughter in the event there is no son." He took another sip of coffee before returning his cup to the saucer.

"Cits, I suppose," she muttered. "If it were up to me, I would remain single rather than marry someone who is ill-bred. I daresay I can exist without a fortune. But I need enough for Mama and Harriet." She gave him a defiant look, hoping he would have pity on her frustration.

Marcus leaned back in his chair after signaling the footman to bring a plate of breakfast to him. "You have a little time yet. You worry too much. Enjoy your Season. Perhaps the man you want will come to you when you least expect it." His expression was enigmatic to say the least.

Charis rose from her chair, waving her hand at Marcus to indicate that he should remain seated. "Very well, I will do as you suggest, although not without protest."

"Your protest is duly noted." He accepted the plate covered with an ample breakfast. It was more than Charis could have eaten in three mornings.

She slipped from the breakfast room to hunt for her sister. Today Charis intended to take matters into her own hands, regardless of her assurances to Marcus. She would take a nice long walk in the park at the fashionable hour and see what she could catch. Harriet had to join her.

"My lady," Seymour said as Charis neared the stairs, "if you intend to go walking, you now have a maid to attend you. Sir Marcus ordered one be fetched immediately. I expect she is in your rooms awaiting you."

"Thank you, Seymour. I trust you did not have to rise too early to obey his order?" How like Marcus to demand a maid be conjured out of nowhere, then say nothing to Charis.

"Not at all, my lady."

Charis nodded and began her walk up the stairs, carefully holding her gown so she'd not trip. Of course Seymour wouldn't tell her if he had left the house at dawn.

She hoped that Marcus could mellow a trifle. He had

lived alone for too long. It was a pity his parents had caught such a nasty bout of influenza and died when he was but a lad at Eton. It had turned Marcus into a self-reliant man who appeared to need no one. The only person who had influenced his life was her father. That likely accounted for the gift of the estate. It was a pity Papa simply couldn't have given him the title as well for all the good it did Charis.

There was a plain girl in a gingham dress waiting for her just as Seymour had said. Brown eyes gave Charis an apprehensive peep before her gaze dropped to the floor. She was neat and looked clean, a good sign to Charis.

"What is your name?" Charis said, gathering Ruff in her arms so he would cease his inquisitive prowl around the maid.

"Betty, ma'am." The maid again peeked up at Charis as though she expected to be reprimanded for something. What that might be, Charis couldn't imagine.

"Well, Betty, I intend to take Ruff for a walk now. Will you be so good as to join me? I suspect Harriet would prefer to remain at home. She always appears to be occupied with something or another lately."

Betty bobbed a curtsy, then inquired what bonnet was wanted and did milady wish a pelisse, as the morning was coolish.

Once all was set, the pair with Ruff in tow set out for the park. Disdaining the notion that the maid ought to walk behind her, Charis wanted to become acquainted with the girl. Her brown eyes seemed too large in her thin face, and her dress hung on her. But Charis knew that Seymour would not have selected her to serve had she not obtained good references.

Nothing was forthcoming, alas. Charis had to be satisfied that she had company and hadn't been compelled to nudge her sister from her room.

Ruff found an intriguing scent and was rummaging around some ivy when Charis saw Lord Egerton riding her way on a large chestnut gelding.

When he drew alongside, he dismounted to join her where she stood patiently with Ruff.

"So this is the dog Marcus mentioned. Clever little fellow, eh?" He knelt down and, to her amazement, coaxed Ruff to his side with the snap of his fingers.

"He is a good friend and comfort when I want one. Thank heavens he is trained. Marcus would never tolerate anything less!" she said with a laugh.

"Ah, there you very much mistake him. In spite of that cool exterior, he is a nice man." Lord Egerton rose to face her, an assessing expression on his face.

"If you say so. I confess that at times he does surprise me." She tugged at the lead, and Ruff obediently trotted along as she walked. Lord Egerton also walked with her, holding the reins with his horse trailing along behind.

They strolled along for a time, chatting about little or nothing when he asked, "You ride, of course?"

"I fear not. I fell badly as a child and never could be persuaded to remount," she admitted. She waited for the old saw about getting on the horse again as soon as possible and all the other advice she had heard more times than she could mount. None came.

"Pity. It is a pleasant way to spend an hour or two. Perhaps you may be persuaded to attempt it again one day?"

"Perhaps. Tell me, do you think Marcus intends to marry Lady Alicia?" Charis inquired with great daring. She knew it was not proper to put poor Lord Egerton on the spot, but she guessed that he'd not reply if uncomfortable with the thought.

"Somehow I doubt it. Although he said something once about needing to acquire a proper wife."

"I hope he doesn't. He deserves someone finer." Charis studied the walk ahead of her, unwilling to face her companion for the moment. It wasn't like Charis to vilify another woman to anyone, much less a gentleman. Lady Alicia had almost become an obsession with Charis, with a determination that Marcus not marry the woman.

"I agree with you there. I do not know her well, mind you, but I find her excessively proper and a trifle critical.

Marcus may say he wants a proper wife, but there is proper and then there is proper, if you see what I mean."

"How true," Charis agreed.

"He is very fond of you, your family, that is."

"Is he?" Charis said, her skepticism ringing in her voice. "It is good of him to tolerate us in his house."

There was no answer to this remark, and they walked along in silence for a few minutes. Charis absently continued her thoughts, "I sometimes wonder where he goes in the evening. We see very little of him." Lord Egerton was remarkably easy to converse with, she discovered.

"I can tell you that he joins his glee club this evening. He enjoys music. Singing, in particular."

"Which club is it?" Charis asked as though not the slightest interested. She vaguely recalled Lady Alicia saying something about a glee club when she came to dine. Charis had thought it a fabrication.

"The Nobleman's and the Gentleman's Catch Club," Lord Egerton replied promptly. "They always meet on Thursday evening."

"What sort of place will allow all that singing to go on for hours?" she wondered. "They must make a fearful noise."

"Why, the Thatched House Tavern in St. James's Street in very happy to have them. The Prince Regent is a member as is the Duke of Clarence, so it is no scruffy group! Women are not allowed, sorry to say." His mouth tilted in an attractive and somewhat rueful smile.

"What a pity, I enjoy listening to music."

His horse obviously restless, Lord Egerton was on his way with a polite farewell and the information that he would enjoy seeing her later.

The two women returned to the house. Charis took Ruff to her room, and Betty followed. The maid took her bonnet and light pelisse away, leaving Charis to her thoughts. How she would like to go to hear the singing this evening. It was impossible! There was absolutely no way she might. But the thought lingered in her mind throughout luncheon and into the afternoon. She was absentminded and only her mother's sharp reprimand brought her forth from her thoughts.

"You are not with us," Harriet whispered under the cover of their mother welcoming Lady Penston and her daughters. "Did you achieve anything with your walk?"

"Nothing, I fear," Charis replied, earning a quizzical look from her sister.

The call proved delightful, and Charis was glad that her mother was bosom bows with Lady Penston, thus resulting in the daughters as new friends.

Harriet agreed to go for the afternoon stroll in the park. Betty went with them, adding to their respectability.

The first person they saw was Lord Pilkington. He seemed so pleased to meet Charis that she was put quite in charity with him. He was ever the dandy, but so kind.

"Dear Lady Huntingdon, how charming you look today. I vow you put every other lady in the shade. Not that you ain't a pretty creature, Lady Harriet, but your sister is in the pink of looks." He bowed over her hand even as she wondered how he managed it, given the tight coat he wore.

"May I join you, dear lady?" he asked Charis with a delightfully respectful address.

Her low spirits bathed in the balm of his kind words, Charis nodded. Harriet fell back to walk beside Betty.

It was a lovely afternoon, and the park overflowed with pedestrians as well as those on horseback and in carriages. She recognized Lord Egerton on his chestnut. Marcus rode that black brute she had seen before. There appeared to be no spare flesh on her cousin. He was lean and well muscled from what she could tell. He was the perfect Corinthian, she thought bitterly.

"Your cousin is out and about, I see. Thought he might squire Lady Alicia this afternoon. They sat and played cards a good part of the evening at Almack's last night."

"Did he?" That explained what had kept him so occupied and out of sight at a place he deemed dull.

"Yes, indeed. I saw him later at White's. We had a bit of balloting, don't you see."

"For new members? I wonder how that is done? I think it a dreadful shame if a fine gentleman is not permitted to join." Charis bestowed a smile on Lord Pilkington that made him preen.

"We meet upstairs in the room above the bay window. The Court Guides, Red Books, Peerages, and new publications are in there as well as the boxes, you see. Rummagy place. One box is for yes, the other for no. The steward announces the names of the candidates, and we vote—a white ball if we approve and a black one if we don't."

"So one who is not approved is black balled. I think that is cruel." Charis glanced up to see his face assume a perplexed look.

"No worse than begging to get into Almack's and having one of the lady patronesses turn you down," he replied with perfect logic at last.

Charis sighed. He had her there. "That is most true," she replied when she could think of no rejoinder.

Suddenly Marcus was at their side, riding up through the throng of people with seemingly no effort at all. "Good day, Charis, Pilkington. Enjoying the air?"

She laughed at that. How silly an observation what with the abundance of horses. At times the smell was so strong she was tempted to hold her nose. But then she was not overly fond of horses and perhaps that made her less tolerant.

"As much as is possible, cousin," she replied with a certain constraint. She could not forget that she was in London on sufferance, not after the way he had behaved last evening, quite as though she was little more than a duty.

His mouth quirked as though she had amused him. "Carry on, then. I shall see you both later."

Once he was out of hearing, Charis inquired, "Lord Pilkington, are you also a member of the Nobleman's and Gentleman's Catch Club?"

"Dash it all, of course. It is the thing to be a member if you have a decent voice. Prinny himself joins us when in the mood, you know."

"I had heard he is a fair musician," Charis ventured to say. She thought the Prince Regent a far better person than generally held by so many. Perhaps he had his excesses, but it seemed to her that they were magnified by the gossips and the newspapers, most of which seemed to detest the man.

"Fair, indeed, ma'am. He does right well on the cello, you know. Pity you cannot hear him. Pleasant voice." Lord Pilkington lapsed into a reverie for a few moments before recalling he escorted Charis.

"The glees are sung in three parts, are they not? Does anyone ever have a solo?" Charis inquired casually.

"Not usually. I say, my lady, you are a splendid companion. Dashed if I know another woman who is interested in the glee clubs."

"I suspect it stems from the women being excluded. What you are forbidden often becomes of no interest."

He looked rather doubtful at that. "Seems to me that when I was a lad, the things I was forbidden became what I most wanted."

"But in this case it is hopeless. There is no way a woman could sneak in to listen." Charis twirled her parasol and inspected a pretty shrub nearby.

"No, I suppose not. Proprietor is right careful about it. Why, I heard tell the Duchess of Devonshire once persuaded a gentleman to allow her to listen in, and I think the chaps caught on and got so angry they stormed out and the glee club fell apart."

"That must have been some years ago," Charis offered thoughtfully. "I wonder if they are as adamant now? And why would it be so terrible?"

His lordship became a bit red in his face and looked exceedingly uncomfortable. "Well, to tell the truth, my lady, a few of the songs are a trifle vulgar, if you see what I mean. Not fit for a gentle lady's ears."

"But the serving wenches have no problem, I suppose," she replied with a catch of a laugh.

"No. They laugh at 'em."

"It has been such a lovely stroll, sir. But all nice things must end, I suppose. It is time for us to return."

He insisted upon escorting them to their front door. Once inside Harriet rounded on her sister. "Of all the boring men, he takes the prize. How could you waste a perfectly good walk on him!"

"Do you know, I thought him utterly charming," Charis said with a smile and sauntered up the stairs to her room, deeply in thought.

Later that evening Charis declared she had a headache, retiring to her room quite early, insisting that all she wished was peace and the quiet of her bed.

Not much later, had anyone been around, she could have been seen tiptoeing down the back stairs. The servants were occupied with their own dinner at this hour, and no one was about when she slipped out the back door. Not that they would have thought much of the young woman garbed in a simple brown skirt, white top, and a floppy mobcap atop her head. Not a curl of dark red hair showed and little of her trim figure, for the clothing was too large, being left from a previous maid who had decamped with the footman of the house next door. Charis had unearthed it in the attic.

A short walk found her a hackney who was willing to take the lady—never mind her garb, he knew a lady when he saw one—to her requested destination.

Charis gulped back her fears and left the security of the hackney when she was deposited before the Thatched House Tavern. It was not so far from the gentlemen's clubs and thus had a better than average clientele. Tonight it was overflowing with gentlemen of every description.

Scurrying around the edge of the room, she found the door that led to a hall and stairs. Supposing this to go to the room where the glee and catch club met, she ran lightly up, any sound of her steps covered by the raucous noise from the main room. She knew success at the second door she tried, the first being a closet.

It was but a simple matter to find a recess. Hiding was something else.

"Here you," demanded a harsh voice at the door. "See to the chairs. The gennelmen be parti'clar about the chairs."

"Yes, sir," she mumbled, hoping to disguise her upper-class accent. Hastily she set about arranging the chairs in rows that she devoutly hoped would be right.

Within minutes the clatter of footsteps on the stairs brought awareness that her hunt for a hiding place was about over. Unless she found a spot, she was doomed. She saw no other way out of the room. But there *was* a small cupboard across the room. What it housed she didn't know, but it was worth a try.

Chamber pots! She had never calculated on that!

Hastily she looked elsewhere, then dived for a corner in the shadows of the recess. She crouched and hoped for the best!

The doorknob turned, and a group of gentlemen streamed into the room, commenting on the odd arrangement of chairs, but chalking it up to new help.

They most surprisingly got down to singing almost at once. Charis, concealed in her corner, listened with pure delight at the wonderful blend of voices pouring forth from the assembled throats. Familiar tunes and ones new were performed one after another. It seemed they spent no time in gossip or chitchat. They were here to sing, and by Jove they sang.

A catch was sung, the words flowing in succession, like a round. Some were beginning while others were ending, and it all was rather amusing.

Her legs grew cramped, and she longed to stand or stretch, but that would definitely call her to attention, so she remained where she was and hoped they didn't sing forever into the night.

It was Marcus who suggested they were finished for the evening. He said something about a race the next day.

The others were clearly perplexed, but agreed good-naturedly. The men straggled from the room, humming and in general sounding in a good mood.

At last it seemed all were gone. Charis rose from where she had curled up, feeling horridly stiff. Hesitantly she peered around the corner to discover her cousin mere inches away from her.

"I trust you have an explanation for this insanity!"

Chapter Eight

They stared at each other in silence a few moments. She could not think of a thing to say; her brain was surely not functioning. In fact, she doubted she could say a word if compelled.

Marcus looked so forbidding. She would not be the least surprised were he to shake her much as Ruff shook a mouse he had caught. She felt about as vulnerable. His mouth stretched in a grim line. If he was not about to yell at her, he looked as though he really wanted to—while at the same time shaking her to bits and pieces.

Then with an exclamation of exasperation he pulled her roughly from the recess, draping his cloak about her slim form, and ignominiously hauled her down the flight of stairs before she could think of a reply to a question he doubtless knew had no answer. He was aware of a way out that did not go through the tavern, and within moments she was on the street. Without a chance to say a word, she was bustled into the carriage that awaited him.

"Well!" she declared in shocked accents.

"Well, indeed, cousin." He had chosen to sit across from her and now stared at her, his arms crossed, looking like a statue in some park. The only difference in her mind was his eyes were alive with anger and he still breathed.

"How did you know I was there?" She had not thought of a good defense yet and stalled for a bit of time.

"It was my turn to direct the group this evening, and I soon noticed a bit of fabric peeking around that corner.

It took but a casual walk across the front of the room—all the while directing—to catch sight of your face. I shudder to think what might have happened had any of the other men seen you. Thank God Prinny was not there tonight. As it is, they all wonder what race I mentioned, which no one else has heard of, that was so bloody important, I called the meeting short."

"Was it that bad?" she asked with a sinking heart.

"Worse. Need I point out that you would have been socially ruined if discovered there?"

"But the music was wonderful!" she insisted.

"And what would you have done had we begun a more lusty tune, may I ask? Merely blush? Or would you have swooned in a heap." The derision in his voice truly cut her to ribbons.

"What sort of poor-spirited creature do you think I am? I'll wager that I have heard just as bad around the stables and garden," she snapped back at him.

"I'll fire the lot of them!" He looked more outraged than her maiden aunt the time Harriet let her pet mouse loose in the house.

"Do not think of such a thing! All the people who work at Huntingdon are good people. They tend to forget about a quiet girl who is always around. I seem to blend into the background, for they totally ignored me when I was younger and sought to escape the house."

"And you thought you might do so tonight?" His voice dripped with acid, as angry as she had ever heard him.

"Well, no one else saw me. And I must say I think it is quite unfair that you get to hear all that wonderful singing and a lady cannot." She crossed her arms, and the cloak slid from her shoulders. Unfortunately, it also pulled with it one side of the overly large top she wore. Nervously she tugged the white fabric up her arm to her shoulder, hoping that no more than her arm had been exposed. She was afraid to look.

What more he might have said was set aside for the moment, as they had reached Huntingdon House. He wrapped his cloak around her again, then ushered her quietly into the house. Seymour was not around at this hour. Likely Marcus had ordered him to retire early. It would be something her cousin might do.

She had little choice but to go before him into the library. He closed the door, then urged her into a chair. He took the one facing it after stirring up the fire a bit.

"I wanted to hear you sing. Simple as that," she said at last, figuring that a straightforward excuse was the best.

"Who told you where we meet and what day?" Marcus demanded.

She shrugged her shoulders, allowing the cloak to slip, only this time she made certain the white top did not go as well. That would never do. "I picked up the information here and there."

"You will not tell me?" He looked like a cat ready to pounce on a tasty mouse.

"Rather—I believe it is not necessary for you to know who said anything. It is not a secret, after all. and I knew that ladies are not allowed to attend," she added with a defiant look.

His mouth twitched slightly. "And so because you were forbidden, it became all the more desirable."

"It would be nice if you sang at home sometime. I truly do enjoy a fine male voice." She gave him a wistful look.

"Oh, Charis," he groaned, "what am I to do with you?"

"Find me a husband, and you will no longer have to worry about me," she replied promptly, although it was not what she would have liked to say.

"I wonder who would be up to looking after you?" he rubbed his chin with a well-shaped hand while studying her. She felt like some rare insect.

Charis had a notion or two who might handle her, but she kept her ideas to herself. The silence continued a bit, then—deciding he was finished with her at least for the moment—she rose, curtsied, and turned to the door. "Good night, Cousin Marcus." He was right behind her.

"Leaving so soon? How do you propose to get to your room in that getup?" He had gone around her and now leaned against the door frame, gazing at her like she was an infant given a puzzle to solve.

"No one is likely to be around at this hour. I shall be just fine." She hoped she was correct. She had not thought of this aspect.

"I'd best walk you up."

"No!" The last thing she wanted was to have him at her side after this dreadful scold. Well—perhaps it was not a scold, but she felt so small. "It is not necessary. I have slippers on, and no one should hear a thing."

He captured her upper arms, studying her face with a searching gaze. At last he shook his head and let her go.

For a moment she had been sure he would kiss her again. And she did not know if she wanted that or not.

She shut the door behind her and tiptoed to the stairs with as much haste as she could muster.

About to place a foot on the first step going to the second floor, she paused. She was certain she heard laughter. Laughter? Impossible. She hurried up the stairs and along to her room.

Once in her room, she quickly removed the purloined garments and stuffed them in the back of her wardrobe. She did not bother to wash, just tumbled into bed and pulled the covers up to her chin. And prayed. Fervently.

Marcus laughed until tears ran down his cheeks. He pulled a square of linen from his pocket and wiped his face, then turned to pour a tot of brandy.

It had been priceless—to see her standing looking so petrified. He had been tempted to wrap her in his arms rather than his cloak—but that was not a part of his plan. And then when that cloak slipped to reveal so much of her creamy shoulder, he had been hard-pressed to stay on his side of the carriage. But it had done his anger a world of good to haul her from the room and down to the carriage. The little fool!

What a worry it had been—that she might be discovered. The fat would have surely been in the fire! There was not a man around who would overlook such a solecism. He would have had her on his hands forever had that happened.

He shook his head and grinned. One thing for certain, living with Charis was not dull. He tossed back the brandy, then sat down to contemplate what had to be done if his plans were to succeed.

Not one to cower in her room, Charis rose to face the day with her resolution firmly in place.

"Will your willow-green muslin do this morning, ma'am?" Betty asked as she stood by the wardrobe. She still looked like a meek mouse, but perhaps not as hungry.

"What? Oh, indeed." It scarcely made any difference to her what she wore. Marcus did not notice, and Mama did not care.

"Is Harriet up?" she asked Betty, while being hooked into her gown.

"Indeed, milady. Scribbling at her paper, she is." The maid urged Charis onto a chair, then brushed her short curls.

Charis frowned, puzzled. Scribbling? She hurriedly rose and walked across the sitting room to knock on her sister's door.

"Enter," Harriet called. "My, you look as though you did not sleep very well. Are you all right?"

"Betty said you were scribbling."

"A letter to Susan, our neighbor at home. It seems strange not to see her when we have grown up together. It's a pity she could not afford a come-out in London.

Charis relaxed. "For a moment I thought you were making good on your threat to write a book."

"You do not think I could?" Harriet looked highly offended and perhaps a bit hurt.

"Actually, with your imagination, you might do well. I just think that Marcus does not need any more catastrophes on his hands."

"What happened? Something dire?" Harriet jumped up from her chair. "Tell me everything."

"Let us go down for breakfast. I can explain as we go." This she did in brevity, leaving out a good deal.

The girls settled with their usual tea and toast, conversing quietly on an unremarkable topic that no one—meaning Marcus—could find objectional.

There was a stir outside the door, and then Marcus entered the breakfast room. While the footman hurried to pour his coffee, Marcus casually walked to the foot of the table, pinning Charis with his gaze.

"I trust there will be no repeat of last evening?" he said in that deadly calm voice that shook her to her toes.

"No, Cousin Marcus," she replied obediently. It was safe enough to promise that, for she had been able to hear the men sing. She had no need to go again, did she?

"If you sang here, we would enjoy it very much," Harriet added, bravely meeting his gaze.

"So she let *you* hear of her tale, did she? And what did you think of it?" He sat at the head of the table, sipped his coffee, and then began to make inroads on the hearty breakfast placed before him by the efficient footman.

"I think it vastly romantic. Imagine hunting in secret for those garments, then finding her way to the Thatched House Tavern. She had to arrange those chairs, you know. I suppose the tavern owner thought her a maid. Anyway, she did get to hear the singing. By her account, it was most wonderful. What a pity you caught her out!" Harriet concluded indignantly.

"Oh, indeed. It would have been disastrous had she been found by one of the other men," he said dryly. "I am pleased to know that you give up that particular interest. I will have no more risky ventures, do you hear?"

Charis nodded and rose. She fled from the room, with Harriet right behind her.

"Well, there is no need to go there again, anyway, is there?" Harriet mused as they entered the music room, which they had found was a delightful place to be left alone.

"No. I wonder if we received invitations to any more balls or parties. Wait here and I shall look." Charis quickly walked to the entry hall table where Seymour placed the sorted mail.

There were several pieces that had the look of an invitation. There was also a folded note written in violet ink on lavender paper in the stack destined for Marcus. Glancing around her and seeing not a soul, she filched the letter from the pile and tucked it beneath the letters for her mother.

Once down the hall, she stuffed the lavender missive down the front of her gown, hoping that the violet scent would not linger until she had a chance to remove the letter in her room. Then she plucked the flowers from a vase, poured a bit of water on her dress, replaced the flowers, and returned to the music room.

"What on earth is on your dress?" Harriet demanded. "You look like one of those women who dampen their skirts. Better not let Marcus see you like that."

Charis looked down as though she had not the foggiest notion of her dress being wet. "Oh, dear, I must have spilled tea on it. Here, take the letters for Mama, and I will run up to change this." She thrust the mail into Harriet's willing hands and rushed from the room. It was a good possibility that her sister would not guess at her reason, nor catch the scent that was beginning to permeate her garments.

Fortunately, Mary was out of the rooms. Charis hurried through the sitting room and into her own room, closing and locking the door behind her. She pulled the offensive letter from inside her dress and stared at it.

Dare she?

She dared. Carefully using her silver letter knife, she slid it beneath the wafer that sealed the missive. It would be a simple matter to glue that down again.

Once the page was unfolded, she found the rather creative writing hard to read. At last she figured out that dear Delilah wanted more from Sir Marcus. Whether it was money or jewels, it was impossible to tell. But she threatened him with retribution. What sort of reckoning she had in mind was beyond Charis.

However, this letter had an address in it, where the scheming woman wanted the money or jewels delivered. Picking up a pencil she made careful note of it on a slip

of paper. She put that in her drawer. Satisfied she had
what she needed, she debated what she ought to do with
the letter. She did not want Marcus to give this stupid
woman another farthing nor the most insignificant
jewel. Nothing!

She paced up and down her room until she decided
that she had no right to keep his mail from him. She
would simply have to hope that he was so busy that he
did not have time to deal with the greedy female at present. Perhaps if Harriet might be persuaded to beg his
assistance, Charis could seek out this woman. She would
give her an earful!

It went amazingly well. To glue the wafer down was
but the work of a moment. Returning the letter to her
cousin's stack was simplicity itself. She merely slid it beneath the others, then went off to find her sister.

Getting Harriet to help might prove to be the sticky
part of her plot. However, Harriet was in great sympathy
once Charis offered the explanation that she'd devised.

"Poor Marcus, to be so put upon. I believe he is far
too good-hearted. I know he was severe with you, but,
Charis think of what might have happened had someone
seen you! You would have been the latest scandal, out-
shining Caro Lamb! Of course I will help you depress
the pretensions of this dreadful woman."

"You must say nothing to our cousin," Charis insisted.
"He must believe you wish his company above all things.
If you can keep him occupied for an hour, that ought to
be sufficient."

"I wonder what one wears to confront a scheming
woman?" Harriet mused.

"I do not want to appear so well endowed that she
can think to seek money from me. But, on the other
hand, I do not want to seem penniless, either—which I
am of course, but she need not know it."

They settled on a simple gown of printed percale that
had a pretty bit of lace at the neck and clever detailing
on the sleeves. "The bonnet can be this one with the
green ribbons. It is plain, yet modish," Charis concluded.

Harriet left to devise a plan that would require her cousin's presence.

Marcus picked up his mail, discovering the lavender missive at the bottom. He tore open the thing, scanned the contents, and then tossed it in the fireplace, where it burned at once. Glad to be rid of the annoying letter, not to mention the scent, he settled to face the remainder of his mail—invitations, a few bills from various shops, and correspondence from the steward at his holdings as well as the Huntingdon estate.

When his secretary came in, he found the letters neatly arranged with notations as to what was to be done in each case. Wilkins asked a question regarding a vague point on one of the directions, then left for his office.

"I shall be back later to sign papers or consult with you if such is needed," Marcus said before he left the room.

He encountered Harriet in the hallway, looking very distressed.

"Oh, Marcus, how good to see you. Could you help me? I do not know where to go, and I feel certain you would know."

"Go for what?" he inquired with a touch of suspicion.

"Music. Since you sing, you ought to know just the place to buy some music for the pianoforte. Even if I found the address, I doubt our maid would be the slightest help. I would like someone who knows something about the pianoforte and what is popular now." She beamed a happy smile at him, and he scolded himself for being mistrustful.

"What about your sister? Surely she would be competent to assist with the music. I have a number of things to attend to this morning."

"She does not have the faintest notion of where to go. I rather think she is supposed to see Madame Clotilde. Oh, please, Cousin Marcus. I would so like some new music. It should not take above an hour at the most."

"Well, I imagine I could look over the vocal music as

well. The men were just saying last evening that it would be good to learn a new piece."

"You are the dearest of cousins," she replied with a happy grin. "I will meet you here whenever you say."

Marcus glanced at the tall-case clock. "About thirty minutes ought to suffice."

"I shall be here waiting for you." She hurried up the stairs, disappearing from view in a trice. She rarely asked anything of him, so this was the least he could do for her. Besides, it would give him a chance to look on his own as well.

Within the allotted thirty minutes, he had completed the finishing touches to his attire and went down to the entry to find Harriet waiting for him.

"Where is your sister?"

"Getting ready to go out. I do not think she intends to be long. It depends on how long it takes at Madame Clotilde's."

Charis stood by the window that overlooked the street, watching to see until the carriage had left. It would be nice to have a new piece of music to practice. Harriet had come up with an excellent excuse. Perhaps it would be well to take lessons from her.

Back in her room, Charis pulled the slip of paper from her desk drawer, tucked it into her reticule, and hurried down the stairs after saying good-bye to Mama. Since that lady was reclining on her chaise longue absorbed in one of the books she liked to read, there was little response.

It was sheer luck that Seymour happened to be elsewhere when she went to the door. Even the footman was busy elsewhere. Going to the stand where she had taken the hackney last evening, she found the same man and carriage.

"Please, can you take me to this address?" She dug out the slip of paper and read it off to him.

"Indeed, miss. Your maid?"

Charis gave him a look that let him know it was none of his business if she did not have her maid along with her.

The creature named Divine Delilah lived in a plain, small house in the less respectable part of London. The small brass knocker had been polished and the steps neatly swept, which was to her credit. She employed a decent maid, at any rate.

"Please wait here for me. My errand should not take me very long." Charis met his doubtful look with equanimity.

It took far more courage to lift the knocker and let it fall than she had expected. When the door opened to reveal a young maid, her head swathed in a mobcap of generous proportions and garbed in a very plain gingham dress, Charis almost ran back to the hackney.

"I wish to see the person named Delilah," Charis said in the most intimidating manner she knew.

It worked, for the girl opened the door at once and led Charis to a small sitting room off the main hall. Without a word, she disappeared. Charis barely heard her steps going up to the next floor. There was a bit of distant conversation, then the maid returned.

"She'll be right down, she will." The maid bobbed a curtsy, then vanished down the hall to the back of the little house.

Charis walked around the room, finally staring out of the front window. Not that she could see much, for it was heavily curtained with lace. Hmm, the lace was not cheap stuff, either. Delilah must have expensive taste in all things. With the exception of that ghastly scent she used, of course. And even that might be costly. It was merely strong. Charis wondered how anyone as particular as Marcus could have anything to do with such a one. Perhaps she had some redeeming quality?

A swish of skirts at the door caused Charis to turn in that direction. She inspected the creature called Delilah. Average in height, hair carefully tinted with henna—unless Charis missed her guess—and eyes that were like blue glass chips, she was still a beautiful woman. She was a bit too plump, but that was hard to determine considering the foaming negligee she wore. Charis nodded, but waited for the creature to say something so she could judge her voice and manner.

"You wanted to see me about something?" she said in a curious but not unpleasant voice.

"I did. You sent a letter of request to Sir Marcus Rutledge, I believe?"

"What's it to you?" Without inviting Charis to be seated, she sashayed to the small sofa, where she arranged herself in a dramatic pose. She draped her skirt carefully over her knees—crossed as no lady would do.

"I am his cousin. You *must* leave him alone." Charis stared down at Delilah with what she hoped to be an aristocratic mien.

"Ha! You and who else are goin' to make me? He was most miserly with his farewell gift. I expect better of him." The woman screwed up her face in a belligerent way.

"He had already given you something? Then I would say you are lucky. My cousin *is* truly miserly." Charis took out a linen handkerchief to dab at nonexistent tears and sniffed in what she thought was a convincing manner before she continued. "Why he got every farthing of our estate. I exist at his sufferance. All I have now is a paltry allowance, when before I lived very nicely."

Delilah gave Charis a sharp inspection and appeared to decide that she was telling the truth. "He has plenty of the ready, ducks. Perhaps you have to appeal to him in the right way? You're a bit on the thin side, but I reckon in the dark he wouldn't mind." She nodded her head as though confirming an idea. "That's the ticket. Get him in your bed, girl. A man's always susceptible to a bit of loving."

Charis swallowed with difficulty. "That is not the point. The point is that you may as well stop asking him for money or jewels. You will not get them."

"Well," Delilah replied with resignation, "there was no harm in trying."

Charis walked to the doorway and paused when Delilah spoke again.

"You aren't bad-looking in a way. I fancy you could

catch him if you pleased. Then you could have what you want."

Charis darted a nervous glance at the woman, mumbled something in reply, and left the house as quickly as decently possible.

"Home, my lady?" the jarvey asked, elevating Charis to her proper title without knowing.

"Oh, yes, please. Huntingdon House at once." Then she realized that she could not simply drive up now, she was too upset. "Change that," she called out. "Take me to Madame Clotilde's shop on Bond Street." She sat back against the squabs and contemplated the harrowing interview she had just experienced. Letting out a sigh of more than relief, she thought she had succeeded. That dreadful woman would no longer importune Marcus. Although to give her due, she attempted to help Charis! Inviting Marcus into her bed to obtain a larger allowance? When pigs flew.

At Madame Clotilde's she gave the jarvey a generous sum and thanked him. "You are most kind, sir," she said as she stepped away from the hackney.

"Call on me any time, milady. It'd be John Jarvey at your service." He tipped his hat and he was gone.

Inside the dress shop Charis slowly walked to where the mantua-maker was seated at her little French desk. The moment she realized who had entered her shop, she jumped to her feet.

"Ah, my lady. The gown is ready to be fitted. How providential you are here. Perhaps Sir Marcus told you of his surprise, *non?*"

"Could I try it on now? Really?" Charis pretended that she knew all about the gown of which Madame Clotilde spoke. She followed her to a dressing room to wait until an assistant returned carrying a confection of gold tissue.

"You are right, I did not order this, so it must be a surprise from my dear cousin. How delightful!"

Charis seethed with frustration. She had told him she did not think it proper for her to wear such a gown. The fabric slithered over her head to fall into graceful folds about her admittedly slim from. Was she too thin?

"Am I too thin, madame?"

"Not in the least. You are all that is fashionable, my lady. Sir Marcus has excellent taste, does he not?"

The gown was one to dream about. It was certainly nothing Charis had ever expected to own. "This is not a trifle too sophisticated for a girl my age?"

"Girl? You are a woman, my dear. This gown will be the making of you. There is not a man alive who could resist it."

"Really!" Charis breathed. "Well, in that case I shall wear it to the Silverstone's ball. The marchioness is such a lovely person, I wish to do her credit."

"You will outshine all others." The gorgeous gown was slipped from Charis, taken away to be boxed while Charis put on her simple percale morning dress.

If the mantua-maker thought it peculiar that Charis was out and about in such a dress, she said nothing, of course. She summoned a hackney, which fortuitously was John Jarvey again, and Charis directed him to her home, this time for sure. It had been an enlightening day so far. What else could happen she could not guess.

Chapter Nine

Harriet and Marcus returned just shortly after Charis was safely in her room. She heard their voices in the hall. Marcus continued to his room while Harriet entered the little sitting room with suppressed excitement.

"Well? Did you do it!" she whispered before the door was quite closed.

"Indeed," Charis replied mendaciously. "I usually complete what I set out to do. Oh, Harriet, she was *such* a woman. I cannot believe our cousin had anything to do with someone so vulgar. I suppose you might liken her to an overblown rose—yet beautiful for all that. She was certainly no bud!"

"But did you persuade her to . . . you know?" Harriet demanded.

"Yes, I succeeded very well, I should say. When I told her how shabbily I am treated and I, his cousin, she realized that it was unlikely she would reap another farthing from him." Charis pulled out her handkerchief and dabbed at her eyes as she had done for Delilah.

Harriet shook her head in awe. "Sister, I am all admiration. What a pity you could not go on the stage. I declare it is just like a book. Marcus ought to be very appreciative for what you dared to do on his behalf."

"Dearest, he must never know! I suspect that gentlemen do not like ladies, even relatives, to know anything about the demireps they favor. It is true she is scarcely respectable, but she was not deplorable. Pity she has to use such strong scent," Charis concluded absently.

"Not very ladylike?"

Charis grimaced at the memory. "Not in the least."

Then, reluctant to speak more of Delilah, she gestured toward her room. "Come, let me show you the surprise from Marcus. Recall I did not order the gold gauze he wanted me to take? Well, I gather he stopped in to order it for me without my knowledge. I will have to take back every unkind word I said about him." She dragged Harriet into her bedroom to see the gown lovingly displayed on the bed.

"Oh," Harriet breathed in astonishment, "it is beyond anything beautiful. You will sweep every gentleman off his feet when you wear that."

"We are to attend the Silverstone's ball this very evening. I will wear it then!"

Harriet beamed her delight. "I will be happy to observe the mad rush in your direction once we arrive. I shall bask in reflected glory." Harriet winked and left the room.

They had the afternoon to prepare, and fully intended to do their new gowns justice. Harriet had a pretty creamy white gown to wear with dozens of tucks and dark green ribbon trim. She declared it utterly smashing.

Charis decided she ought to walk poor Ruff, who had sulked at being left behind this morning. Opening the sitting-room door, she set him down before she had quite attached his lead. The dog escaped her hands and skimmed off along the hall to a door that stood ajar.

She tore after him. She had promised Marcus that Ruff would not bother him, and now the dog aimed for the door that led to his room!

Ruff was able to slip through the opening with ease. Charis opened it farther and reached out to grab the dog, falling onto her knees to catch him.

"Well, on your knees before me, Charis? That really is not necessary, dear girl."

Charis looked up and gulped. There, standing before her looking like a god from Olympus, was her cousin. Only he was far different from his usual sartorial perfection. Although he wore biscuit breeches and boots, he was shirtless! There was a shocking expanse of bare skin, well muscled and lightly tanned as though he had been sparring in the sun. Never had she been so close to a gentleman in such a state.

"Ruff," she gasped as she grabbed the dog. She clutched him against her, ignoring his wiggles for freedom.

Marcus descended from his great height to squat before her, touching the little dog lightly on the head to calm it. Ruff licked his fingers, wagging his tail with joy.

Charis did not know where to look. She wanted to stare at that amazing muscled torso. She had seen the Elgin marbles, of course. Marcus stunned her senses with the reality of what those carved figures might have been.

"Need help getting up?" His voice, musical and low, teased her ears with a sensation amounting to touch.

She could not have moved to save her life. When Marcus cupped his strong hands around her elbows and raised her to her feet, she wondered if she would be able to stand.

Thinking it safer to look at his face, she raised her gaze to meet his. "Th-thank you. Sorry Ruff slipped in here. I was about to take him for a shirt, ah, I mean walk, and he got away from me. I'll go now. Th-thank you, again." She was babbling and could not seem to stop. Her fingers fought to reach out to touch that warm, smooth skin, to feel the texture. She must be far beyond hope to hold desires like that! But what would it be like to be crushed against him?

"Are you all right, Charis? You seem a little flustered." He smiled at her, and again she thought of how devastating his smile was—a dazzling marvel of perfection.

It was too much for her overheated senses. "Well," she retorted, "I do not see you in such a state as a rule. My goodness, Marcus, the sight of you only half dressed is enough to send any gently bred girl into spasms!"

"How fortunate you are made of sterner stuff, my dear." He leaned forward to place a brief kiss on her forehead, then shooed her from the room with a gentle push.

He closed the door behind her, and Charis simply stood there for a few moments, catching her breath. If she had adored her cousin as a young girl, her feelings toward him now were quite different. Never had she been so aware of him as a man, as someone utterly desirable.

Was she a wanton woman to think such things? She clipped the lead on Ruff and walked down the stairs absorbed in her revelations, moving as though in a dream.

Betty joined her, neatly bonneted and prepared to leave the house. She handed Charis her bonnet, then her gloves before nodding to Seymour to open the door. They might have been ready to go for the walk, but Charis was still in a daze.

"Be you all right, milady?" Betty inquired.

"What? Oh, indeed. I am quite well, thank you," Charis replied briskly, coming to her senses. It was all very well for her to become truly aware of her cousin's attractiveness. What good did it do her? All he could talk about was finding her a husband.

This time her sniff was in earnest, and she applied the handkerchief to good use.

Betty said nothing but kept an eye on Ruff.

The walk in the park was the best thing she could have done, she decided. Watching as Ruff chased a squirrel, then trotted proudly along the path, soothed her senses. Her life had to continue on its path. What else could she do?

Ahead of her she spotted Lord Baylor walking with Isobel Penston. Not wishing to meet them when her mind was still in a disordered state, she turned abruptly and reversed her direction.

"Lady Huntingdon, what a lovely surprise to see you here. 'Pon my word, you are a pretty sight for the eyes." Lord Pilkington rode up to where Charis slowly walked Ruff, allowing him to run to either side of the path and sniff all the intriguing smells.

"Good day, sir. I thank you for the charming words."

He dismounted to join her much as Lord Egerton had done, to walk with his horse trailing along behind him.

It seemed a docile creature as one might expect Lord Pilkington to ride.

They exchanged polite nothings for a time before Charis inquired, "Do you attend the Silverstone ball this evening?"

"Everyone who is anyone will be there, dear lady. I trust I may have the pleasure of at least one dance with you. I vow I would be in black books were I to request two." He chuckled, his light tenor voice not displeasing. It could not compare to the rich baritone of her cousin's voice, of course, but she was hopelessly partial there.

"You will have your dance and perhaps two if possible," Charis answered gracefully.

They continued to chat until Charis decided she had better return to the house and bid the kindly gentleman farewell for the nonce.

"He seems kind, does he not, Betty?" she idly asked the maid.

"Indeed, milady. A kinder gentleman one could not think."

Well, thought Charis, a kind man was better than a stupid or cruel man if one were thinking of a husband. And it was necessary she look at all the men she met in that light. After this episode with Marcus, it was imperative she leave Huntingdon House as soon as possible.

If Marcus appreciated the cold beauty of a woman like Lady Alicia, he was hardly to think twice about Charis, other than his obnoxious little cousin who needed help.

She thanked Betty, then set Ruff down, keeping his lead attached to the collar. She wanted no more accidents of any sort.

About to go up the stairs, she encountered Marcus and his secretary in the hall. She feared she blushed at the memories that flooded into her mind as she looked at her cousin. Even garbed correctly in his tight-fitting blue coat, the stylishly patterned waistcoat, and a cravat tied in incredible simplicity, he was disturbing.

"Afternoon, cousin. Did you eat anything? I did not see you at luncheon."

"I was not hungry," Charis replied. She glanced down

at Ruff. The dog strained at his lead, wanting to go to Marcus. Tail wagging and panting with seeming delight, the terrier adored the man who rarely even looked at him.

Was it a case of like dog, like mistress? She grimaced at the thought.

"Walked the dog, instead? If you plan to attend the Silverstone ball, you had best eat. It takes a good bit of energy to dance every dance. What do you wear tonight?" He gave her a quick glance.

"If you also attend, it shall be a surprise, I think." Charis hurried up the stairs, dragging a reluctant fox terrier with her.

After consuming the light meal that Betty brought up to her, Charis began her preparations. Betty washed her hair, then helped with a slipper bath. Charis applied creams to her skin. The delicate perfume she preferred scented everything. So many of her new friends seemed to like lavender scent. She had always loved the smell of gillyflowers, the spicy fragrance somehow appealing to her senses. Now she floated in a delicate haze of it.

It was not that she intended to be different from the others. She had her own ways and preferences and intended to keep to them.

Once dried, her hair tumbling in unruly curls about her face, she donned her undergarments prior to settling on the dainty chair before her dressing table.

Betty deftly worked the unruly curls into a delightful array, standing back to study the effect when done.

"Help me into my gown, then you may go to assist Harriet," Charis commanded politely. She tried not to be thoughtless or unpleasant to the servants. They were people with feelings, and served better when treated well.

The gown fell into graceful folds about her. The golden hue lent sparkles to her dark red hair and made her skin appear even more creamy.

"You look ever so pretty, milady," Betty said before she left the room.

Wishing she had some truly splendid jewelry to enhance the gown, Charis searched her small case but found nothing appropriate. Perhaps her mother had something she might lend? It was but a few steps along the hall to her door.

Charis paused before it just as Marcus left his room.

"Good evening, cousin," Charis said with a curtsy.

He did not say anything for a few moments, and she began to wonder if perhaps her looking glass had lied to her. Maybe the gown was not the perfection she thought.

"So you found this at Madame Clotilde's when you stopped there? The gown surpasses my expectations. You look very, er, well, Charis." He walked across the hall to pick up her hand and seemed to notice the total absence of jewels. "Wait there, I believe I have something that would go nicely with your gown."

Perplexed, Charis waited where he left her.

It was several minutes before he returned carrying a brown velvet-covered case. He flicked it open as he came up to her revealing a beautiful topaz necklace with matching ear bobs and a rather lovely ring.

Realizing he intended her to wear these, Charis protested, "I could not, Cousin Marcus."

"They belonged to my mother, and I believe she would think you worthy of their charms." He held up the necklace, an entrancing affair with the fine topaz stones cradled in an intricate web of gold tracery. The ear bobs matched and the ring as well, although its setting was more sturdy.

"You truly want me to borrow these to wear to the ball?" She searched his face, studying the expression in his eyes. Satisfied at what she found, she said somewhat hesitantly, "Well . . . I shall be exceedingly careful of them. I doubt Mama has anything half as lovely that I might use. I have a short strand of pearls, of course, but I thought this beautiful gown deserved something special."

He handed the velvet box for her to hold, then clasped the necklace about her slender throat. "The ear bobs you must put on yourself." The ring he eased onto her finger, where it fit as though made for her.

She had expected that ring to be too large. How

strange that it should fit so well. She gave it a bemused look.

Ruff wandered out from the sitting room to sit at her cousin's feet, looking as though he had not made a mad dash down the hall earlier. If a dog could look innocent, he did. He also gazed at Marcus with utter devotion.

"That dog. One of these days he will go too far," Charis murmured, vividly recalling the earlier episode and fighting a blush.

"I believe I deserve thanks. You will stun them all." He grinned at her, his eyes alive with what could only be called mischief.

"I do thank you, and quite sincerely. I thought the gold tissue would make me look like an . . . actress or something of that ilk. I'd not wish to disgrace the family. I fall into enough scrapes as it is," she concluded, recalling the Thursday evening venture to the Thatched House Tavern. That she had also visited a demirep in her home, she dismissed. No one knew anything about it save for John Jarvey, and who would ask him? She forgot that there was one other person aware of her lapse—the Divine Delilah herself.

"We shall forget that blunder. I believe I shall take a cousin's privilege," Marcus murmured.

With that he leaned down to place a light kiss on her willing lips that recalled a previous kiss all too well. It almost got out of hand, for Charis leaned into him, wanting more. He appeared to relish the kiss as well. The sound of a door opening along the hall tore them apart.

He appeared as distracted as she felt. "I did not intend that to happen, that is, to get carried away. Dash it all, Charis, I am going to have to watch you like a hawk this evening. Some fellow is likely to want to make off with you." He thrust a hand through his hair, creating disorder totally unlike his usually disciplined self.

"Thank you, I think," she said while giving him a wary look. If he thought that Lady Alicia would welcome fiery kisses of that sort, he was far off his mark. Charis very much doubted her ladyship would permit them. Maybe a polite kiss on her fingertips would be allowed?

"Charis, that gown looks even nicer *on* you," Harriet said as she joined them. "Oh, where did you get the topaz necklace? It is gorgeous, and I must say it is perfect for that gown. Do you not think so, cousin?" She glanced at him before returning her attention to her sister.

"Marcus has loaned it to me for the evening. Perhaps I should show it to Mama as well. And I can use her looking glass to put on the ear bobs." Charis curtsied to Marcus while giving him an impish smile. She was beginning to have a suspicion or two about her cousin. It occurred to her that perhaps he did not despise her as she had thought. Of course that was a long way from liking and miles from anything stronger. But at least he did not dislike her as she had feared.

She slipped away from them, tapping on the door to her mother's room, then entering when summoned.

Harriet gazed after her, then looked at Marcus with a calculating expression. "If I was a suspicious person, which I am not, I would say there was something between you two more than being cousins. But that is a silly notion, is it not?" She turned to retreat into the little sitting room, leaving Marcus standing in the hall.

He retraced his steps to his room to stare at his reflection in his cheval glass. Never mind that his hair was total chaos, it was what was inside his head that needed examining. Why did he so frequently go counter to his intentions? He meant well in offering the topaz collection to Charis. He could have simply handed her the box and left it at that. Why did he stupidly place that necklace around her throat, touch that satiny skin, feel the tumultuous pulse at the base of her neck when he adjusted the necklace? He had never been one to play with fire. And now? He practically jumped into the blaze!

Tonight would be a trying time. He had to escort Lady Alicia. She had made it plain she expected him to do so. He hadn't minded in the past, for he had no attachments. Now he found her less charming, almost an obligation he would rather not have. But he was an honorable man and did his duty. After all, she possessed great *ton*.

Marcus had imposed on Egerton and Sir William to

keep an eye on Charis. At least he could trust them to toe the line. It was all the rest of the male portion of the *ton* that had him worried. In her golden guise, Charis was utterly irresistible.

Especially when she smiled as she had just now.

When they joined him in the drawing room, Marcus greeted Sir William and Egerton with mixed feelings. They were to have dinner here before going to the ball— he thought it only proper in view of what they did for him.

Marcus was committed to escorting Lady Alicia, but she'd had dinner at home, insisting Marcus ignore his family and obligations to dine there with her, though he did not. It had annoyed him to realize that Lady Alicia was behaving in a so proprietorial manner toward him. He disliked that. In his preoccupation with Charis—and her family—he'd failed to deal with the matter. Now Lady Alicia had assumed she had the right to demand he dance attendance on her. He had not permitted it in the past and would not allow it now. At least not from Lady Alicia. She had been suitable company, a well-bred lady to escort here and there. He tried to imagine kissing her as he had Charis, and quite failed. Alicia was not the woman he wished to marry!

"Egerton and Sir William, happy you were able to join us. The women will be glad of your escort."

Sir William harrumphed and said, "Delighted, my boy. Delighted. Known Anna, Lady Huntingdon, that is, any number of years. Sorry her husband died and left her in such straits. Not that I begrudge you what you've inherited, my boy. Anna said you were like a son to him. Pity he did not have one of his own."

"I fear Charis feels the loss of her fortune keenly," Marcus replied cautiously.

"Well, any chap could overlook that with a woman like her," Egerton said with a grin. "She beats a platter-faced heiress all hollow. She does not need a fortune. All she has to do is walk into a room to conquer all men."

Marcus fought the urge to punch his good friend in

the teeth. Egerton was right. Why did it annoy Marcus to such a degree? Charis stated she wanted a fortune, not love. Marcus wanted more.

A stir at the door brought in the three ladies. Harriet looked demur in her pretty white gown, while the elder Lady Huntingdon was elegant in a simple lavender gown of some lustrous fabric that did wonders for her skin and hair. She was still a handsome woman, and it seemed as though Sir William was of the same opinion by the looks of things. The way he bowed over her hand and admired her appeared highly flattering.

Charis entered the room hesitantly, as though fearing reaction to her golden splendor. Considering the dreadful black things she had been wearing when first arriving in Town, she likely felt conspicuous. Egerton quickly dispelled that with his fawning compliments.

"My lady, you are as shining as the sun itself, glowing in the best of looks, I vow." He appropriated one of her hands and walked at her side to stand near the fireplace. If he had drooled, Marcus would not have been the least surprised.

But then, Charis was a sight to behold. She *did* glow, dash it all. The topaz set had been the perfect touch to her appearance. He probably would have half the men in London at his desk on the morrow, begging for her hand.

Seymour paused in the doorway to announce dinner. Sir William held out his arm for the elder Lady Huntingdon. Egerton gleefully (Marcus thought) escorted Charis. Marcus as a mere baronet offered his arm to Lady Harriet, who as the daughter of an earl far outranked him.

The dinner went much as dinners were inclined to go. The food was superb, thanks to the outrageously paid French cook in the kitchen. Marcus glanced at Charis to see that her gentle mouth was curved in delight at Egerton's flattery. He recalled the feel of her mouth beneath his and had to sharply remind himself that this was not his intent and that he hoped she would find a good husband. Egerton was one of the best. So why was he not rejoicing that his good friend seemed so taken with her?

They ate leisurely, enjoying the various dishes. There

was little point in hurrying, as they well knew the ball would not begin early and there was no reason in arriving at the dot of nine. Besides, Marcus wanted most guests present when they arrived. He would escort Lady Alicia first, instructing Egerton to get there a trifle later. Marcus felt compelled to see his cousin's impression on the *ton*. She's had modest exposure prior to this evening. One could scarcely count the limited number at Almack's as an introduction to Society at large. Whether she knew it or not, this was her unveiling. The gold tissue gown could not have come at a better moment.

He did not pause to consider why he felt as he did, nor did he consider how Lady Alicia might react to Charis in her gorgeous costume.

At last it was time for him to leave. Lady Alicia was sufficiently annoyed that he had declined to join her for dinner at her home. He did not want to stir her anger.

He reminded Egerton when they were to depart, then with a word to Seymour he left the house most reluctantly, thinking he would rather be with them, even if he escorted Harriet.

Lady Alicia was not pleased with him this evening. Apparently his wealth and looks—which he admitted were better than average—did not compensate for some notion she had in her head. What it could be, he did not know and was not about to ask.

The speed at which they covered the streets to the Silverstones' house compensated, it seemed. She was all cool graciousness as they made their way up the stairs and into the large ballroom.

Greeting her hostess and host with her habitually superior attitude made Marcus flinch inwardly. He'd wager Charis would be more gracious.

Once they were absorbed into the throng of guests, Lady Alicia greeted her particular friends, dismissing Marcus as though he were a mere nobody instead of one of the wealthier men in Town. It was at that moment that he knew he did not wish to continue as her escort. He had been irked before. This was the outside of enough! Their parting would require tact and care, but part they would.

A faint stir at the entrance caught his attention. Sir William escorted the elder Lady Huntingdon with great composure, looking gratified to be with her. Lady Harriet followed immediately behind them, as was proper.

Charis came into view with Egerton, and Marcus noticed that there was a lessening of conversation as one man after another caught sight of her at the top of the stairs.

How proud he was of her! Her curtsy was perfection itself. No princess could have looked more regal walking down the few steps to the ballroom. Egerton beamed at her as though he'd created all that beauty.

Forgetting to dance attendance on Lady Alicia, Marcus forged his way through the sudden gathering of the single men—and a few married as well—to his cousin's side.

"Charis, I am happy to see Egerton brought you here safe and sound." Egad, if that did not sound foolish. It was something some greenhorn would say, surely.

She smiled at him as though he had been witty. "Indeed, he is most kind. You have some very nice friends, Marcus. I like them all." She waved a gloved hand at those closest, smiling shyly at them and probably capturing the hearts of those nearest at once. Could a goddess do otherwise? Pilkington was there. That lad fell in and out of love a half dozen times a year, and it looked as though Charis was his latest fancy.

Before long the men most favored had been promised one dance with the star of the evening and returned to wherever they had been before.

Marcus stepped forward to her side. "I trust you saved me a waltz as promised."

"I did." She tilted her chin up as though he might argue. "It is the fourth dance of the evening. Lord Egerton has the second waltz." She tapped his friend on the arm in a playful manner. "The naughty gentleman insisted."

Marcus could have cheerfully throttled his friend, then recalled that he was to dance the cotillion with Lady

Alicia, and she'd have his head on a platter if he was late. He bowed politely. "I shall see you later, then."

Lady Alicia was not best pleased with him. "I see you had to make certain that the poor chit you generously allow to stay in your home has a partner or two." She sniffed, then latched on to his arm.

Marcus smiled inwardly. Pity Lady Alicia could not see the slip of paper with every dance marked with some peer's name after it. He'd wager it was filled better than hers. He had not failed to note that fewer men hovered about her, and wondered if her spiteful tongue had something to do with it.

The cotillion proved a trial, for Lady Alicia appeared distracted. She took a wrong step more than once, and Marcus soon realized that she was keeping an eye on Charis. It was rather amusing, really. Of course, Charis outranked Lady Alicia, and she likely found that hard to forgive. But there was a genuine glow of delight about Charis that was fresh and heartwarming.

His second dance was a duty one with the Silverstone daughter. She was a sweet little thing, timid as a mouse.

When it came time for his waltz with Charis, he found her surrounded by every unattached male who could get close. He made his way through the group to her side. "I believe this is ours?"

Charis gave him a delighted smile. "It is."

She licked suddenly nervous lips. All these men around her were intimidating. Thank heavens Marcus was to take her away. Then she remembered how his arms had felt about her. It would be just fine. Marcus would see she came to no harm and take care of her. He had done that years ago, and looked after her well now. His kisses she ignored for the moment. For now she focused on the bliss of waltzing with Marcus. Other matters could come later.

The dances that followed would be a comedown, she knew. He was perfection when he danced. She glanced up at the chiseled features. There was more to him than met the eye. She could not imagine any other man ordering such a flawless gown, and then lending the topaz jewels to set it off. He might look daunting, but inside he was warm and thoughtful. She just knew it.

The remainder of the evening went in a whirl of partners, each one more fulsome in his compliments than the one before. It was a heady experience. She was delighted that Harriet had acquired a court of her own. All in all she found the Silverstones' ball to be far beyond her expectations.

Her mother was standing with Sir William when she caught her elder daughter's eye. At her beckoning nod, Charis joined her, as did Harriet and Lord Egerton, who had been her partner for the last dance.

"I believe it time to depart. It has been lovely, but all good things come to an end." With that, she went to express her pleasure to her host and hostess, as did the others. They took their leave, not without the woeful notice of a number of gentlemen.

Marcus also observed the departure. He suggested to Lady Alicia that the hour was late. Oddly enough she went without an argument.

All he could think of was to get home. He left Lady Alicia with unseemly haste.

Charis awaited.

Chapter Ten

Charis was still in a golden haze when she went down to breakfast the next morning. Actually, it was closer to noon and luncheon, she supposed. There was food on the sideboard, and she found rolls and cheese, then requested a pot of tea. She pulled a chair close to the table so to prop her chin on her hand while she contemplated her wild success of the previous evening. She had earned dark looks from Lady Alicia, who apparently thought it scandalous that Charis should be so besieged. It had been great fun!

All her life she had longed to be the belle of some ball, and now she had. Thanks to the gold tissue gown and her pretty hairstyle and the susceptibility of the gentlemen present, she had enjoyed a smashing evening. She went over the various dances and the gentlemen she had met, wondering if any of them might be suitable as husbands. She was prepared to wed almost anyone, but she preferred to have a husband she liked if she couldn't have the one she wanted.

Not long after, Harriet wandered into the room. She selected similar foods, and after pouring a cup of tea, joined Charis at the table. "If we were in the country on such a pretty day, we could take our meal to the arbor and enjoy the flowers," she said wistfully.

"You miss the country so much?" Charis wasn't terribly surprised. Her sister had always felt strongly about their country home, and although she had been delighted to come to London, it was plain it wasn't what she had hoped it would be.

"Yes. I think I shall look for a gentleman who likes

living in the country. There must be one somewhere," Harriet concluded pensively.

"We could take Ruff for a walk in the park. And while we stroll along the path, you can help me think of a means by which we can expose you know who." Charis dropped her voice to a whisper at the last of her suggestion.

"You mean Lady A?" Harriet whispered back. "Why are we whispering?"

Charis rolled her eyes. "Our cousin has a way of hearing what we say when we least expect it." Her ears alert, she heard steps approaching and gestured to the door. But it was only Seymour, and the girls chuckled.

"Is there something you wished to tell us?" she asked the stately butler as he paused in the doorway.

"Sir Marcus has left the house. He wanted me to inform you that he wishes to speak with you when he returns. He said it was rather important." What may have been intended as a request sounded far more like an order from on high.

Both girls nodded, utterly mystified by the message.

"We are usually around the house, more or less," Harriet murmured. "I wonder what the problem is? I think Seymour meant you. Marcus never wants to talk with me. I never get into trouble."

"It sounds ominous," Charis said thoughtfully. "I think I should like to postpone any discussion with our cousin. I believe I am for the park. Perhaps a spot of shopping? Something. I cannot explain, but I doubt whatever he has to say is anything good."

She searched her mind and tried to think of something he might scold her about, but really couldn't think of a thing. Of course there was the matter of the Divine Delilah. But who knew about that? Harriet did, but she would never utter a word to anyone.

With stealth that would have done a thief proud, they tiptoed about and were shortly out of the house, Ruff prancing along to enjoy the treat.

They were not the only people who wanted to take pleasure in the out-of-doors on such a fine day. In addition to the usual nannies and governesses supervising their charges, there were young ladies with maids trailing behind them and gentlemen pausing to chat a bit.

"I say," Harriet said, "I believe this was a splendid notion. There is another fox terrier. Even Ruff may find a friend." Harriet pointed out the other dog, but the owner was not inclined to let them meet. Charis shrugged and kept Ruff close to her side,

"Look, I see Isobel and Barbara not far away. Perhaps they know something that we do not. Lady Penston always hears the latest gossip before anyone else does." Meaning their own mother, of course. Charis glanced at her sister, and they walked more quickly.

The other girls were delighted to meet friends. They walked on together, talking about the ball and all that had occurred.

Isobel twirled her parasol, allowing the fringe to dance wildly. "I understand that a certain Lady A is not best pleased today. Rumor has it that she gave a particular gentleman a telling off last evening. Not that I actually saw this, mind you. I heard Mama talking about it with one of her friends. They always think you don't understand what they are discussing, but there is only one Lady A who is being gossiped about presently. This means it will shortly be the *on-dit* of the day around Town."

"It would seem that we may not have to do anything after all," Harriet murmured to Charis when the sight of Lord Baylor astride his chestnut captured Isobel's attention.

"Miss Penston, may I walk with you?" Lord Baylor said. "Such a lovely afternoon for a lovely lady." That three other women were present seemed to escape him. He only had eyes for Isobel. He dismounted to walk at her side.

Barbara left her sister, who still was not far away, to join Harriet and Charis. "You both looked so nice last evening, especially Lady Huntingdon. Lord Egerton said you were like a golden goddess."

"How lovely of him. But you must call me Charis.

Even after a year I find the title strange to my ears. Considering that we spent all our time in the country, I suppose that is not surprising."

Charis was happy to see that Isobel had found such an eligible beau. Lord Baylor possessed a tidy fortune and would inherit a vast estate when his father died. Since his father was not labeled a spendthrift and considered a good landlord, that estate was likely to be highly valuable as well. Lady Penston would not be displeased at the connection.

"It is such a lovely day. It seems a shame to spend it inside a house," Harriet said with a happy look around the park.

"Why do we not have a picnic? We could order a carriage, and Cook would fix us a little nuncheon to take along," Charis suggested, thinking it would be a way of avoiding what she suspected would be another confrontation with Marcus. "I think it would be a delightful way to spend an afternoon."

"I say," Lord Baylor inserted, "Egerton and Pilkington would likely want to join us."

Charis glanced at Barbara and back to Lord Baylor, who seemed to catch her thoughts. "And Portchester as well. You all know these fellows, and it would be a jolly way to spend the afternoon. We could drive out to Richmond Hill."

Charis nodded her agreement. Eight people would make an agreeable outing. She could bring Betsy if necessary.

It was agreed that they would gather in two hours at the Penston residence. Isobel insisted they be allowed to bring one basket, leaving the other for Charis and Harriet.

It was a good thing that Huntingdon House was not far from the park. The Penston abode was close as well, so the girls hurried to their respective homes, making requests of the cooks first of all, then changing into suitable dresses and footwear for a picnic in the country.

The elder Lady Huntingdon thought it fine that her girls were to go on a jaunt with a party. She had acquired

a new gothic novel and was inclined to spend the afternoon on her chaise longue, reading. "Most appropriate.
The picnic, I mean," she concluded as she returned to
the book at hand. "Really, it is amazing what variety of
books they have." At Harriet's questioning look, she
added, "At Hatchard's, dear girl."

It was surprising how quickly the Huntingdon cook
assembled the ingredients for their outing to Richmond
Hill. Within the allotted time, the girls left from the rear
of the house with a footman lugging the basket. Not
wishing to take one of her cousin's carriages, Charis summoned a hackney and was pleased to see John Jarvey
respond. She gave him their destination, and they set off,
the footman hanging on behind to assist with the basket
once at Penstons'.

In due course a laughing, chattering group collected at
the Penston residence.

Lord Pilkington said, "It is jolly good that you didn't
ask Vane to join us. He'd be another hour making himself ready." The other men chuckled at this truism.

Not wishing to linger, Charis suggested they be off as
soon as might be. The gentlemen, seeming flattered that
their company was so agreeable, made haste to assist the
four young women into the two landaus chosen for the
expedition. The two large baskets were stowed away, and
then they were off—but none too soon to suit Charis.

She held her breath as Cousin Marcus and Lady Alicia
came toward them from the opposite direction. The best
part of London wasn't all that large, so it wasn't surprising to see them. Surely he would not stop the carriages
to drag her home. Would he? Stop them he did.

"Sir Marcus, how do you do?" Lord Baylor cried. "We
are off to Richmond Hill for a picnic. Won't you join
us? The more, the merrier!"

Charis met her cousin's gaze a trifle defiantly. She
lifted her chin. Whatever he had to say could surely wait?

"I am certain Cook has sent enough food for a small
army. What say you, Lady Alicia? Shall we join them?"
Marcus cocked an eyebrow at his passenger, as though
testing her.

Harriet exchanged a wary look with Charis.

"Yes, of course. It would be a delight, I am certain."

It seemed to a concerned Charis that the picnic held all the appeal of a sour plum to her ladyship. And Charis did not desire her cousin to join them. Alas, it was too late. Marcus skillfully turned his team, and in short order joined the little parade leaving London headed for what Charis had thought would be an escape from Marcus. The only blessing was that it would be unlikely that he could corner her in the park. She hoped.

The weather was perfect for an outing in the country. They drove past the pretty market gardens and country houses, skimming along the road at the great pace of eight miles per hour, and at last reached the park boundary.

Marcus drew up alongside the carriage, where Charis sat next to Lord Pilkington. "I have a ticket allowing use of the park—unless you already have yours out," he said waving a paper card in the air. At a nod, he proceeded to the gate, where he showed his ticket to the gatekeeper, and the three carriages were allowed passage.

Charis wondered if her cousin was ever without what he required. If there was anyone who always seemed to have what he wanted, it was Marcus—even a silly ticket.

Once inside the park, they soon found an agreeable spot. Charis helped Lord Pilkington arrange the cloth from her basket, and then she and Harriet set about unloading the bounty while Isobel and Barbara did the same with their basket. Soon a repast fit for a king was placed in readiness.

Charis managed to ignore her cousin as much as possible, which was a trifle difficult under the circumstances. Why did he have to happen along at the precise moment they were setting out? And whatever made him think that Lady Alicia would like a picnic? She was like a hothouse rose set among the daisies.

"Lucky we met Sir Marcus. I didn't have my pass with me, nor did Portchester. Forgot it. I fancy the chap at the gate might have let us in, but you never know."

"To be sure. My cousin is always to be found where

he is needed," Charis replied without heat. But far too often he happened to show up when not desired.

They all ate with enthusiasm, and before Charis knew, the various bowls and plates were empty, ready to be stowed in the basket. Being out-of-doors had given most of them an appetite. She had nibbled, worrying about whatever was to come from her cousin. She didn't forget for a moment that he held the purse strings. Her allowance, what there was of it, didn't go far in London.

Harriet wandered off with Lord Portchester, who endeavored to explain the intricacies of driving in the country to her. That she paid him little heed to admire the bucolic beauty in the park seemed not to disturb him in the least. It seemed he just enjoyed talking to someone.

Isobel and Lord Baylor restored the bowls and plates coming from the Penston kitchen to that basket, then sat quietly talking.

There was a slight altercation between Barbara and Lord Egerton when he chose a path that led away from the group. She insisted upon being close, and he graciously yielded.

"I say," Lord Pilkington said to Charis as the others paired off, "this was a splendid idea."

Keeping an eye on her cousin and Lady Alicia, Charis absently agreed. "It is nice to be in the country and still so close to Town." Marcus led Lady Alicia toward Charis and her escort, and she wished them elsewhere.

"I expect that someday it will be open to everyone, the way things are going."

"Heavens, I do hope not," Charis replied. "Just think what hoards of people would do to his lovely landscape. No, I doubt it will ever come to that."

"There's talk about draining the low part to make pasture or gardens," Lord Pilkington mused. "It might add a certain something. Heard they plan to plant more trees. Oaks, most likely."

"Let them do that if they *must* do something."

"Do what?" Marcus inquired as he and Lady Alicia walked up to join them.

She gave him a wary look, not trusting his genial manner.

"The park," Lord Pilkington replied. "We wondered what the future of the park might be."

"Admirable topic. Charis, if I might have a word with you?"

"We were just about to go for a walk. Surely you and I can discuss whatever it is you want to talk about later?" She turned to Lord Pilkington with an appeal in her eyes that he was only too happy to oblige.

"Dash it all, yes," Lord Pilkington inserted. "Too nice to discuss anything serious."

"You think I mean to read a scold?" Marcus countered.

Charis rose to confront her cousin, thinking to escape with Lord Pilkington and get the better of Marcus. "You usually do, cousin. We shall see you later."

"I had hoped that Pilkington here might show Lady Alicia where the mound is located. You know, the place where they believe some ancients are buried? It is over there not far from where Portchester and Lady Harriet are walking."

Charis calculated that Lady Alicia had not been consulted regarding this plan, as she looked furious for just a moment. When Marcus turned to her, she smiled sweetly and said, "There is nothing I should like more. Please do take me, Lord Pilkington. At least I shall have some conversation out of you." She tossed Marcus a look, then accepted Pilkington's reluctant offer of his arm and escort.

"I do not believe she wanted to see the mound," Charis observed.

"I daresay she didn't. When did this picnic come up? There was no such thing in the offing this morning as far as I knew." Marcus crossed his arms and stared a hole through Charis.

"You do *not* know everything in the world," Charis retorted. Then she thought better of her sauciness and went on, "We met in the park this morning. Harriet had been bemoaning the city and wishing for the country. I thought it would be good to get out into the country, or as near enough. I suggested it and all thought it a splendid scheme."

"So it was not to elude me?" he queried, his eyes narrowing at her explanation.

"Why should I do that?" she replied with wide-eyed innocence.

"Seymour told you that I wished to speak with you?" he continued with persistence.

"Indeed," she replied mendaciously.

What Marcus might have said after that was not to be known, for Lady Alicia screamed, enough—as Harriet said later—to wake those buried within the mound.

"Good grief," Marcus muttered along with a few other words Charis chose to ignore.

They swiftly hurried to where Lady Alicia stood screaming her head off. She pointed to the ground and began to sob, throwing herself against Lord Pilkington, accepting his handkerchief with a sniff.

"What in heaven's name is going on?" Marcus demanded.

Lord Pilkington gave a grimace, then said, "Garden snake. She saw that little thing—wouldn't hurt a flea—and began screaming to beat all hollow."

"You poor thing," Charis said to Lady Alicia, thinking the woman had to be the silliest creature alive.

"A snake?" Harriet asked as she and Lord Portchester arrived on the scene. "Was it an adder or something of that sort?"

"It was a garden snake," Charis replied straight-faced. "It would seem that Lady Alicia has an aversion to snakes of any kind."

"I imagine you would prefer to go home now, my lady," Marcus asked with seeming forbearance.

"Oh, yes, indeed I would," she cried. "Give me a city party any day."

"I don't see any snake," Harriet muttered to Charis.

"I fancy it is long gone by now." Charis watched with satisfaction of a sort as Marcus led the very upset lady to where his carriage stood. He spoke briefly to his tiger, and within a short time the horses were hitched back to the carriage and the pair left the park.

And yet there was a hollow feeling deep within Charis as she watched the two disappear from view. She had wanted this, hadn't she? She hadn't wanted Marcus to be with them, watching her, scolding her for who knew what.

"I am sorry she had to leave with him," Harriet said. "I know you aren't really fond of Marcus, but I truly hate the thought of his being married to that woman."

"He wouldn't!" Charis gasped as a light dawned within. "Oh, no!" He couldn't marry Lady Alicia. He should marry her, Charis. She would take care of him far better than that scheming, heartless woman would.

Exposing the true character of Lady Alicia became more important than ever before. Somehow, some way Charis would think of a means to do so. It would be necessary to be creative, and she was very good at that.

The departure cast a pall on the group, and it wasn't long before the rest of them decided to leave as well. Charis felt she had postponed the dreaded meeting with Marcus for a brief time. At least he could not blame her for the snake!

Charis entered the library with apprehension. Marcus had called for her not long after they returned to the house. Looking at where her cousin sat behind his desk, her fears rose. If he had looked stern at the picnic, he looked positively forbidding now.

"Goodness, Marcus, you look as though you could do serious harm to someone. I cannot recall such a fierce scowl. Did I do something to displease you?" She had decided to take the offensive by bringing his annoyance out at once. There was little point in prolonging her suspense.

"You might say that I am displeased. Actually, you might even call it anger." He picked up a lavender, highly scented letter from his desk to wave at her.

"Oh, no," Charis said with a sigh of dismay, sinking onto a chair before the desk. This scene bore all too strong a resemblance to many incidents during her time at the Select Young Ladies Academy. It had always amazed her how narrow a viewpoint the directress had. All Charis had done was try to help people, and it had always got her into scrapes. She never could understand how her efforts were so utterly unappreciated by the lady in authority.

"Oh, yes, dear cousin. Just what sort of harebrained scheme did you dream up to bring forth this letter?" He continued to wave it about, and Charis caught a whiff of the perfume. "She says that since I am a heartless ogre who will not even pay for your things, she decided not to ask for anything else from me. At least I think that is what she writes," he admitted with a glance at the page.

"Umm," Charis agreed, "her writing is a bit creative."

"What do you know about her writing. Have you been reading my correspondence? *And* you have *not* answered my question. What did you tell her?" He stared at Charis with a threatening frown.

"I read her previous letter to you and her outrageous demands. So I made up something so she would believe you would never send her another farthing or the smallest jewel. I was not going to let that . . . that woman bleed you anymore!" Charis jumped to her feet as Marcus rose to his full and intimidating height. One thing for sure, he was not the slightest bit like the directress. "I merely wanted to help you."

He closed his eyes briefly. When he reopened them, his gaze pierced her to the heart. "Do you have the slightest idea what would have happened if it became known that you went to her home?"

"The Divine Delilah? No. Well, I suppose she is considered a demirep, but, I must say, I think you could do better. Have you ever seen her in a good light?" Charis shook her head. "Tsk, tsk, cousin. A handsome man like you? Wealthy, too. I should think there would be fallen women begging to be your, ah, er, friend. Although I admit she seemed sweet-natured," Charis concluded doubtfully.

He closed his eyes once again, then shook his head.

"I cannot believe we are having this conversation. Charis, you are not supposed to know that women of this type exist, let alone talk about them with a gentleman. You would have been ruined! This makes the glee club incident pale in comparison."

"I do not see why. In the first instance I merely wished to hear some lovely music. In the second, I wished to help you escape from the dunning of this creature."

"Let me set you straight, my dear cousin. She would have received not a farthing more from me no matter how many of these appalling letters she wrote. I merely toss them into the fire—as I will do with this one." He suited his words to action, and within seconds the letter burned merrily away.

Charis wondered if the scent went up the chimney. "I am glad to know that. But I didn't. That is, I had no way of knowing, and when I read her demands, well—"

"You *opened* my mail!"

"I saw the distinctive paper and writing, and worried about you," she said dryly. "Silly of me, I know, but I did. I replaced it at once, although I was tempted to toss it where you did." She glanced at the fireplace to see the objectionable missive reduced to ashes.

He took a deep breath, crossed his arms, and stared at her a few moments before replying. "I ought to beat you. Lord knows you deserve it. You are a trifle too old for that, however." He looked as though the idea still appealed to him, and she took a step away from his reach.

"Besides, I outrank you," Charis pointed out obligingly. She also outranked Lady Alicia but decided now was not the time to mention *that* woman. "I do think we ought to do something about your choice of women, though. As I said before, you could do better." He didn't seem to appreciate her concern for his love life or lack of it.

"Do you know there were three young chaps here this morning wanting to pay their addresses to you? Three no less! And I denied them! I took a look at them—one by one—and knew you could wrap them around your little finger and make life miserable for each of them. Besides, I doubt there was one of them who could handle you."

"Three? Who were they? I suppose you won't say. Pity you turned them down. You want to remove me from your home, do you not? That hardly seems the way to go about it. Besides, I am not the least bossy. I am always polite to servants. I am faithful to my friends and relatives—protective, too." She swallowed with difficulty, then forged ahead. "Marcus, find me a husband! I thought after last evening I might find one or two at the door. I never dreamed you would *disapprove* of *three*." She paused a few moments. "I trust they came from good families?"

"They did," he admitted.

"But you considered them weak?" she queried sweetly.

"I did. You require a man with more backbone than they possessed, even if you put the three of them together."

"I believe I might have been able to judge that for myself," she complained, giving him an annoyed look. "Do you know—I do not understand you in the least?"

"Good. We shall keep it that way. The last thing I want is to be understood by you."

"Oh." Charis walked to the door, then paused. "Was there anything else you wished to scold me about, cousin dear?"

"I am certain I will think of something else once you are out of here. Lord help me, Charis, what will I do with you!" Marcus stared at her, his face unreadable.

She smiled, walked past the door, and closed it gently behind her so he couldn't see her wipe tears away with her fingers. She walked along the hall, bumping into Seymour because her eyes were blinded. "Sorry, Seymour," she murmured.

"My lady, is there anything I may do for you?"

"No." She gave him a wan smile, then dragged herself up the stairs to her room, where she indulged in a good cry.

*   *   *

Marcus looked up as his butler entered the room. "Yes, Seymour, what is it?"

"The young Lady Huntingdon was most upset, sir. She is crying, as a matter of fact. I was most sorry to see that. I have known the family since I first went into service as a lad. I'm that sorry to see the young lady so distressed."

Placing his pen to one side, Marcus rubbed his forehead. She was more than polite to his servants. She had the entire lot of them wrapped around her little finger, just as she would have done to those moonstruck lads.

"I was greatly perturbed by something the countess had done, Seymour. She had earned a scolding, and she knew it."

"Indeed, sir." Seymour was rigid with his disapproval.

The butler bowed and left the room, but Marcus full knew that he had disappointed the faithful retainer. What more could happen?

Chapter Eleven

They endured a very quiet evening during which Harriet entertained her mother by playing several games of cards with her while Charis ostensibly read a book.

Unfortunately, it was followed by a restless night, for Charis spent a lot of time tossing and turning and not much in sleeping.

She plumped her pillow for what was the umpteenth time before deciding that perhaps a book would settle her mind. Could she find a novel that would compel her interest enough so she could forget her cousin's harsh words?

With a sigh she admitted she probably deserved them. But she had meant well. She had known she ought not go to Delilah's house, but she had wanted to help Marcus. As well, she admitted she was curious to know what sort of woman this creature might be. Delilah proved to be opulent, lush, walking with the decidedly languid air of one sure of her attraction.

Well, her own figure was slimmer, and she dare not walk in that manner. Some inner sense told her it would be deemed *fast*. On the other hand, Charis was little more than a catchpenny countess, dressed to attract a purchaser, got up merely to sell herself to a wealthy buyer who wanted a countess and nothing more. It was a hard truth to acknowledge, but truth it was. And she wondered what the difference was between her and those women who sold themselves for a coin. Was she any better?

Past tears, she slipped from her bed, donned a sensible dressing gown, then took her still-lit candle and left her room. Tapers yet burned in the hall, witness to her cousin's absence. He had not been home for dinner, nor had she seen him since she left after her fateful dressing down. It was a simple matter to walk down to the library, light a few more candles, then peruse the section where the novels were shelved. Ruff followed her down the steps, sat near the shelves, and studied her with a puzzled expression. After a time he gave a little growl, and Charis tensed. Faltering footsteps in the hall brought her gaze to the door.

"Cannot sleep, cousin?" came a mocking voice from the doorway as her hand hovered over a novel by Miss Edgeworth.

Charis stared at her cousin, feeling vulnerable yet knowing she had more clothing on than during the day. "No. I came to find something to entertain me."

"And to take your mind off the scold?"

"True," she agreed. She couldn't pretend that his words had not struck her a cruel blow, but she wouldn't let him see how deeply. "But then, as I was just thinking, I am naught but a catchpenny countess after all. All the world and his wife must know I am dressed and on display to catch a husband." The words were lightly spoken, but reflected the cynical thoughts she nurtured. She had believed it would be a simple matter to come to London and find a husband. That was before she encountered her cousin and the difficulty of wedding a man she did not love.

"Indeed. You and every unmarried girl in London hope for the same. This is the matrimonial bazaar, remember? But it is only a temporary state. Most girls marry and are thus out of the running. The mantuamakers pray for a goodly crop of come-outs each year." He strolled into the room, looking a trifle owlish but not castaway.

Charis pulled the book from the shelf, then turned to leave the room, praying to get past him before he began another reprimand. One had been quite enough.

She thought success was in her hands when he stopped her by simply catching her shoulder.

"You thought me cruel. Am I right?"

She stiffened and looked back at him. "True. I did. I do. How could I not?"

"You must see I had to rebuke you for your actions. I would have been remiss had I not. You cannot do here as you might in the country." He took a step toward her, tilting his head as he considered her. "Tell me, what would you be doing if you were there now? What activity would engage your mind and heart?"

She turned to face him, yet backed to the door. Ruff stood at her side, looking from one person to the other. "I planned to set up a dame school before father died, and it became impossible." At his look of inquiry, she added, "It requires a sum of money. I wanted a clean, dry building and a woman to teach." Her enthusiasm caused her to step forward, one hand gestured in a sort of supplication while the other clutched the book. "I read a pamphlet that said a worker who can read is likely to be more productive. Surely that is a good thing for the estate?"

"I believe I have read something of the sort." He took another step in her direction.

"Well," she said eagerly, "would you consider it?"

"I might," he replied, now standing close to her.

Charis realized her dangerous position about the same time that Marcus touched her chin lightly with his hand.

She jerked away from his touch. How was it possible to want something so very much and yet know you must not want it?

"Perhaps we could kiss and make up?" His lazy drawl told her that he was closer to being castaway than she'd realized. She detected a slight hint of brandy emanating from him. He was dangerous when sober—to be near him now could be truly risky.

"I do not think that a wise idea, cousin." She ought to flee his light touch while she could. Her feet refused to accept the message from her brain.

"But we are only second cousins—not so close as all that, are we?" His words were faintly slurred, but otherwise there was little clue to the amount of wine or brandy that he might have consumed that evening at his club.

"I best go to my room," she protested. Her feet still refused to move. Foolishly, she didn't force them.

Marcus shook his head. His fingers beneath her chin drew her toward him, and heaven help her, she could not resist him. His kiss was a light, cousinly touch, but only for a few moments. It deepened and consumed her with flames of desire. He threaded a hand through her fiery curls and demolished her will to resist him.

It was only when he smoothed his hand over her back and felt the texture of her dressing gown that he drew away. Ruff jumped up on him, whining. Marcus shook his head, turning slightly away from her. "Go to your room. Can you not see I am intoxicated?" His voice was harsh, thickened.

Charis fled. Ruff took one look at the man who stood so still, then went after his mistress, galloping up at her side.

Marcus followed her to the door, watching. The candle illuminated her dark red curls until she reached the landing and shortly disappeared from sight.

Egad, what a fool he was to play with such fire! His mind was befuddled with wine and brandy, true. But he knew better, regardless. Her gentle mouth looked bruised, and he could not lightly dismiss the hurt in her captivating green eyes.

What he was to do about the situation he didn't know. One thing certain, he must sever the connection with Lady Alicia. She had little appeal, unlike another who inflamed his desire and made him ache with longing. Alicia had once seemed agreeable company—but no longer!

In her room Charis glanced at Ruff, dropped the book on her bed, then walked across the room to build up the fire a little. A few bits of coal would add warmth and comfort, she was sure. She felt shivery.

"This is madness," she informed the dog. "I *must* find a way out of this house. I cannot allow him to kiss me whenever he wishes." That she had not been unwilling, she ignored. She hated to admit the powerful attraction he had for her. He was more likely to wed Lady Alicia than his vexing cousin.

Her most likely way out was marriage. But to whom? Lord Pilkington? He seemed kind and gentle, sympathetic but not maudlin. He had exhibited just the right note when Lady Alicia had watered his cravat. And, Charis recalled, he had not fussed about the ruined state of that cravat once Marcus and Lady Alicia departed.

Marcus had been splendid with Lady Alicia. He had been polite and comforting, escorting her from the scene without a bit of seeming regret.

Charis did not like snakes—they were slimy, and adders were dangerous. But she would not have screamed to wake the dead if she had spotted a little grass snake. She would far prefer chasing peacock butterflies. Perhaps that said something of her character? Too tired to contemplate her nature at this hour of the night, particularly after the encounter with Marcus, she set the Edgeworth novel on her bedside table. Ruff jumped up, then curled into a little heap at the foot of her bed. Charis dropped her dressing gown aside, snuffed out her candle, and slid under the covers, seeking the oblivion of sleep.

Come morning she brought Ruff downstairs with her, handed him to a footman for a walk, then sought the breakfast room, hoping to find Harriet.

"You did not sleep well, did you?" her sister said after regarding Charis in the morning light.

"I have slept better, thank you. Do you have any plans for the day?"

"Barbara Penston and I thought we might take a walk in the park. Isobel is going for a drive with Lord Baylor."

"Her mother approves?" Charis queried.

"Indeed, she does. You know what an excellent catch he is."

"I do. Would that I could do as well," Charis replied with a rueful grimace.

The elder Lady Huntingdon entered the room, greeting her daughters with an absentminded smile, a book in hand. "Where is Marcus?"

"I would imagine he is still sleeping. I believe he returned home rather late last night. If he was at this club, he might have consumed sufficient wine or brandy that he sleeps later today," Charis explained with a degree of self-consciousness.

"I think we are driving him from his own house," Harriet commented thoughtfully.

"True," Charis agreed, then munched a bit of toast without butter or marmalade, a thing that her sister noted with surprise.

Harriet studied her sister. "I believe you would enjoy a walk in the park today as well."

"By all means, go, dear girls," their mother said at once, surprising them that she had paid the slightest attention to their conversation. "You must be out and about to catch the eye of a gentleman."

Charis dropped her crumb of toast on her plate and rose from the table. "In that event I should dress for presentation. After all, I am here to display my wares."

She left Harriet behind to go to her room.

"She is upset," Harriet said thoughtfully. "I think she is discovering that it is no simple thing to catch a husband."

"No one ever told her it would be," replied her ladyship. "Simple, that is. She will come out well in the end, I should say." She opened her book and began to read.

"I could wish she felt as confident," Harriet responded as she rose from the table to go to her room.

She met her cousin at the bottom of the stairs. "Good grief, Marcus, you look dreadful. Foxed last night?"

"Harriet, please. You are not to say such things to a gentleman." He gave her a pained look, then moved away.

Harriet was not to be deterred. "We intend to go to the park with Miss Barbara Penston. Even though it is late morning, we thought it might help Charis."

He paused and turned to stare at her. "Help Charis?"

"There might be a gentleman riding in the park who

will take one look at her and be smitten. It is not unknown to happen, I believe."

"Only in novels," he snapped.

"You do not believe in love at first sight?"

"I do not believe in love, period." With that pithy retort, he went on his way to the breakfast room.

"Touchy, touchy. I wonder if he has the headache or if there is something else troubling him?" Harriet murmured as she ran up the stairs and hurried to the shared sitting room.

Charis, dressed in a new and lovely creation of willow-green sarcenet trimmed with a Vandyke border in white and dark green at the hem and collar, was in the act of selecting a bonnet, when Harriet knocked before barging into her room.

"Well, that ought to bowl someone off his feet. What a fetching gown. Do you think you might see anyone we have met?" Harriet plumped herself down on the side of the bed to watch her sister.

"Lord Pilkington said something about riding in the park this morning. I do not know how early he goes, but perhaps he was also out in the wee small hours last evening and rides late?"

"How did you *know* Marcus was out late last night? For you did, unless I miss my guess," Harriet declared.

"I went down to fetch something to read and was in the library when he returned. I picked up that novel by Miss Edgeworth. Have you read it? Is it interesting?"

Not about to be sidetracked, Harriet asked, "Was he corned, pickled, and salted? Or merely a bit elevated?"

"I suspect he was a trifle muddled. I cannot imagine our fastidious cousin becoming foxed." Charis set her bonnet at the proper angle, then collected a parasol and reticule. "I am ready. Fetch your things and we can go."

Apparently deciding that Charis would say no more, Harriet left, obediently returning with her parasol and reticule. Harriet's gown of sprigged muslin became her well, and as to her bonnet, the narrow brim revealed a determined chin below a gentle mouth.

Once they had collected Miss Barbara, the three young

ladies continued on to the park. By this time it was early afternoon, and the nannies and governesses were sprinkled here and there, watching their charges.

The young women ignored them, concentrating on the latest gossip and keeping a sharp eye out for anything of interest—that being a gentleman they had met.

"There is Lord Pilkington riding with Marcus," Harriet said quietly.

Not wishing to meet her cousin, Charis was at a loss as to what to do. She could hardly bring Lord Pilkington up to scratch if she didn't spend more time with him. Yet did she want Marcus to watch her efforts at flirting? He would most likely summon her to the library to offer her lessons.

Harriet watched her sister blush with interest. "I'd give a guinea to know what you are thinking, Charis."

"Do not be silly. It is merely the sun."

"If you say so," Harriet replied, clearly unconvinced.

Charis was saved from further questioning by the arrival of the gentlemen astride their fine horses.

"Good morning, Sir Marcus and Lord Pilkington," Barbara said, looking quite winsome in her pale blue muslin dress.

Both men dismounted, taking reins in hand to walk beside the young women who were bewitchingly fetching.

"Harriet, I've not seen you in that before. Most becoming," Marcus said after a quick perusal of his young cousin.

"I think Charis looks nice," Harriet said modestly after properly thanking her cousin.

"Oh, indeed" was the gallant reply from Lord Pilkington.

Charis glanced at her cousin. She did not seek his opinion, yet she wondered if he would say something.

"I believe Charis knows what I think of her . . . attire," Marcus said with a raised and knowing eyebrow.

She longed to do major mischief to that handsome face of his. "You are too kind, Cousin Marcus."

"Good chap, always say so," Lord Pilkington obligingly offered.

"We ought not keep you both from your ride," Charis said, hoping her cousin would leave and Lord Pilkington would somehow remain.

"We can spend a few minutes basking in beauty," Marcus said. "The park is overflowing with lesser charmers."

Charis thought she detected a bit of mockery in his tone and shot him a narrow look. She wanted to tell him to bask elsewhere, but that might look odd to Barbara. That lady seemed to think there was no one superior to Sir Marcus. He seemed to epitomize all that was the cream of Society as far as Barbara was concerned. Pity she didn't know the other side of the bewildering creature.

At that moment Lady Alicia came into view, superbly mounted on a fine chestnut that she controlled with ease. Charis had to admit she looked dashing as she rode up to join them.

"What a lovely day," she said in her most lofty manner.

"Undeniably true," Charis replied. "It has been."

Lady Alicia shot Charis a look that was as kind as one she might bestow upon that green snake should she see it again. Clearly, no love was lost between the two ladies—which suited Charis right down to her toes.

"Sir Marcus, surely you find strolling along the lane a trifle tame. Will you not join me for a little run?" Lady Alicia coaxed.

Charis watched her cousin with care, and thought she detected a slight hint of annoyance on his face before he turned to face Lady Alicia. "With great pleasure, my lady," he replied politely.

Tossing a triumphant look at Charis and ignoring the other young women completely, she wheeled her horse about and began to ride away, obviously expecting Marcus to join her at once.

"I shall talk with you later about that project," Marcus announced to a mystified Charis.

"Project? How intriguing," Lady Alicia said, turning back to join them at once. "And what manner of project could you have with your little cousin?" There was a sneer in her voice that was undoubtedly calculated to annoy Charis. It did.

Charis counted to ten and waited to see what Marcus might say to this.

"Why, it is an excellent scheme to start a school on the estates in the country," he said while watching both women. "We have to discuss the size of the school, the type of building, qualifications for a teacher, and so forth."

"Good show," Lord Pilkington said. "My mater started a dame school in the village, and it has done no end of good."

"Well, I think it a pack of nonsense!" scoffed Lady Alicia. "What good can come of teaching the peasants to read or write? Gives them ideas, that's what it does. It is a complete waste of good money."

"What would *you* have them learn, Lady Alicia?" Charis inquired.

"Nothing!" her ladyship snapped.

"Other than the job they are intended to perform?" Charis said with an innocent look at her regal ladyship. "It would be a pity if a worker put poison where it should not go, simply because he could not read a label."

"They know what is what," her ladyship sputtered. "Come, Sir Marcus, let us be off."

"When you have no good reply, it is best to retreat," Charis said quietly. However, she spoke loud enough so that Lady Alicia heard her and sent Charis a nasty look.

"Until later, Charis," Marcus called, giving her a rueful smile.

Lord Pilkington made his adieus as well and took off in another direction.

"Forgive me, but I truly dislike that woman," Barbara said, sending a gloomy look after the pair of riders.

"What a pity you do not ride, Charis. I have no doubt that you would prove to be vastly superior to her high and mightiness." Harriet giggled.

"It would be lovely," Charis admitted. "But I fear I am too old to learn now. I waited too long."

"Is it ever too late to learn something you want to

do?" Barbara inquired as they caught sight of two more gentlemen wending their way in their direction.

"Lady Icicle would laugh at any attempts to do what she does so well," Harriet said with a grin.

"Oh, Harriet, what a deliciously wicked thing to say!" Barbara replied, laughing.

"I wonder," Charis mused, then stopped when Lord Egerton and Lord Portchester rode up to greet them.

"I say," Harriet said to Lord Egerton, "do you think it is ever too late to learn how to ride a horse?"

"Who needs to learn?" he inquired with a glance at Charis.

"My sister. Unlike many people, she didn't get right back on the horse when it tossed her. Although to be sure, it would have been difficult—for she broke her arm and sprained her ankle."

"That must have been painful," Lord Egerton said to Charis, sympathy clear in his voice and on his face. "But perhaps you might try?"

He showed a nice regard for her being, Charis thought. He would likely make a fine husband, and no doubt she ought to consider him an excellent prospect.

"Never do," Lord Portchester contradicted. "Take someone like Lady Alicia Dartry . . . nearly born in the saddle. Raised to ride. It would be humiliating for any woman to barely hang onto a mount when in public."

Charis decided that Lord Portchester was beyond consideration as a prospective husband. Again, the thought occurred to her that he would be an excellent mate for the thoughtless Lady Alicia.

"Perhaps there is a school for riding? I thought I heard someone say there is one here in Hyde Park?" Charis asked politely, not because she truly wanted to learn, but she did not want to appear fainthearted.

"Opposite Gloustershire House on the east side of the park, there is the Gloustershire Riding House," Lord Egerton said. "Captain Fozard is the name of the chap who runs it. Takes private pupils, and I believe the fee is about a half guinea unless you take a course of lessons from him when I think it is less."

"Thank you," Charis said, smiling up at Lord Egerton. He truly seemed nice. "I shall have to think about it."

"Wise thing to do," his lordship said.

The gentlemen rode on, and the young ladies continued with their walk. Harriet and Barbara chattered away sixteen to the dozen.

Charis remained rather quiet, contemplating the figures on horseback that rode on the other side of the rail, which had been erected for the safety of persons on foot. Could she dare to cross that rail, learn to ride again? She had thought about it from time to time, always backing away from the actual deed. Her mother did not care what she did in the slightest, and her father had never compelled his daughters to do what upset them. Maybe if she took lessons from one not related to her, not someone who was an employee—like the elderly groom at the country estate who scoffed at her refusal to ride, she could learn.

They eventually returned to the house. It was time to prepare for the afternoon calls.

"Do you think you might take lessons, Charis?" Harriet inquired when they reached their sitting room.

"And use what for money?" Charis replied simply. "I have spent most of my allowance, and I would rather die than ask Marcus for some."

"That's a bit silly, you know. He won't kill you." Harriet sniffed and marched off to her room.

Charis slowly walked into her room, greeting Ruff with absent pleasure. She picked up the little dog, rubbing her cheek against his sleek head as she considered the lessons.

Could she?

The elder Lady Huntingdon greeted Lady Penston with delight when she entered the drawing room. Barbara and Isobel followed in her trail, meeting Charis and Harriet to slip off to the far end of the room. If they spoke in low tones, they could enjoy a most comfortable coze.

"What do you wear to the party at the Minchins'? I trust you mean to go?" Isobel asked Charis.

"I suppose it would not do to wear the gold tissue again," Charis said with a wry grimace. "I dote on that gown, and it seems silly to wear something once and not again when it was probably a costly item."

"You didn't order it for yourself?" Isobel looked intrigued.

"Marcus surprised me, ordering it shortly before the ball. Perhaps I can alter it somehow?" Charis mused.

"Well, it created a sensation. I doubt you can find a gown half so impressive if you try!" Barbara said with a nod.

Resolved to do something that would enable her to make use of the gown again, Charis decided it would be difficult. That was the problem with such a distinctive garment. It would be remembered—particularly by a woman like Lady Alicia. Wearing the gown again without a major alteration would be like asking for one of her ladyship's famous set-downs. Charis wondered if Marcus had ever been treated to such a spectacle. She doubted it.

Other women came, stayed the proper length of time, then departed. Lady Penston had remained far beyond the usual calling time by reason of being asked to stay.

"I have been out of touch too long," the elder Lady Huntingdon protested. "I welcome your news, dear Lady Penston. You must make me *au courant* with Society."

Charis smiled at the formality between the two older women. However, it was what they had known while growing up. Manners tended to stay with you even as you aged.

At last the callers all departed, and Charis was free to go to her room. She intended to take out the gold tissue gown. Surely there might be something that she could do to make it wearable again—and without comment.

Harriet and her mother had gone to their respective rooms while Charis browsed in the library, hoping to find a copy of *La Belle Assemblee* or another like publication that would have fashion plates. It was too much to hope her cousin would not come home. She heard his now-familiar step in the entry hall and braced herself.

"I do seem to find you here often, cousin. Does the room have an attraction for you?" Marcus queried from the doorway.

"Not really," Charis replied not quite truthfully. "I merely hunted for a journal that would have a few fashion plates in it. I want some ideas," she concluded absently.

"I thought you had quite enough of those." He walked slowly into the room, and Charis likened it to the prowl of a cat.

"It seems a lady cannot wear a dress twice—no matter how fine it might be—if she is not to be considered a pauper or worse."

He paused and frowned thoughtfully. "What do you intend?"

"Well, I do like that gold tissue gown and thought to alter it in some manner, only I have little talent for that sort of thing."

"Yes, I seem to recall those dreadful things you wore when you arrived here. If that was an example of your dressmaking skills, I agree with you. Why do you not take it to Madame Clotilde and have her change it? Seems the obvious thing to do."

"Could I?"

"Why not? And while we are on the topic of clothing, I would take you to my tailor and have you measured for a riding habit."

"What makes you think I intend to learn how to ride?"

"Shall we say that I know you?"

Chapter Twelve

Marcus followed through on his word. The next day he escorted Charis to Madame Clotilde, where the problem with the gown was explained. Charis would have preferred to go by herself; however, her cousin seemed impervious to all suggestions she made in that regard.

"Rubbish. She will attend the Countess of Huntingdon all the better for Sir Marcus Rutledge being with her," he insisted without the least arrogance in his manner.

Of course he was correct, the odious creature.

"Are you ever wrong, cousin?" Charis asked when Madame Clotilde had left to find a sketch to show them. It was difficult to be out of charity with him when he managed to accomplish precisely what she wanted with an ease that was downright aggravating.

"At times I find I've made an error in judgement. It happens infrequently, and usually I can rectify it without too much difficulty." He made the admission with the assurance of one comfortable with his decisions and life. Also, one whose wealth allowed him to do as he pleased.

Charis wondered when and how an error occurred but decided it was better not to ask.

Once they left Madame Clotilde's shop, Marcus headed for the tailor shop.

"I could have merely sent him my measurements, you know," Charis said quietly.

"He is most discreet, and you will be fully clothed, of course," Marcus countered.

Evidently a note had been sent to Stultz indicating that they would pay a visit, for there were no other gentlemen about and the man appeared to be expecting them.

The tailor measured her for the habit, and then Marcus selected the fabric—an exquisite deep green wool that Charis had instantly coveted when she viewed it.

"You take a great deal upon yourself, cousin," she said, not wishing him to think he could have his way without consulting her on the matter.

"Admit you like it. Nothing else would become you half so well." His smile was slow and intimate, and threw her into confusion.

The tailor took the bolt of cloth, along with the order, to the rear of the shop, and they prepared to depart. Charis paused to study Marcus. What possessed him to behave as he did? She wished she knew. "And what if I find I loathe riding? What if I turn out to be totally inept? This expensive habit will prove a total waste."

"I shall teach you. You will prove to be an apt pupil," he said with his touch of arrogance.

By this point they were on the pavement. Charis stopped in her tracks, gasping at his audacity. "Never! You will *not* teach me to ride. I have it on good authority that it is dreadful for a husband or relative to school one to ride. I cannot imagine anyone more intimidating than you," she said, a bit more frank than she had intended, wincing at her slip of her foolish tongue. She hoped he would ignore it.

"I am not intimidating," he argued.

She closed her eyes for a few seconds, then flashed them open to send him a scathing look. "You could give royalty lessons."

"Sorry. I must learn to be more humble when I'm with you," he replied, not sounding in the least meek. He assisted her into his carriage, took the reins from his tiger, then set off, driving to an inch as usual.

Charis gave up. It would be impossible to convince him that she found him daunting. So absorbed in her thoughts was she that she completely missed seeing Lady Alicia going in the opposite direction with Lord Portchester.

"I see Portchester is trying to cut me out," Marcus observed as he feathered a corner on the way home.

"What?" She glanced behind them to glimpse Lord Portchester's distinctive carriage and a lady passenger wearing a bonnet that had been seen on Lady Alicia any number of times.

Charis settled back to face forward, not looking at her cousin to see what his expression might be. "Well, you need not fear I shall try to patch that up. The last thing I would wish on you is a connection with that woman."

"Truly? She is considered quite the desirable catch," Marcus said with smooth urbanity.

"Then, allow Lord Portchester to have her. They are two of a kind, you know. I cannot think she would be good for you." Charis closed her eyes again when she realized she had overstepped the bounds she had vowed not to break.

"Why?" He sounded innocently questioning.

Not trusting his ingenuous query, Charis said, "If you cannot understand that, you are truly hopeless." She longed to tell him that Lady Alicia was even more autocratic than he and possessed the nastiest disposition Charis had ever seen.

The drive continued in unbroken silence as each of them digested inner thoughts.

"Where do you go this evening?" Marcus inquired as they arrived at Huntingdon House. He handed the reins to his tiger, then assisted Charis from the curricle.

"The Minchins are giving a party. The Penstons are going as well, so we will be a jolly group." Charis shook out her skirts, closed her parasol, and walked up the few steps to the door. Seymour was in attendance, for it opened at once and she was bowed into the house. Marcus followed.

Once in the hall, Charis paused to look at her cousin. "Shall we see you there?"

"Lady Alicia requested I escort her and her mother some time ago," he admitted.

"I know I promised I'd not say a word, but you really ought to persuade Lord Portchester to perform the honors." Her smile was a trifle forced as she admitted she had just done what she had said only minutes ago she would not do.

"I wonder why you are so concerned about my love life? I cannot fathom what your motive could be," Marcus murmured once out of Seymour's hearing range.

"You are a relative," Charis claimed, grasping at a familiar straw. "Of course I care what happens to you." She added with an attempt at flippancy, "But then, we can always move into the dower house should you marry."

"Really? And have you a particular candidate in mind so that is unnecessary?"

Aware he watched her face like a hawk, Charis assumed the mien she had practiced while at school when required to confront the headmistress over a misdemeanor. "Lord Egerton appears to be a kindly gentleman."

"Ah, yes, you relegate Portchester to Lady Alicia."

"He has little kindness and talks too much—I have learned more about his carriages than I could wish to know. But then, she talks about the endless round of parties she attends. As I said before, they are well matched."

"Surely there must be someone else."

"Lord Pilkington is consideration itself. I like him very well." Find the conversation more than a little difficult, Charis moved to the stairs.

"What do you plan to wear this evening, Charis? I ask so that I shall be able to spot you in the throng of people." He leaned against the newel post as she paused on the first tread of the stairs. His lazy half smile proved hard to resist.

If she'd intended to snub him, it was impossible. "I have a pretty apple-green aerophane crepe over a white taffeta slip."

"Yes, green becomes you—as I have noted before."

It was amazing how he could hold her with nothing more than his voice. She shook herself free from his spell and hurried up the stairs to her room.

Harriet was in the sitting room, leafing through a periodical with an air of innocence that gave Charis pause. Before she could question it, her sister brought forth a query of her own.

"Did Marcus persuade you to be measured for a riding habit?"

"Yes," Charis responded dryly. "It is to be in darkest green, for he declares it suits me best."

"Well, and so it does. Did you buy a few habit shirts and leather gloves, and what about a hat? I should think a black one with a green scarf would be very dashing."

"You think I need to be dashing? I wonder if Lord Egerton would approve. Or Pilkington, for that matter."

"Are you certain they are the only ones who are important?"

"I have relegated Lord Portchester to Lady Alicia. Do you know that we saw them driving together? I chanced to see a glimpse of them as we turned a corner. No mistaking her, for she wore that bonnet with the strange plaid ribbons on it."

"He might have been taking her to the bookshop. I have observed she tends to prevail on gentlemen to assist her in errands," Harriet said with a wry face.

"Well, with any luck at all he will do it forever."

"I thought she intended to wed Marcus."

"Perhaps she did. Maybe she still does, for she requested he escort her this evening to the Minchin affair. It may be she believes it wise to have two beaux to her string?"

Harriet chuckled as intended.

Once at Minchins', the apple-green aerophane crepe over the white taffeta proved to be a smashing success if the respectable cluster of gentlemen surrounding Charis was any measure. She took their compliments with pink cheeks and wide smiles.

Lord Egerton was the first to beg two dances, followed by Lord Pilkington. Others did so as well. When Marcus walked up to her, her dance list was almost full. She did not demur when he withdrew the paper from her hand. She knew full well that it was useless to counter him.

"Hmm, a waltz and the supper dance." He signed his name after both.

At this effrontery Charis did object. "Marcus, I expected you to seek out the lady you escorted here for the supper dance. You will be obliged to sit with *me,* you know." She glanced at where Lady Alicia stood chatting with Lord Portchester. They seemed equally enthralled with one another. She flashed her eyes back to her cousin to see if he had noticed. If he had, it seemed he did not care. Could he be encouraging the connection?

"I am aware of what I do." He gave her a look that sent tingles to her toes and back.

"I doubt I shall ever understand you," she complained.

"I thought I told you I did not wish you to understand me," he countered, his brows raised in mockery. He handed her the slip of paper, then sauntered off to speak with some of his particular friends.

"Oh," she exclaimed softly while stamping a slippered foot in exasperation.

Lord Egerton claimed his first dance, and Charis saw nothing of her cousin until it came time to demand his waltz. She stood next to her mother, waiting.

The elder Lady Huntingdon ceased chatting with Lady Penston long enough to nod to Marcus when he took Charis's hand to lead her away.

"Your mother seems to truly enjoy Lady Penston's company," he observed as he gathered Charis in his arms.

The last thing she wanted was to discuss her mother or her friendships. Charis nodded briefly, but said nothing.

It seemed that was agreeable with Marcus. He drifted around the floor holding Charis a trifle closer than was proper. She did not bother to scold him on it, as he always had some logical excuse for doing precisely what he wished.

Marcus inhaled the delicious scent of gillyflowers that belonged to Charis. She was like a feather in his arms. A charming, much sought after feather, he amended. He wondered how much longer his resolve could hold.

Thank goodness Charis was taking her time about her selection, and even seemed indifferent to what her choice might be. It gave him hope that ultimately he would have his way. This was one time he could not be certain that he would succeed as he usually did when he planned a complicated scheme. His plan was risky, uncertain.

She was quicksilver, elusive, and at times it was impossible to guess what she thought or would do. What madness to insist upon a waltz. Yet he could not have tolerated another gentleman holding her like this. He looked down at the mass of dark red curls with a silly little rose tucked in their midst. He would have liked to bury his face in the softness of her curls, and a lot of other things he had best not think about if he was smart.

When the dance concluded all too soon to please him, he properly returned her to her mother's side, bowing over her hand. "I shall gather you up for the supper dance," he promised before leaving her. He did not want to know who her next partner would be, and yet he paused to note that Portchester claimed her hand for a reel.

"Sir Marcus," a silken voice said, insistent in spite of the low tone. Her hand plucked at his sleeve.

"Lady Alicia. I trust you are enjoying the party?" He deftly removed her hand and smoothed down the sleeve.

"A paltry thing. Too few people for it to be called a ball, I suppose. I had expected the Minchin affair to be grander than this." She waved her fan about to encompass the pleasant room with modest decorations befitting someone who did not possess a vast fortune but did like to entertain a number of friends.

"I believe they are wise to confine their party to what they can afford. Too many entertain far beyond their means." Marcus thought Charis correct when she said Lady Alicia rather suited Portchester. He was finding his escort role more and more difficult to play.

"Fetch me some lemonade. I find it far too hot in here." Her petulance was not becoming to her.

"Please?" he was goaded into saying. He had observed

more than once that the autocratic lady failed in simple courtesy.

"Do not be silly, Marcus." She tapped him on the arm with her fan in a familiar manner, simpering coyly.

He disappeared with a rapidity that doubtless made her blink. She was not accustomed to men deserting her. Good manners compelled him to return with the demanded lemonade. He did not, however, have to remain.

"I must claim my partner for the next dance."

"And who tears you from my side?" she asked with an arch tone he disliked.

"Lady Harriet, as a matter of fact. My little cousin is blooming and fair to become a diamond." He bowed and walked off before she could think of a reason to detain him. As far as he was concerned, Portchester was welcome to her. Now, if he could just think of a way to convince the man of that.

Charis had returned to her mother, following the dance with Lord Portchester, and was about to be paired with Lord Baylor when Marcus walked up to take Harriet's hand.

"Let us form a set," Marcus suggested.

Lord Baylor instantly agreed while the young ladies merely exchanged glances.

The pattern of the dance was familiar. Charis allowed her mind to wander while she performed the various steps.

"Pay attention," Marcus murmured when he briefly stood next to her. "The supper dance is next. We will not bother to return to your mother."

Raising very surprised brows in reply, Charis could only nod before they were once again separated. It was a sprightly dance, and she marveled at how graceful Marcus was in spite of his height and impressive physique. Those pale biscuit breeches fit his muscular legs in a way that must make less fortunate men quite envious.

It puzzled her that Marcus did not wish to observe the ritual of properly returning her to Mama. If nothing else, her cousin was correct in his manners.

Lord Baylor escorted Harriet to Mama once Marcus

explained that he was his cousin's partner for the supper dance.

Isobel partnered Lord Baylor for the third time, a thing that a number of people noted. Custom had it that a gentleman asked for no more than two dances in an evening. To ask for more indicated a closeness that hinted at an engagement at the very least. Charis hoped this was the case for Isobel. She scarce had eyes for anyone else.

"Your little blond friend does well for herself," Marcus observed as he swung Charis into a waltz.

"Indeed. Marcus, this was not supposed to be a waltz. The program indicated a cotillion." She narrowed her eyes, studying his face. "Did you by chance have something to do with the change?"

"Why should I wish to waltz with you? Perhaps they merely confused the program. I believe that is the dance that follows supper."

He was right, but she had a niggling feeling that he had persuaded the musicians to change the order. He had passed that way shortly before he chatted with Lady Alicia. That Charis had kept track of him all evening was ignored.

The dance floor was crowded with more than one couple looking confused at the alteration in the program. A gentleman bumped into Marcus and apologized. Then Marcus pulled her against his chest, nearly suffocating her in the process. Mercy, her nerves were in a tumult. It was difficult enough to be close in his arms. To be plastered against him was pure torture.

"Marcus!" she objected. Glancing up at those chiseled features, she could only wonder what went on in his mind.

"Dashed fool was about to trample you to bits." He released her a trifle, but not nearly enough.

"Thank you . . . I think. Is there still a danger? I shall swoon if I do not get air." It was not air she needed, it was distance from Marcus. How could she proceed with plans for Lord Pilkington or Lord Egerton if her cousin's appeal overcame her at every turn?

He made no reply, merely waltzing her to where there were tall doors that opened out to a narrow balcony. In seconds she found herself inhaling cool air, but with her cousin's arm still around her shoulders.

"Thank you." Charis trembled, but not from the cool air. Why did his touch disturb her so? Maybe she *had* adored him when a child, yet she was an adult now. She knew better than to be attached to her cousin.

"I could not have you swooning in my arms. I much prefer to have a lady awake on all suits in such a circumstance." He looked down into her eyes, touching her chin lightly with one gloved finger.

She could have sworn the look he gave her was tender and held regard. But the light was dim, and she was uncertain.

"Those green eyes seem a bit cynical. Why, I can only wonder." He trailed his finger along the edge of her jaw, and Charis felt a sensation unlike anything she'd known. She wanted to lean into him again, feel safe and yet know that magical touch.

"I confess I was wondering what it meant to be awake on all suits while in your arms," she retorted, stung to a rash reply as always when he teased her.

"I do not think you need to worry about that, my dear. I fancy you would do well enough should the occasion occur." He tilted her face up, then placed an all too brief kiss on her lips.

"Marcus, what if someone saw us. They might jump to the wrong conclusion," Charis whispered when she could reclaim her mind.

"And that is what?" He toyed with an errant curl while closely watching her.

"Why, that you are interested in me, and not in a cousinly manner," she quipped. Her lighthearted voice was hard-won. He teased, and she knew full well that she must look elsewhere. He had made that plain enough. "Cease playing around with my fondness for you."

"You have a fondness for me?" He froze, studying her closely.

"I always have had," she replied simply.

A noisy couple left the house to join them on the balcony, and Marcus swiftly escorted Charis back inside while muttering a few words under his breath that she preferred not to hear.

The waltz had ended, and everyone wandered in the direction of the room where a supper had been set out. A long table was loaded with every delicacy one might wish. Small tables had been arranged here and there, with a proper amount of dainty chairs for the diners.

Marcus found her a chair at a little table nearby, and then he collected plates, filling them with an assortment of foods designed to satisfy any appetite. He set her plate down, joining her at the table and sitting far too close. Within moments Lord Baylor and Isobel joined them.

Charis noted that Marcus did not seem pleased at the company.

"When do you begin your riding lessons?" Isobel wanted to know once she had settled.

"My habit is not ready, and I do not possess the proper boots," Charis replied, in essence reminding Marcus that he had forgotten that essential.

"Good grief," he murmured with a wry look at her.

"True," she answered with a grin. "However, I thought I might borrow something and take a lesson at that establishment in Hyde park."

"Mr. Fozard's place? I understand he is very good," Isobel said. "If he can train the Westminster Volunteer Cavalry, he ought to manage you." Isobel laughed at her friend's expression of dismay.

"I trust it will not be as bad as all that!" Charis exclaimed.

"Not in the least," Marcus smoothly inserted. "Since I intend to supervise your lessons, there will be no need to pay Mr. Fozard, even if he does train the Westminster Volunteers."

"I thought you had given that up," Charis declared.

"Whatever gave you that notion? I think we will have a fine time of it." His eyes seemed to promise a great deal more than riding lessons, but perhaps she was imagining things. She seemed to do that a lot lately.

"Well, if it is anything like the time you decided I needed to learn how to swim, I have my doubts." To the others she added, "I thought he would drown me at the very least."

"But . . . you did learn to swim—after a fashion." Marcus shot her a look full of mischief.

"Did you not refer to my ability as a dog paddle?" Charis said sweetly.

It was difficult to believe that her granite-faced cousin, who raked her over the coals more often than not, could indulge in this childhood memory.

"You will learn to ride better than you dog-paddle, I assure you."

"Best be prepared with soothing baths and a balm," Isobel cautioned.

"Well, as to that, I did ride as a child until I had that dreadful fall. And do you know Harriet was able to cope with that horse most ably? He dared not toss her! I found that particularly hard to take," she said with a grimace that made them smile.

Marcus laughed, and the people at the next table stared in amazement. "You will do, cousin. You will do."

Following the supper, Charis joined her mother and Harriet.

"You seemed to have a jolly group," Harriet observed.

"I did not see you," Charis replied.

"Barbara and I were joined by our partners, and they were most pleasant. It is good, I think, to have a variety of friends."

"That is true," Lady Huntingdon said. "The more friends you acquire, the better chance you have of finding a husband who agrees with you."

Charis nodded her concurrence with this view, but wondered just how one set about meeting more gentlemen. It seemed to her that she was in what was called a set, and that they tended to group together whenever at a party. Not that she disliked them, with the possible exception of Lord Portchester. And the trouble with him was that he was a prosy bore. Yes, he would suit Lady Alicia to a tee.

When the hour drew late, the elder Lady Huntingdon declared, "I would leave now. There is much to do tomorrow."

Charis gave Harriet a mystified look, but promptly obeyed her mother.

"What are we to do tomorrow?" Harriet inquired after they had bid Mrs. Minchin a good evening and waited for their carriage.

"Shopping for boots. Marcus said Charis needs a pair, and I daresay she does if he says so."

"Marcus says I am to shop for boots on the morrow?" Charis inquired with not a little astonishment.

"No, he'll take you. Said you have not the slightest idea what is best for you. In boots, that is."

The carriage arrived, and Charis had no more opportunity to question her mother, who began to talk of something else entirely.

She was prepared come breakfast, and Marcus entered the room. "I suppose I must buy a pair of boots."

"Yes. I cannot believe I forgot. You'll need habit shirts and a hat as well. I am losing my touch, I fear."

Somehow she doubted that but agreed with docility which earned her a thoughtful look from Marcus.

So following the late breakfast, she set out with her cousin in his curricle to a boot maker he said was the finest for women's riding boots.

She did not doubt it any more than she doubted that Mr. Stultz made the best riding habits. She had heard that the military gentlemen, even the Prince Regent, ordered garments from Mr. Stultz as well as many women.

The boot maker measured her foot, showed her a selection of leather, then agreed with Marcus which would suit her the best.

Once outside, she turned on him. "Just once I should like to make a choice on my own!"

"You shall, dear cousin. You shall." He guided her into the carriage, then collected the reins from his tiger.

Within seconds they were off to Grafton House, where Marcus assured her she would find excellent habit shirts and whatever else she pleased. "The hat I shall buy for you." When she protested, he smiled. "A present from me."

As if everything she owned had not come from him. He was being his usual high-handed self, but she yielded with grace. Why not? He would get his way regardless. And he would be so charming about it, she would not care!

Chapter Thirteen

As predicted, the hat proved to be as charming as she expected. The black beaver had a somewhat mannish look, only much shorter in height. A dashing length of dark green chiffon twisted about the hat that would doubtlessly sail behind her when she rode at any speed. It was utterly gorgeous and quite what she would have chosen had she been allowed.

And that bothered her a little.

"It is lovely, Marcus. Precisely what I would have selected had I been permitted," she acknowledged.

"It is a present." He held out the entrancing hat, and when she did not immediately take it, he placed it on her head.

She was woman enough to wish she could view the confection he had bought her. She had no doubt it looked elegant, but she would not preen before the looking glass with Marcus present. She removed it to place on the desk for the moment, and faced him resolutely.

"Are you saying that I shall have to reimburse you for the remainder of my clothing?" she asked with a dangerous green glint in her eyes.

"Not at all," he said in a manner to soothe a fractious child.

"Well?" She tapped her foot, waiting to see what he said in reply.

"Think of the clothes as an investment. To catch a husband you need the proper lure. What you wear is certainly alluring, my dear," he said, casting her a provocative look that succeeded in vexing her greatly.

"As I said before, catchpenny it is," she snapped, hurt by his words as much as his attitude.

"I looked in *Dr. Johnson's Dictionary,* and he calls a catchpenny a worthless pamphlet merely calculated to gain a little money. You are exquisitely gowned and presented nicely, but scarcely to gain money." His eyes held mischief, and that was too much.

She was utterly furious and contained her anger with difficulty. "No, I must attract a husband! I am got up to sell, and I must not forget it."

She pushed past him, intent upon leaving him and the blasted hat as fast as she could.

"Charis . . . the hat." He picked it up, offering it to her with that amused look still on his handsome face.

"Keep the bloody hat!" Charis stormed up the stairs and, once through the empty sitting room, slammed her bedroom door behind her. It was no use. She could not possibly deny it any longer, no matter how hard she tried. She was in love with the most heartless man in London. No, in all of England! How could she be so completely stupid? He could not wait to be rid of her. And she wanted nothing more than to fall into his arms and stay with him forever.

She fell across her bed and pounded her pillow in frustration. There was no point in tears. She'd already cried buckets of those and accomplished nothing but blotchy cheeks.

"Charis?" The low, husky, and distinctively male voice she foolishly adored came from her bedroom door. She had not heard it open.

Shocked, Charis sat up and twisted around to see Marcus, her hat in hand, standing in the doorway.

"What are *you* doing here?" she challenged.

"I am sorry my teasing upset you. I brought up your hat. Please wear it when we go riding."

"Cousin? Can that be *you* who is sounding so humble? I cannot believe it." She slid from the bed to confront him, accepting the hat with patent reluctance. She placed the hat on a small table and then returned her gaze on him, surprised he remained.

"You are not a catchpenny countess, you know. Any man would be fortunate to win your hand. I told your father that his will was madness. It was not what I wanted, believe me, Charis."

She looked down for a moment—irresolute, uncertain. "I do not think I ever truly believed you had anything to do with that infamous will. Perhaps father's mind became a trifle unbalanced toward the end. Who knows?"

He reached out to touch her chin, tilting it up so she was more or less forced to meet his gaze. "Friends?"

She closed her eyes a few seconds. Friends? Was friendship better than nothing? Raising her gaze, she attempted a smile. "Very well, friends."

"I should have recalled that you have a temper. That red hair and those green eyes of yours ought to remind me. You usually have it in tight control. In all fairness, I must confess you look magnificent when angry."

"What an old saw that is," she said with a hint of bitterness. "I've heard it before."

"But not from me, I think. Kiss and make up?"

She did not know what to say. He was here where he ought not be and saying what he ought not say. Why not?

"Very well." She attempted to seem prosaic and feared she sounded breathless instead. She tilted her head to meet his.

It was not a mere kiss. *That* would have been prosaic. His kiss was magic, a stunning of her senses, an assault on her heart. And it was far too brief.

She stood silent, unable to find words to utter when he released her from the captivity of his touch.

"That's much better. I would not wish a chasm between us. Would you?"

She shook her head. "No. That would be dreadful."

"Well, then, I am off. I'm trying to promote an interest." He watched Charis closely with those dark blue eyes that could turn her to mush.

"And naturally you must go." Charis was proud of her calm, even voice. "Best hurry."

He studied Charis a few moments longer, then apparently satisfied with what he saw, he strode from the bedroom, leaving the door open behind him.

Harriet popped out from her little room, a puzzled look on her face. "Did I hear Marcus just now?"

"He brought up my hat," Charis replied lightly.

"Oh, I must say it is smashing. All you need now is the habit."

"Indeed," Charis said, thinking that she had already acquired a habit that was not going to be easy to break.

A week passed with Charis avoiding her cousin as much as possible. Naturally, that state of affairs could not continue without comment. Marcus cornered Charis in the library, where she sought something to read.

"Why do I have the feeling I have fallen from favor? And after we cried pax, too," he demanded. He crossed his arms and stared at Charis with more than a little curiosity.

True, he demanded nicely, but nevertheless it was clearly not an option as to whether she reply or not. She had no choice but to think up something.

"I? Avoid you? Never. You have not fallen from favor. I have merely been busy."

"Seymour informed me that your habit was delivered from Stultz. I propose we begin your riding lessons today. I have a nice docile mare for you, so you need have no fear on that score."

"Today?" She swallowed with care and licked suddenly dry lips.

"You are not nervous about this, are you?"

"Where am I to have these lessons? I had thought the privacy offered by the riding school ideal." Could she shake off his insistence of lessons from him?

"Hyde Park is quite wooded along the road to Uxbridge. You ought not meet anyone while there. Gloustershire House School is on Park Lane, and you would be far more subject to view coming and going from there."

She could think of no more objections to his plans.

"Very well. When?"

"Why not now?" he said, challenge clear in his voice.

"I shall change at once." She forgot the book she had selected and left the room without looking at her cousin. She did not have to, for his chiseled features were engraved on her heart.

The little boots were a problem, but Betsy proved helpful there, and although the dark green habit fitted her more closely than she liked, she could not deny it flattered her. Her waist looked trim, and the hat set off her dark red hair admirably. She adjusted the green chiffon that fell over the brim, and gathered up her leather gloves and whip.

Allowing the skirt to trail behind her, she marched down the stairs to the entry hall, where Seymour looked at her with approval on his kindly face.

She tugged at the jacket to adjust it slightly. The taffeta lining felt stiff in spite of the fine lawn of the habit shirt. She caught up the skirt, walking into the library where she could check her appearance in the looking glass. Were the hooks that fastened the jacket to the skirt firmly in place? She thought so. Betty had assured her that all was as proper. She caught sight of her cousin in the looking glass.

"You look charming, cousin."

Charis whirled to face him. "Thank you. I trust that I may prove an apt pupil. Perhaps some gentleman will catch sight of me on Rotten Row and decide he must buy me."

"I do not suppose you could forget that business of the catchpenny countess, could you?"

"I could try," she said without inflection.

"Come." He held out his hand.

Charis walked from the room, hoping that she did not look as nervous as she felt.

Seymour saw them out, offering Charis a reassuring smile. She smiled back.

There were two horses before the house, held by the groom. Both looked enormous. She was impressed right down to the heels of her sensible boots.

Recalling a few things she had learned as a child, she walked to the left side of the horse, placed her right hand on the pommel, and took the reins in her other hand. Having Marcus assist her up to the saddle was unnerving. When she felt his hand on her leg, she almost jumped. Only her determination to see this through saved her from making a total fool of herself. She calmed her fears and adjusted her body, hooking her right knee over the pommel as she remembered, aligning her body with the spine of the horse.

"Good," Marcus said while smoothing her skirt down.

Did he linger a tiny bit? No, it was merely her nerves getting to her.

Once assured she was comfortable on her sidesaddle, they set off toward the park at a pleasant walk.

"By the by, the creature's name is Belle. You are comfortable?" Marcus asked.

"Yes." She glanced over to him, admiring the way he sat on his horse, a veritable advertisement for perfection.

"Then, relax. I can feel your tenseness over here. If I can sense it, your horse can as well."

"That is all very well for you to say, cousin. Becoming accustomed to riding again is something else entirely. Even with a gentle Belle!"

"You are frightened?" He was surprised.

"I am terrified," she confessed. "My blood has turned to ice, and no part of me wants to work as it should."

Holding the reins as she knew was correct, she turned her head to look at him, wondering how he would accept her admission.

"I see. That makes the lessons a trifle more difficult, but you seem to have remembered a fair amount of what your father taught you."

"Not Father. He had little time for me. It was the groom who led me through the terrors of riding lessons. I began somewhere around three with a pony, then progressed to a pretty little mare named Goldie. I shall never know what it was that triggered her fractiousness that day she tossed me. I had to live with the results for weeks."

"But you healed admirably. I confess I am surprised that the earl did not oversee your lessons."

She responded to the interest in his voice with a shrug. "I was not a son, nor was Harriet. She was supposed to have been Harry, and I was to have been Charles. He turned to you for the son he never got."

"I'm sorry, Charis. Yet you turned out well. He should have been proud of you."

"So proud he cut me off with an allowance that an opera dancer would scorn." She sniffed and wished she dared let go to dig for her handkerchief tucked into her sleeve.

"Just what do you know about opera dancers?" He was amused. Charis could hear it in his voice. At least he did not chew her to bits over her slip.

"One of the neighbor lads thought to brag about his stay in London and told me how much a prime opera dancer obtained from her protector. That was a few years back, of course. I fancy they receive more today. 'Tis a pity I cannot dance like that. Perhaps I could train to be a bareback rider?"

He coughed into the back of his superbly gloved hand. "I doubt they earn more than your allowance. You forget I know the details of that will. And I have authority to increase it if prices rise."

He waved his hand to indicate they were to turn to the left, and Charis obeyed, thankful for the gentle gait of her mount. "Indeed, costs do have a tendency to go up, never down. I confess I am amazed he thought of it." She glanced at him, then added, "He did not, I'll wager. It was your idea."

He did not deny her allegation.

The first lesson went surprisingly well, all things considered.

"Charis, you continue to amaze me. I would have thought you would have forgotten all you knew, and you certainly have not." Marcus stopped her after a time, suggesting she get down and rest a bit.

"I suppose once it is beaten into you, it becomes a part of your system." Charis grinned at him to disguise her aching. If she felt like this now, what would she be a few hours later?

"You exaggerate. I imagine that groom was as wrapped around your finger as all my servants are now."

Startled, she looked up at him. "Well, if he was, it was greatly hidden. He was severe and demanding. I well recall practicing those stupid figure eights for hours. I was to walk, trot, and canter the school horse for days, weeks, forever, it seemed until I pleased him. I cried with relief the day he said I could ride Goldie."

Marcus gave her a troubled look before changing the subject. After a while he set her back on the horse and took her through a routine of sorts, testing to see how she did at a trot.

"We shall canter tomorrow if you feel up to it. For now, we quit. Come, let us go home."

Nearly moved to tears at her reprieve, Charis gave him a brave smile. How fortunate that Belle was a docile creature, not given to odd starts and fidgets. Charis had no desire to cut a swath along Rotten Row. Should she do a decent walk, she would not object.

"Lady Alicia rides well, does she not?"

"Yes," he admitted, "she is an accomplished horsewoman. But I doubt if a single one of their servants gives a fig about her."

Surprised at this admission, Charis remained silent, not certain what she could say to that. She did not think she had the servants at Huntingdon House wrapped around her fingers any more than at the country house.

In short order they reached Upper Grosvenor Street and turned up the street in the direction of their house. Charis stiffened when she saw Lady Alicia riding toward them, her posture as perfect as her control over the great beast she rode.

She nodded to Charis, who supposed she ought to be humbly grateful not to be ignored. She was not. She heartily wished Lady Alicia to China.

"I see your lesson has gone splendidly—your friend mentioned it. At least you are on the horse and not carried home in bits and pieces." Her voice carried a silky tone that rubbed Charis the wrong way.

"True. Perhaps it attests to the devotion of my instruc-

tor. I could not ask for a finer one." Charis bestowed a
smile on Marcus that appeared to dazzle him. At least
she devoutly hoped it did, for she intended such.

Lady Alicia did not appear at all pleased with the
praise Charis heaped on her cousin. She ignored Charis
again and inquired, "Sir Marcus, have you given any
more thought to a ball? I think it about time you entertain. With your aunt in residence, there is no excuse,
you know."

Charis stared at the spectacle of Lady Alicia attempting to be coy. It was not a pretty sight. She awaited
her cousin's reply with interest. Should he be in favor of
such an entertainment, it meant a lot of work for her,
not to mention Harriet and their mother. His answer also
might serve to reveal his attitude toward Lady Alicia.
Charis had not known him to relish being told what he
should do.

He turned to Charis. "What say you? A ball? Would
you enjoy one?"

"If that is what you wish, I can see no reason why you
could not have a ball. The house is admirably suited for
entertaining. Mama has spoken of the wonderful parties
they used to have there." Charis waited, barely breathing
in anticipation of his decision.

"Then, we shall. As you say, the house is well adapted
to entertaining," Marcus said, exchanging a hooded look
with Charis.

"How soon?" demanded Lady Alicia. "You must
choose a date that is not taken by some grand event."

"Two weeks, perhaps. I must consult with my aunt."
Marcus signaled his horse to move forward, and Lady
Alicia perforce was compelled to either join them or con-
tinue her ride to wherever she'd intended to go.

"Well, do know you can count on me for help, Lady
Huntingdon. I am well versed in entertainments suitable
for Society." She smiled at Charis as though she were
not too bright.

Charis nodded serenely, then followed Marcus closely
to their home, leaving Lady Alicia off to wherever. Inwardly she seethed with annoyance.

A groom hurried forth to take their mounts. Charis watched them disappear around the corner with relief.

"Shall we go inside?"

"By all means, cousin," Charis said through gritted teeth. Gathering her long skirt in one hand, she went before him and headed toward the stairs.

"Lady Alicia meant well by her offer. Do you feel able to cope on your own?" he queried mildly.

"She is an insufferable toad!" Charis said, quite beside herself with anger. "As though my lady mother did not know what is proper for Society! I would sooner accept the help of that opera dancer!" With that pronouncement, she majestically marched up the stairs, leaving Marcus standing in the center of the hall, mouth agape.

Harriet met her in the sitting room. "Was it very bad? Do you ache?"

"Yes and yes. I am so furious I could spit tacks!"

"At Marcus? From your riding lesson?" Harriet asked, clearly confused.

"No, not Marcus. It is that dreadful Lady Alicia. She had the effrontery to imply that Mama could not know what is proper entertainment for a Society ball!"

"What ball?" Harriet wanted to know as she helped Charis from her habit.

"We met her just around the corner, and she demanded to know when Marcus was going to give a ball. Said he had no excuse what with his aunt in the house."

"And Marcus agreed?" Harriet said with almost a yelp.

"Indeed he did! Perhaps two weeks, he said." Charis stepped out of the skirt to the habit, handing it to Betty to put away. She did not want to see it again until necessary.

"Good heavens. Well, we can put his secretary to good use with the invitations. Mama will know what to do as far as arrangements. She has had a ball here before, I imagine." Harriet spoke in her usual way, enthusiasm mixed with anticipation.

"Harriet, what would I do without you?" Charis said

with a sigh. She washed her hands and face, drying with care before applying her gillyflower-scented cream.

"Best tell Mama at once."

Charis agreed, and as soon as she had changed into a simple muslin day dress, she went with Harriet to their mother's room.

The countess was not the slightest dismayed at the news. "I have been waiting for something of this sort," she admitted.

"You have?" Charis squeaked.

"Yes, it is not so surprising, is it? He has not been able to entertain all his friends and acquaintances since he inherited this house." The countess waved a hand to encompass the building while looking very thoughtful.

Charis told her the offer from Lady Alicia, and dear Mama was quite as scornful as Charis might have wished.

"Need help? I should say not! With the excellent staff plus that secretary Marcus employs, we shall do very well on our own. Who does she think she is?"

"The future Lady Rutledge, I fancy," Charis replied in a small voice.

"Nothing set there that I can see. She is far too pushy to snabble your cousin, in my opinion." Lady Huntingdon rose with regal grace, then swept from her room issuing instructions to her daughters all the way down the stairs to the library, where she sought out her nephew.

"Marcus, dear boy. Charis says you intend to give a ball. Excellent notion. Give me your list, and I shall see to it all—that is if you wish," she concluded modestly.

Charis and Harriet exchanged dumbfounded looks. This was their absentminded mother who seldom finished a sentence properly? Had she merely needed a project to bring her to life as Charis had thought?

"Sir William is to call this afternoon. Perhaps I can prevail upon him to lend his assistance. I doubt very much I shall need Lady Alicia. The girls said she had offered to help, but there is no necessity for her to lift one of her dainty fingers." Her ladyship flicked her own fingers in the vague direction of her daughters as she spoke.

Marcus looked stunned.

"I imagine your secretary will have lists of all your friends. Check with him should you wish to add others, such as Lady Alicia," the countess concluded blandly.

Charis almost choked. What a masterful set-down for Lady Alicia. It was a pity she was not present to hear it.

Marcus blinked, then his usual suave manner asserted itself. "I will summon Wilkins at once, my lady. As you say, he will know who ought to receive invitations. And the date?"

"Three weeks will be ample—unless there is a reason for haste?" She smiled serenely at her nephew and waited.

"No, no reason at present, anyway."

Charis wondered what he meant by that hedging.

"Good. I shall discuss matters with er, Wilkins, and consult you on the precise date later. Not a Wednesday, I think," her ladyship murmured as she left the room.

"This is a side of your mother I've not seen before," Marcus said as he watched her ladyship disappear down the hall.

"Nor I," Charis replied with a shake of her head.

"Well," Harriet added, "I think she simply did not have enough to do before. Marcus, you have offered her something with which to occupy her hours. A project! Praise be!"

"And she will have Sir William to assist."

"The tone of your voice implies that he has been seeing something of Mama." Charis marched up to Marcus, her eyes questioning. "Is that true?"

"So Seymour mentioned. I trust you are pleased. Your mother is not in her dotage yet. It is pleasant for her to have a gentleman friend." Marcus leaned against the desk, arms crossed, and studied Charis with a curious expression in his eyes.

She dropped her hands to her side and considered the matter. Papa had not been much company for Mama. When she had failed to produce a boy, he had turned to the company of his cousin and later that cousin's son,

Marcus. Small wonder if Mama had felt neglected and retreated into her own daydreaming world.

"I should be so fortunate as to have a gentleman friend," she mused. "Yes, I am pleased for Mama."

"You would wish for a gentleman friend?" Marcus inquired, uncrossing his arms to stroll to the fireplace, where he leaned on the mantel. He had not ceased to watch Charis, and she began to edge toward the door with the thought of escape in mind.

"Well, yes, that would be nice. I do think one ought to be friends with the man one marries, you see, and if I must choose a husband, as I must soon, it ought to be someone with whom I can be at ease." She felt breathless after her somewhat long explanation.

Harriet slipped from the room, leaving Charis to face her inquisitive cousin alone.

"Have you decided on the lucky fellow yet?" He stared at her like she was an alien creature.

"No." Her voice came out in a whisper, and she repeated herself more firmly. "No, I have not. Perhaps I may be able to make a decision by the ball? Of course that is a presumptuous thing to say, is it not? The best I can do is hope that the one I want also wants me." A stab of unhappiness hit her when she remembered the man she truly wanted did *not* want her, could not wait for her to leave.

"I cannot imagine any man not wishing to have you as his own," Marcus said quietly.

"Oh? Well, I can. I have a temper, as you well know. You once wondered who in the world could handle me. Do not tell me you have forgotten, for I have not." Now it was Charis who crossed her arms before her, feeling almost defensive.

"Did I really say that? I must have been in a fit of the blue-devils that day. I 'handle' you, do I not? If I can, another should as well."

Charis closed her eyes briefly, then turned to exit the room. "I must remember that. It ought to help me choose, do you not think? Let me see—Lord Egerton or Lord Pilkington? Surely one of them should do."

"Charis . . ." Marcus called after her.

He was too late to stop her flight.

Marcus walked to the front of the house where he could see out the window to the street. Except he did not see. He stared blindly, wondering how on earth he was to solve the problem handed him by that bloody will.

"You wished to see me, Sir Marcus?" Wilkins said from the doorway.

Marcus wondered how it was that no matter where he happened to be in the house, his servants could always locate him. "Yes. I am giving a ball, Wilkins. I am told it is past time that I did so. The elder Lady Huntingdon is taking charge with the assistance of Lady Harriet and the younger Lady Huntingdon." Lord, if that did not sound complicated. "You are requested to find any lists of my friends and so forth. Report to her ladyship for additional instructions."

"Indeed, sir. Is there anything else?"

"Increase the allowance for Charis, Lady Huntingdon. It seems prices have been rising."

"Quite so, sir. May I do the same for Lady Harriet? She has spent her allowance and likely needs more."

"Of course," Marcus replied with a wave of his hand. Once his secretary had left, Marcus rubbed his forehead. Perhaps he ought to discuss this problem with an old campaigner like Sir William. He'd been a general, although to be sure he had commanded troops and they had obeyed him implicitly. Somehow, Marcus doubted Charis was that docile.

She had smelled of gillyflowers when she came down. The scent still haunted him. What was he to do? Within three weeks he must solve the matter. He would not put it off any longer. Portchester to the rescue!

Chapter Fourteen

It seemed that planning the ball for Marcus had put new life into the elder Countess Huntington. She bustled about the house, consulting with Wilkins regarding the guest list, the musical arrangements, and the like.

"After all, dear girls, the musicians who were the thing when I last gave a ball may not even be living now," she explained when Charis took her to task, fearing that her mother was overdoing.

Sir William seemed to appear at the house more and more, causing Charis to wonder if he was merely helping her mother plan the ball—although how he might do that was beyond her—or if he truly had an interest in Mama as Marcus implied. It was an unsettling thought.

The housekeeper brought forth the crystal and linen that had long been in storage. Mama endlessly discussed the sort of flowers to use until Charis welcomed her cousin's suggestion that she have another riding lesson.

Donning the habit that had been brushed and pressed, Charis thought she might probe into the true reasons why Marcus agreed to a ball. There had to be something besides wanting to repay invitations he had received. Did he perhaps intend to announce an engagement to Lady Alicia? The truth was of course that Charis did not trust Lady Alicia one whit. Her dear cousin could easily find himself in the position of a compromised man, with Lady Alicia cleverly arranging the trap. She might be as annoying as a gnat, but she did have the ability to turn things to her own benefit. This, even if he nudged Lord Portchester her way.

Charis needed to know more. Her cousin must not

be ensnared by that heartless woman—no matter what it took.

After she adjusted her hat, she gathered up leather gloves and whip before joining Marcus in the entry.

"I see Sir William is here again," he said as they walked from the entry to the street, where the horses awaited them.

"What would happen if Mama were to marry him?" Charis said with a hint of worry in her voice.

"She would change her name to Lady Kingsley. There would be one less Lady Huntingdon around," he said. He assisted her to mount, then mounted his own steed. They walked the horses at a sedate pace until they reached Park Lane, where they turned right toward the Uxbridge Road side of Hyde Park.

"It seems to me that in that event I have a stronger reason for finding a husband. Surely Sir William would not want to have two grown girls as well as Mama!" Charis tried to relax as Marcus suggested, but found she was as tense as the string on a harp.

"I thought you were trying to make up your mind as to whether you ought to marry Egerton or Pilkington," Marcus queried as they crossed the road to the Cumberland gate.

She went before him, thus allowing her to school her features before he came alongside her once again. "Did I say that?" She smiled for his benefit, then stared ahead.

"Unless my memory is seriously wrong."

"Mercy, all this talk of a ball has put it out of my mind," Charis said most untruthfully.

"Hmm."

"Marcus, why did you decide to give the ball? Was it truly to repay those who have entertained you? Or was there another reason?" There was little point in beating around the bush with Marcus. Sometimes being direct brought results.

"Why do you think I decided to give this ball?"

"You are answering my question with a question. I do not think that is fair."

"I have my reasons, but I do not have to list them for your benefit," he retorted at his most austere.

Charis subsided at once. One glimpse of that severe face, and her questions dried up. She had probed too far. But she could not imagine why he was touchy on a simple matter like the ball. Unless he had an ulterior motive!

Once well into the park away from the public eye, Marcus again put her through her paces, studying her as she trotted then cantered. It was odd how the things she had been taught as a child came back after so many years.

"What do you say we head over to Rotten Row?" Marcus inquired after a time. "I believe you can manage a sedate walk in the park. Nothing daring, mind you. I'll confess, I am surprised at how well you do."

"So am I," Charis admitted.

They cantered along the path that led from one side of the park to the other. Within short order they had reached the end of Rotten Row. Charis found herself on the other side of that railing. And straight ahead rode Lady Alicia! Small wonder, her ladyship rode here every day.

Naturally it was too much to hope that her ladyship did not cast her gaze about and miss seeing them. At once she wheeled her horse to join them.

"Have you set the date for your ball?" she instantly demanded as soon as she reached them.

Actually, she spoke to Marcus, totally ignoring Charis. That was agreeable, but Charis gritted her teeth at the notion of her poor cousin falling into the clutches of this woman. Nevertheless, Charis awaited her cousin's reply with interest.

"It will be in two weeks. I persuaded Lady Huntingdon that she was entirely capable of organizing the affair by then. After all, she has my entire staff at her disposal."

He glanced over at Charis, who had paused to listen, then suggested they walk the horses so not to obstruct the path.

Without saying a word, Charis nudged her horse to a

gentle walk. Gradually she was able to relax and look off to where those who strolled along the wooded paths turned an occasional eye on the riders.

What did Lady Alicia have up her sleeve? Charis had taken one look at her and calculated that she had s... plan in mind. She wore a devious expression. But what?

Returning to a more immediate problem, how could Charis persuade one of the gentlemen she hoped to wed to propose to her? She had no experience at this. Heretofore, she had done all she could to avoid a proposal. Now she needed one. She would not remain a burden on Marcus much less Sir William even if she had no more than a mild liking for either of the gentlemen in question.

"Ah, Lady Huntingdon," Lord Egerton exclaimed as he rode up alongside her. "I am pleased to see you join us—and so very well. I must say, Rutledge is a remarkable teacher."

"She had been taught as a child," Marcus inserted. "You do not easily forget that."

"How charming," Lady Alicia said, riding up on the left side of Charis and her mount. "What a lovely habit, Lady Huntingdon. The color suits you admirably."

Charis was leery of her unexpected friendliness, merely modestly nodding as she murmured her thank you.

The conversation was unexceptional for a time. Then Egerton fell back to discuss some matter with Marcus. Once the two gentlemen were deep in their discussion, Lady Alicia leaned toward Charis and softly said, "That is excellent fabric." She glanced behind, then reached over as if to finger the cloth. "Lovely. We shall see how well you do, my dear."

Charis dared not look behind, uneasy on her mount.

Out of the blue Belle kicked out and bolted.

Suddenly Charis was tearing along Rotten Row at a dreadful pace. It was not done to gallop here, but Charis wagered that Belle was far beyond that. She always thought she possessed enough strength to persuade her horse to halt when desired. Belle had other ideas. She had the bit between her teeth, and there was no stopping her.

Calls and remarks bellowed as she passed everyone on the Row, all the while trying her best to bring her poor beast to a stop. If any were concerned, none rushed to her aid. She had about succeeded when Marcus galloped up and seized the bridle, turning the horse slightly.

Belle stopped so suddenly, Charis lost her seat. She sailed off the horse to land on her side, knocking the wind out of her and wrenching the ankle that had always been weak since that first nasty sprain. What a good thing she had managed to kick her foot free of the stirrup! She had a momentary vision of being dragged along, bouncing her head on the ground or some such thing. It was not a pretty picture.

After she regained her breath, and not moving more than necessary, she checked her feet and arms bit by bit, moving each just a little. It seemed she suffered no great damage, other than a throbbing ankle—again.

"You little fool!" Marcus hissed in her ear. "Anything broken?" He knelt at her side and looked as though he could have cheerfully wrung her neck. He immediately inspected her feet. When she winced as he touched her right foot, he pulled off her boot before the ankle swelled even more. Painful as it was, at least her boot did not have to be ruined by being cut away.

"No thanks to you," she snapped, realizing at that moment that she had a rib or two that ached in addition to the rapidly swelling ankle.

Lord Egerton joined them, taking the other two horses in hand from a kindly bystander.

He had been followed by Lady Alicia, who tittered a dainty laugh as she rode up. "My dear, I guess you did not recall as much as Marcus thought you had. What a pity. It was not well-done of you to resist calling attention to yourself."

Charis shot her a look that should have withered her to dust. What a perfectly odious allegation to make.

"I do not suppose you will be in any condition to dance at the ball now, will you?" Lady Alicia looked overjoyed at that possibility. Charis could see it in those cold blue eyes that raked her with such glee.

"I heal quickly," Charis replied, clenching her teeth against the pain. It would be lovely to snap out at the thoughtless Lady Alicia, but she could not. At least, not in the middle of Rotten Row with who knew how many riders, not to mention onlookers on the pedestrian path, watching and listening. And Marcus could not possibly have noted how Lady Alicia had looked at Charis. He probably thought her just fine.

"Egerton, could you help me with Lady Huntingdon?" When he agreed, Charis was lifted to her feet at once, one gentleman on either side of her.

"I do not believe I can walk, cousin," Charis managed to grit through her teeth. She did not wish to faint, but it was a thought that appealed at the moment.

"Perhaps she can sit on that horse, and you can walk her home," Lady Alicia said with sweet helpfulness.

Charis detected a hint of spite in that voice. Oh, she was going to relish getting the better of this woman. Somehow she'd do it. The trouble was that it had to be nasty and not public. Sneaky, underhanded, and a just retribution. What a pity Charis was not given to doing things like that. But she was very tempted. She thought it quite suspicious that Belle bolted immediately after Lady Alicia had leaned over to touch her habit.

"Can you?" Marcus asked Charis.

"Of course. It is my right ankle, I do not precisely need it while riding, do I?" Charis managed a tight smile and hoped she did not scream with pain.

Being lifted onto the saddle almost did her in. She said nothing. Not bothering to put her left foot in the stirrup, she concentrated on remaining conscious until she reached the house.

With Lord Egerton riding on one side and Marcus on the other, holding his cousin's reins, they carefully proceeded. Lady Alicia fell in behind—and who asked her was more than Charis could figure.

"I had no idea that Lady Huntingdon was so delicate," Lady Alicia said in her high, fluting voice. "One becomes accustomed to the rigors of riding, and it is easy to forget that there are frail women attempting to ride when perhaps they should be at home . . . tatting." Lady Alicia had enough sugar in her voice to satisfy the entire tea-drinking population of London.

It was impossible for Charis to reply. She had all she could do to sit upright. Never had the distance to the house seemed so long. She seized the pommel tightly in one hand, while clutching Belle's mane with the other. She was quite certain that neither Marcus nor Lord Egerton had any notion just how wretched she felt. With Lady Alicia laughing and telling amusing stories, it was possible they paid little heed to Charis. However, she noted with satisfaction that they frowned and looked concerned.

Her cousin's tiger came running forth to take the horses, staring at Charis with wide-eyed wonder.

Marcus reached up to take her at the waist, lifting her down with surprising ease. At her wince when he was about to set her on her feet, he swept her into his arms and strode into the house, snapping orders to Seymour as he went.

Egerton suggested to Lady Alicia that they look in later to see how her ladyship went, and Seymour closed the door at once.

The butler bustled off to the rear of the house.

Marcus carried Charis up the stairs. At the first landing she gave up to her long repressed desire to escape the pain, and fainted.

When she roused, it was to find Marcus hovering over her with Harriet and her mother standing at the foot of her bed.

"I do not usually faint," Charis said, mustering her dignity.

"Where is the pain, and pray do not conceal anything from me," Marcus barked.

"Willow bark and a posset," her mother murmured, then drifted away.

"I have pain in my rib cage and my ankle, mainly," Charis replied, trying to figure out how many other places she hurt that could be revealed to her cousin. "I would enjoy a bath, but I will settle for a wash and some cold compresses on my ankle," she concluded with a beseeching look at Harriet.

Marcus rose to his impressive height and stared at her as though assessing the completeness of her answer. "Your ribs?" He leaned over her, gently probing her rib cage and watching as she winced and grimaced.

Charis shut her eyes tightly, hoping she'd not faint again. What a pity she was so miserable, but to have Marcus concerned for her well-being was gratifying.

"I'll send for Dr. Knighton at once," Marcus declared before he marched from her room.

"What happened? I mean really. I cannot imagine you falling off a horse again," Harriet said, pulling off the left boot, then the stockings with tender care.

With a darted glance at the doorway, Charis beckoned her sister to her side and whispered, "The horse took off as though she'd been shot. Needless to say, I had a hard time stopping poor Belle. I believe I provided gossip for everyone within sight. Harriet, I suspect that Lady Alicia had something to do with it, but it probably would not be easy to prove. She admired my habit, even touching it, and that is not in keeping with her character."

"But you did eventually halt," Harriet said.

"Had Marcus not been precipitate, I'd have managed. That dolt grabbed my reins, and Belle stopped on a farthing. I sailed off, and it was as though history had decided to repeat itself. At least I did not break any bones this time. This is quite painful as it is."

Harriet eased the jacket from her sister, then debated what to do about the rest of the habit.

"Do not even think of cutting this habit!" Charis cried. "It must have been expensive. Bring up the skirt and ease it under me."

With Betty's help, Harriet managed to slide the habit up, under, and away from Charis. It was a difficult, painful, slow process, but the habit was not cut.

"You are as pale as a ghost, dear sister. Do you think you can manage a nightgown?" She whisked the habit shirt away.

"My dressing gown. And for goodness sake, Betty, remove these stays. Even though they are short and soft, they are killing me."

In minutes Charis was clad in her shift and a soft cream dressing gown. It was a good thing, too, for shortly after that Marcus barged into her room, looking like thunder.

"My tiger says there is blood on your horse—the left flank to be precise. Do you have any idea how it got there?"

"Well, I did not put it there, you may be certain," Charis said, gasping at the pain from talking too vehemently. "Perhaps a wasp? Poor Belle."

"Have you not done enough today?" Harriet said, looking as though she could cheerfully conk her cousin on the head.

"What do you mean? I did not frighten her horse." He looked all injured male innocence.

"I doubt it helped when you yanked at the bridle. What did that leave Charis? Her seat was precarious at best—tearing along at a gallop. I must say, Marcus, I thought better of you." She made a shooing motion with her hands. "You had best leave before you frighten poor Charis to fainting again."

He appeared to notice his cousin's state of undress at that point and left the room at once, muttering something under his breath.

"His face actually turned red," Harriet said with surprise.

"I do not know why he bothered to summon a doctor, much less Knighton. I cannot afford *his* bill!"

"I suspect our guilty cousin will pay up and be glad to do so." Harriet chewed her lip, looking worried.

"Why did this have to happen now?" Charis began, then ceased, for it hurt too much to talk.

"Indeed," Harriet said, clearly cross at the accident that resulted in such pain.

"How embarrassing. I looked like a stupid girl who ought not have been on a horse, let alone in Rotten Row!"

They sat in silence for a time, contemplating the ramifications of the calamity.

"I most likely cannot dance at the ball, either," Charis said at last, recalling the comment made by Lady Alicia. "In fact, she even remarked about it, feigning sympathy for my injury. Tatting! She said I ought to remain home doing tatting, of all things. I hate tatting," Charis grumbled.

At that point Dr. Knighton entered the room with her mother right behind him. Charis wondered what Marcus wrote to have him rush over. He took exception to the number of people in the room and told Betty and Harriet to leave for the moment.

It was just as Charis estimated. He wrapped her rib cage quite tightly, and surprisingly it eased her pain a good deal. He actually admired the cold compress her mother had brought up, suggesting it be continued. When he suggested cupping, both Charis and her mother disagreed.

"She has done this before, sir. She heals quickly, and I doubt she has suffered enough to warrant cupping," Lady Huntingdon explained.

Reluctantly agreeing, the doctor left, and Charis could hear him talking to someone as he went down the hall. Probably Marcus, she surmised. Her cousin would want to know every detail. Well, at least she could stay out of his way now. He'd not feel obligated to give her riding lessons after this. Charis wondered how long it would be before she dared ride once more.

Ruff jumped up on the bed, a bit of paper in his mouth. "Dog, what do you have now? Give it to me," she demanded.

The dog reluctantly released his hold on the crumpled paper.

Charis tried to figure out what he purloined. The letter was in her cousin's handwriting. She could not make out the body of the letter with Ruff's teeth marks all over it, but he signed it, "Your loving Marcus!" Precisely *who* did he write this to and what could be done about the chewed missive now? On the other hand, perhaps he had discarded the paper, and Ruff had thought to have a bit of fun with it. The dog could not take it from the desk. But had he written this to Lady Alicia? Horrors!

She shut her eyes to doze for a bit, the portion of letter beside her. Ruff curled up next to her in his customary little ball. The willow bark concoction Mama gave her appeared to be effective. Her pain was easing, or perhaps it was merely the luxury of snuggling in a fine bed?

It was the sensation that someone watched her that brought her eyes open later. When she looked up, she found Marcus studying her face.

"I do not believe my face was scratched. Or was it?" She raised a hand to lightly touch her skin.

"No. You are as lovely as always. I sought an answer to a puzzle." He pulled a chair closer to the bed and leaned toward her, inspecting her face and hair until Charis wondered if he had told her the truth about her face. He reached out, almost reluctantly, to smooth her hair back. How gently he touched her!

"Why the horse was bleeding?" She eyed him warily. He did not seem to be in a good mood.

"No—although I wonder about that as well. I do not guess you will tell me?" He continued to watch her, precisely like the hawk she had likened him to before.

"I truly could not say, but I'd guess it was the wasp." She kept her suspicions regarding Lady Alicia to herself. She was not going to say a word against the lady until she knew which way the wind blew—perhaps not even then.

"We have no knowledge of what caused the blood on Belle's left flank, still I cannot accept you charged off deliberately as Lady Alicia claimed. Perhaps, as you say, it was a wasp. It is not like you to desire to call attention to yourself. But, it is not going to be easy to salvage your reputation—gossip being what it is."

Stung, Charis chewed her lip a moment, then said, "I do not believe I want to talk to you any longer. Please go away." She nudged the scrap of paper where he could not see it. The last thing she wanted was to confront him now.

"It is as well that you will most likely not be able to dance at the ball," he concluded as he rose.

At that precise second Charis knew that come what may, she would be at the ball and not as a spectator. She would dance! She would show Marcus!

"Look at the lovely flowers Lord Egerton sent you," Harriet cried softly as she entered the room.

"It's enormous!" Charis said, impressed at the size and beauty of the offering.

"Well," Marcus said nastily, "I can guess which fellow will win your hand."

"I do not base my choice upon a gift. He merely feels sorry for me. He did see me fall, you know. And he was a help getting me home from the park," she reminded gently.

Marcus did not reply. He stalked from the room, and shortly Charis and Harriet recognized the slam of his door.

"My, he is in a temper, is he not?" Harriet mused.

"A frequent state since we have been here," Charis added with a grimace.

"Let me wash your hands and face for you. I know you must feel grubby," Harriet said, wringing out a face flannel in tepid water.

Charis submitted, then asked, "My face truly is not scratched? Marcus said it was not, but stared at me so I feared he lied to keep me from worrying."

"No," Harriet said with a shake of her head. "You are as pretty as ever. I imagine Lady Alicia envies you not a little. She does not have your gentle mouth for instance. Rather, hers is more like a prune. But then she is so disapproving that is no surprise."

"What can we do to make her reveal her true nature further? Marcus listened to what she said about my supposedly wanting attention in the park. As though I would behave so on purpose! It makes me realize how little he knows me, in spite of our being cousins and having seen a fair amount of each other over the years."

Harriet wrung out the cloth and placed it on the edge of the basin before she spoke. "*I* know you would never do anything so stupid. But regarding Lady Alicia—Marcus may not be as dim-witted as you think. Lord Portchester is seen with her more and more. I trust you plan to attend the ball. I heard what Marcus said, you see."

"You know me better than he does at any rate. I shall rest and keep my foot elevated and accept any potion Mama hands me if it will mean going to the ball."

"Bravo!" Harriet cried eagerly. "What about a gown?"

"Madame Clotilde promised to do something with that gold tissue gown. I suggested changing the neck a trifle and perhaps altering the trim. She is so clever, I feel no one will be certain it is the same gown."

"What do you want to wager that Lady Alicia will make some nasty little remark?" Harriet said dryly.

"I do not care at this moment."

She was spared additional comment by the arrival of Betty with a fine vase of spring blooms, quite as magnificent as the one brought by Lord Egerton.

Harriet pulled out the card to read, " 'I am devastated at your injury. Please feel better soon. Lord Pilkington.' Well, both of your beaux have sent flowers."

"I'll warrant that is more than Marcus will do," Charis said, grumpy and feeling out of sorts that had nothing to do with the pain in her ankle or her ribs and other assorted hurts.

Harriet said nothing to that, but replaced the cool cloth on her sister's ankle, then covered her with a light shawl.

The light from the window had faded into twilight by the time Charis awoke. She stirred, and Betty was at her side to assist her with necessary help.

Charis was resting as well as might be expected when there was a sound from the adjoining sitting room.

Betty hurried to the bedroom door to look out.

"Is she feeling any better?" inquired a familiar and masculine voice.

"Marcus, you may as well come in. I am awake. Betty will find me something to eat."

When he entered her room looking a trifle awkward—

an attitude she'd not have associated with him—she smiled.

"I brought your mail. A note from Miss Penston and missives from both Egerton and Pilkington." He glanced about to note the second bouquet of flowers. "As though their floral tributes were not enough."

Charis tore open the letter from Isobel, scanning it quickly. "My, how news travels. She heard of my accident and wishes me well. She would like to call. Please send a footman with a message to her that I would enjoy it above all things. She is so dear and cheerful."

"Are you implying that I am not? You must confess that it is not a happy situation." He spotted the crumpled and chewed paper that peeped out from under her side. Before she could stop him, he pulled it out, glaring at her as he recognized it.

"What's this? How did it get here? I thought I'd tossed it away." He looked utterly furious.

"Ruff found it. Having trouble writing love notes? Perhaps you need lessons," Charis said without thinking.

"If there are any lessons to be given, I would wager you would be the one to receive them."

He leaned over her. She wondered if he would kiss her. Unfortunately, he also touched her side. Charis yelped in pain.

"Cousin Marcus, what are you doing to my sister!"

Chapter Fifteen

It had surprised Charis how quickly Marcus covered his blunder. Hours later she could still recall the comical expression of dismay on his face when Harriet entered the room to discover him at her sister's side, and so very close, at that. The sound of her gasp had activated him most speedily.

The thought of being compromised with her must have been frightfully dreadful! What skill he used to extricate himself from any possibility of such an occurrence. He had ignored Ruff's growl, turning to face Harriet at once.

"Charis looked uncomfortable. I thought to see what bothered her. I've brought up a book for her to read." He had exchanged a warning look with Charis, dropped three small slim volumes onto the bed, then rose, all in less time than she would have believed.

Charis picked up the first volume. "*Self-Control* by Mary Brunton. How very appropriate," Charis had murmured with an ironic look at her cousin.

"Actually, Lady Alicia suggested it," he admitted. "I know nothing of the contents. She thought it a book to offer guidance or perhaps amusement. I thought it was rather nice of her to care."

Harriet had given Marcus a disbelieving stare but said nothing. She favored the three-volume book by Mary Brunton with a look that held about the same enthusiasm as Charis had bestowed on it.

Now Charis stroked the comforting dog, talking with him as she often did when alone. "I shall not read that dreadful tale," she confided, approving the lick on the hand Ruff gave her. The book had little appeal. She'd flipped through the last volume of the book to see the end, and it seemed to her that the heroine was as stupid as could be. Then she'd read the preface and grimaced. "Ruff, the writer says that in this age of lax morality and the declining esteem of virtue, young women are in need of the lessons her heroine, Laura, presents. Humbug. Not that there do not exist young women who could use a lesson or two in proper behavior. I do not believe I am one of them. On the other hand, perhaps Lady Alicia could benefit from such a book? She assuredly needs something. Her manners are sadly lacking!"

Ruff was clearly unimpressed by this pronouncement, and Charis chuckled. "Wise doggy. Would that others had your perspicacity."

Ruff, as always, agreed with his mistress. "Ruff," he barked in response to her earnest look and scratch under his chin.

Charis thought back to the accident. She'd not blamed the horse for bolting, nor even her own inability to bring it hastily to a halt. She was certain that in some manner Lady Alicia had begun the incident and Marcus had completed the farce by grabbing the reins. Small wonder that Charis had tumbled to sprain her poor ankle.

She heard the swish of skirts in the next room and turned her face toward the door.

"Harriet said that Marcus brought you something to read," Lady Huntingdon exclaimed as she brought in a posset for Charis to drink, then inspected the elevated foot. She picked up the cloth that Harriet had placed over it. "Goodness, it looks frightful. I had no idea an ankle could turn so many colors."

"But, it feels much better. I should think I would be sufficiently recovered to go down to the drawing room by tomorrow."

Lady Huntingdon immersed the cloth in the cool solution, wrung it out, and then draped it across the injured ankle. "Perhaps. However, my love, why not exercise a bit of caution and remain here? You have the sitting room to use as well as your lovely bedroom." She paused, then said with a nod, "Surprise is the thing."

"Surprise?" Charis queried.

"For the ball, dearest." Giving her daughter a sapient look, she added, "Lady Alicia will not expect you to be there."

"And why should that concern her? I may think she takes on more than is her due, but as to my having any affect on her—I rather doubt it," Charis sadly concluded. "Marcus is willing to believe a wasp may have stung Belle, but he still thinks my reputation is beyond salvage."

"What a nodcock! He ought to know you better than that. Now, while you rest your foot, do not rest your brain."

"Rest my brain?"

"Think!" Lady Huntingdon explained vaguely and left the room in a whirl of draperies and the scent of lavender.

Charis wrinkled her nose and did just as her mother suggested. She might seem vague, but she did see more than one expected.

Marcus strolled about the comfortably large house, inspecting the preparations for the coming ball. He had not anticipated that Charis would be laid up with a sprained ankle when he first agreed to the dratted thing.

He paused to stare into space. He could not understand what had possessed him to approach Charis as he had yesterday. Could she guess how attracted he was to her? His plans were so tenuous, depending on her reaction to him, and he'd not had a chance to explore that recently. It all went back to that mad will that left everything to him and so little to her. It had complicated his intentions and schemes beyond belief.

And then there was the problem of Lady Alicia. With Delilah, he had simply sent a parting gift. One could not do such a thing with a lady, however. She was devilishly hard to shake, testing his manners to the hilt. Portchester seemed attracted to her, and Marcus could only hope that Lady Alicia settled for him.

Seymour presented himself to Marcus, looking more important than usual. "Sir William to see you, sir."

Marcus schooled his features into a smile of bland welcome. Goodness knew the chap was around often enough to feel at home in this house.

"Marcus, good of you to see me so early in the day," Sir William said upon being shown into the drawing room.

"Not at all. Could I offer you anything? Sherry? Canary? Perhaps a glass of port? Or would you rather have coffee?"

"Coffee, if you please." Sir William looked uncomfortable, almost sheepish if such a thing was possible.

When they were settled with fragrant cups of coffee, Marcus waited for his guest to embark upon whatever topic was on his mind. He did not have long to wait.

"I intend to ask Anna, that is, the elder Lady Huntingdon to marry me. Known her for ages, and confess I was not saddened to hear her husband had gone aloft. The man never appreciated her as he ought. I shall."

"Fine. You scarcely need my blessing. She may do as she pleases, as you well know." Marcus bit back a delighted grin. How neatly the chap was falling in with his own plans.

"What I do not know are the prospects for the girls. Mind you, they are welcome to move into my place if they wish. But the house is not large, and two more women will strain things a trifle." He gave Marcus a concerned look.

"I feel confident that Charis will be wed ere long. As to Lady Harriet—I cannot say." Marcus set his cup on the saucer with precise care before eyeing the other gentleman. "I daresay my cousin's husband will welcome Lady Harriet into his establishment. She will have an opportunity to enjoy a Season next year without competition from her elder sister, the countess."

"Do I take it that you have, er, inside information?" Sir William studied his future relative with a speculative gaze.

"You might say that, yes," Marcus replied without giving anything else away.

"Well, I suppose that any chap who wanted to marry the younger Lady Huntingdon would feel obliged to seek your approval." Sir William placed his cup and saucer on a nearby table and studied Marcus, a smile lingering on his face.

"You think so? Well, I have turned down a few silly fellows so far. I fancy they feel it necessary to ask a lady to wed—perhaps to get a bit of practice? They certainly should have known I'd not approve of a match with some upstart!" Marcus relaxed his face to grin at his guest in shared amusement.

"Well, that is a burden off my mind."

The two men sat quietly to chat a bit longer, then Sir William took himself off, no doubt to fetch the family engagement ring or something of that sort.

"One down, two to go," Marcus said to himself as he walked rather jauntily to the library. It was a lovely place to plot.

He had completed luncheon when Lord Pilkington asked to have a word with him. "Better and better," Marcus murmured as he went forward to greet his old friend. He had counted on Pilkington, knowing how he fell into love at the sight of a pretty face.

"I suppose you know what I'm about," Pilkington said when they had exchanged polite greetings and settled down for a chat.

"Can't say I do," Marcus said, his long, capable fingers rubbing his chin. It was a useful ploy to keep himself from grinning.

"Admire your cousin, you know," Pilkington blurted.

"Lady Harriet?" Marcus said in feigned surprise.

Pilkington frowned. "Dash it all, the countess. The young one, that is. You call her Charis. Lovely name, Charis." He gazed off into space for a moment.

"I see. You plan a big wedding?" Marcus inquired.

Pilkington cringed in his chair, obviously dreading such an affair. "I suppose she would want the church and wedding breakfast and everything else that goes with it?"

"Actually, old fellow, I believe she would prefer a quiet wedding in the country. I believe I heard her say she thought a flit to Gretna Green most romantic."

"Did she, by Jove?" Pilkington said in amazement. "My sister was wed in the drawing room. She went into agonies of shyness at the mere thought of St. George's. Gretna sounds even better."

"And you do not even have to worry about banns or an archbishop," Marcus pointed out.

"You really think she would agree to such a scheme?" Pilkington said with more enthusiasm than heretofore.

"You would have to plan matters carefully," Marcus advised. "She has certain likes and dislikes. For instance, you would leave her dog here. Ruff could only make the trip difficult."

Pilkington immediately perceived the sense of that.

"And do not bother with urging her to take a lot of clothes. The nonsense some women want!"

"Oh, indeed," Pilkington agreed. "My sister takes an entire coach full of clothes when she travels. Blasted nuisance. That poor clod she married is under her thumb when it comes to folderols."

"Well, Charis isn't the least that way. Sensible girl, Charis," Marcus replied with a shrewd nod. "Although she does tend to get ill when traveling too long. Best to stop frequently along the way. Better than having a sick female on your hands. But in all other respects, she is a prudent individual."

"I'm glad to know that," Pilkington replied, looking thoughtful. "Mind you, I'd not have thought such a lovely creature would have a sensible notion in her head. Beauty is rarely paired with common sense."

"She is all of that. The romance comes with the dash to Gretna, you see. Of course you would have to learn her favorite foods."

His old friend nodded. "True. What might they be?"

"She dotes on pickled pigs feet and cooked cabbage, for one," Marcus informed him with a straight face.

"You don't say!" Pilkington cried, looking aghast.

"I fear strawberries out of season are another of her favorites," Marcus added.

"My sister as well," Pilkington said gloomily. "When she was in the family way, that was all she wanted to eat for a time."

"Amazing," Marcus said, sounding not a little astonished. He continued to inform his friend of other likes and dislikes as they popped into his creative mind.

Armed with the knowledge, Pilkington rose from the chair. "Wonder when she will be in fit shape to come downstairs."

"I shouldn't wonder but that she joins us at the ball," Marcus replied, looking as serious as ever but with a twinkle lurking in his eyes.

"Lady Alicia said she was certain Charis would never be able to attend!" Pilkington was clearly astounded.

"I believe she underestimates my cousin. Many people do, you know," Marcus said with a half smile. "Never pays to misjudge another." He'd been about to say rival, then realized that might raise questions he had no intention of answering. With a word of encouragement for the imminent abduction of Charis, Lady Huntingdon, he sent Pilkington, or Perry as intimate friends called him, on his way.

The following days passed with the slowness that afflicts someone confined to her bed.

"I am tired, tired, tired of this room, no matter how nice it might be," she complained to a patient Harriet.

"Let's move you to the sitting room," Harriet suggested, quite understanding of her sister's impatience with her captivity.

Charis first insisted upon her best dressing gown, not wanting to be caught in the old flannel thing she had donned while eating. Then she rolled to the edge of her bed, talking to Ruff all the while.

"Dog, do you promise to stay out of my way while I attempt this move? No waltzing about my feet, and for pity's sake, no jumping up on me!"

"Ruff," the dog replied promptly.

"I swear that dog understands everything I say. I do enjoy having him with me," Charis said to her dear sister.

"He is a comfort when we all leave you on your own," Harriet agreed.

Charis didn't reply, for she had swung her feet off the bed and trusted that she could hop to the next room without difficulty.

Harriet disappeared without a word, and Charis stared at the door, wondering if she dared to try it without a supporting arm.

She was contemplating her ankle, now greatly reduced in size and appearing almost normal, when Marcus entered right after Harriet.

"I have no desire to see you take a tumble. Since Cousin Marcus happened to be in the hallway when I looked out, I simply asked him to help," Harriet said.

"You know I am always glad to lend a bit of assistance," Marcus said, his eyes agleam with a hint of mischief.

Charis wondered why she had ever thought him taciturn or remote. True, he still possessed those chiseled features. But she had observed his eyes held the real clue to his feelings. And now he was highly amused about something.

"I'd give a pretty penny to know what is in your mind," she murmured when Harriet went ahead to make certain the small settee in the sitting room had enough pillows.

"I wonder if you would. What if I said I should like to kiss you again? Would you be properly horrified?" He swung her up into his arms as he spoke, his mouth now dangerously close to hers.

"I ought to be proper," Charis reminded him. "You were very angry that day in the park. Did you finally decide that I am innocent?"

His eyes narrowed, and that gleam in his eyes disappeared. "Lady Alicia insists you wanted to show your abilities. I cannot believe that."

"What a pity we cannot find the corpse of the wasp."

Charis drew her head back, creating more space between them. "That insect will be dust by now."

"I'd not seen any wasps about in the park. That is something that puzzles me," he admitted. "I am glad to see there were no broken bones and that your ankle heals well."

"Well, it will likely remain a mystery. Surely you know me well enough to understand I would hate being considered a silly fool, displaying unseemly conduct, particularly in the park. I truly do not know what caused Belle to bolt." Charis hoped she sounded credible.

"It is quite a mystery." Marcus carried her to the sitting room, placing her on the settee with great care. He glanced at Harriet. "Another pillow, I think."

Harriet ran from the room to search for another pillow.

Marcus stared at Charis. "I believe I am owed thanks for my services. Am I not?" he quirked an eyebrow at her.

"Thank you," Charis murmured, not quite trusting the look in his eyes.

With a hasty look at the door to his cousin's bedroom, he placed a quick kiss on her cheek, then stood back when Harriet returned.

"That is not allowed, Marcus, and you know it." Charis gave him a look that ought to have withered him on the spot. Unfortunately, her withering didn't seem to be doing well lately.

Harriet plumped an altogether unnecessary pillow behind her back, then gave Marcus a questioning glance. Without saying a word, she escorted him to the door. "Thank you, cousin. I do not know what we would do without you."

"But I wish we could," Charis muttered.

"Are you angry with our cousin?" Harriet wanted to know when Marcus had gone down the stairs.

"I merely wish we were elsewhere. It is awkward to be living in the same house with the man who inherited all the money we expected to be ours."

"You mean yours," Harriet reminded. "And do not aim those green eyes at me like that."

"Marcus says they go well with my red hair. As to the money, you well know I'd share it with you and see Mama respectably situated."

"As to Mama, I suspect she may do better than either of us. I heard Seymour telling Mrs. Bigley that Sir William had called this morning, and he'd not be the least surprised were an interesting announcement to come from that quarter." Harriet gave Charis a rueful look.

"Oh, Harriet, what would we do then? I feel certain that Mama would accept him. He has practically lived here of late. And Mama looks so happy. Were could we go?"

"Well, we could certainly not remain here, and I believe Sir William has a smaller house than this. There might be room for one, but not two of us—unless we shared a room." Harriet cast a doubtful look at her sister. They were truly spoiled what with each having had a room of her own since infancy.

They frowned and worried and were both out of sorts in no time at all.

Charis hoped that Marcus would allow one of those gentlemen who sought her hand to pay his addresses. Even if there was no love on her part for anyone in particular, it was becoming urgent that she settle on her marriage.

That she loved her cousin, she ignored. It was plain that he didn't care a pin for her, else he would have believed her when she said she was ignorant of what had caused the horse to bolt. He subtly changed the subject, but didn't say he would try to solve the mystery.

The arrangements for the ball proceeded swiftly, with things falling into place very nicely. The elder Lady Huntingdon managed everything incredibly well.

When Charis came down for breakfast the day before the ball, testing her ankle with gingerly care, she remarked on the decorations.

"The flowers come tomorrow morning. Are you certain you ought to be down here, love?" the elder Lady Huntingdon inquired, frowning at her elder daughter.

"I cannot remain upstairs forever, Mama. Perhaps there is some little thing I might do?"

While her mother debated this point, Charis selected a dainty portion of the breakfast offerings before thankfully finding a chair. Her foot was really much better, but she wanted to be careful. She was determined to attend the ball, even if she didn't dance.

"Well, this is a surprise," Marcus exclaimed when he joined them.

"Be assured that I am *not* displaying an unseemly desire for notice, cousin," Charis said dryly.

He didn't reply but merely watched her for a few moments before turning his attention to his food.

Following her scant meal, for she had lost her appetite when Marcus joined them, Charis hobbled down to the library, found a book, then slowly made her way up to the drawing room. Once here, she inspected all that had been done with an approving eye. Her mother had bettered all previous efforts at entertaining.

She sat quietly near a window ostensibly reading, but actually deep in contemplation, until Seymour entered the room. Standing by the doorway, he stated, "Viscount Pilkington to see you, my lady."

"Show him up, please." Charis could have danced with glee. How lovely to have someone else with whom to talk.

"Lord Pilkington, what a pleasant surprise. Now I have the opportunity to tell you in person how much I have enjoyed the pretty flowers you sent me. That was a very nice thing for you to do." She beamed a smile at him.

Encouraged, his lordship strolled over to sit down close to where Charis perched. Within moments Betty entered to occupy a chair by the door.

"As you see, I am proper today," Charis said wryly.

"From what I can tell, you have been proper all while you have been in London." He nodded politely.

Charis considered her expedition to the Thatched House Tavern and the call on Delilah, and hoped he'd not learn of them. It was bad enough that he had heard of her mad dash along Rotten Row. Harriet had gone with Mama to Almack's ever since then. Even though Charis had been abed with her damaged ankle, she doubted she'd have been welcomed at that staid assembly room had she attended. If they knew the whole of it, she would probably be exiled to Canada to join the wild beasts.

"Your cousin tell you I called?" his lordship wanted to know.

"No." Charis gave him a wary look. Called? She wondered what precisely had been said during that call.

He appeared to relax.

"Was there anything in particular I should know?" Charis asked politely.

"Well, Pilkington, old boy," Marcus exclaimed heartily from the door, then striding over to shake his hand in welcome. "Seymour told me you called."

His lordship looked distinctly ill at ease, quite as though he wanted to be elsewhere.

"Lord Pilkington was just telling me that he came to call on you while I was recovering from my accident." Charis thought that was a splendidly clever way to get around saying she had taken a tumble while tearing along in the park.

"Indeed." Marcus gave a sly glance at Lord Pilkington that alarmed Charis no end. Had her cousin actually agreed that one of the gentlemen who formed part of her court could pay his respects? His lordship was a nice person, but she was uncertain she could ever form anything more than a lukewarm fondness for him.

"Well, the ball is tomorrow. Are you both ready?" Marcus inquired.

Charis wondered why her cousin gave his lordship a look she could only term significant. "I am. Madame Clotilde has done herself proud with my gown."

"And I have all in readiness as well," Lord Pilkington declared with an equally wily look at Marcus.

"Excellent, excellent. Well, I shall leave you two so you may pass the time of day."

Unfortunately, Isobel and Barbara entered just after Marcus left. There would be no learning what was afoot.

"I am so pleased to see you up and about," Isobel cried with obvious pleasure.

"How agreeable to have friends come to visit." Charis was sincere. She didn't think she was ready to receive the proposal that hovered on Lord Pilkington's lips. How could she agree to marry him? He had never attempted to kiss her, nor had he uttered any words of fondness to say nothing of love. Well, she supposed it was better to be honest about such things. Why pretend a love that didn't exist?

On the other hand, she had to respect his propriety. He was always the perfect gentleman, even if a bit of a dandy. Perhaps she could learn to deal with him in time?

"We are so excited about the ball. Do say you will be able to attend. It is unthinkable that you would have to remain in your room," Barbara said with a rush and a coy glance at Lord Pilkington.

"I fancy she will be there if I know the least about her," his lordship said with just the right tone of jollity. He rose from his chair, where he had looked increasingly nervous. "I shall bid you all adieu for the moment. Until tomorrow."

He bowed correctly before hurrying from the room, as though Ruff had taken a fancy to his new boots.

The dog came out from hiding to survey the newcomers. Apparently deciding they were acceptable, he hopped up on his owner's lap and settled down for a petting.

"I trust we were not inopportune," Isobel inquired. "Dare I think his lordship was on an important mission?"

"I truly do not know," Charis answered with a laugh that was only a little forced.

"Will you be able to attend the ball? Lady Alicia has told everyone that you cannot attend. She hints that it is your scandalous behavior that prevents you, not the injury to your ankle."

"She does? How utterly beastly of her," Charis declared.

"No one ever gave her an award for being kind and concerned about others," Barbara said dryly.

"I intend to be there if only to thwart Lady Alicia's hopes. You must know she angles for Marcus. We must prevent that at all costs."

"I would like to know how," Isobel said thoughtfully.

"We shall think of a scheme," Barbara declared emphatically. "I cannot abide that pompous woman."

"Nor can I. Although I saw her out with Lord Portchester, and you must agree they are two of a kind," Charis said with a wise look.

"What do you wear?" Isobel queried.

Charis explained about the gold tissue gown in its reincarnation, and they fell to discussing the gowns and hats they expected to wear and to wonder about the others.

"Well, I will wager Lady Alicia will have a gown with a lower neckline than in the past and hang on your cousin until the rest of us are ill," Barbara insisted as Harriet hurried into the room to join them.

"Betty came up to tell me you are here. What a nice surprise. I thought Lord Pilkington had come to pay a call." She turned to Charis for confirmation while wearing a mysterious smile on her lips.

"He did. He left. I shall see him tomorrow at the ball. May I inquire what has you looking so delighted?"

"Well . . . I have written that book that I said I would, and I sold it!" Harriet announced with a modest curtsy. "It is called *The Rogue's Regret*, and I shall be paid for my efforts."

"What!" Charis cried. "I had not the slightest idea. Did you tell Mama? Or Marcus?" she added with caution.

"Mama was a little horrified. Marcus does not know—yet. I will wait until he is in a mellow mood before I break the news."

"Perhaps after the ball? It isn't that I'm not over the moon with your success. It is merely a shock! Congratulations, dearest sister. I am truly proud of you."

"Is Marcus supposed to know you will attend?" Harriet wondered, changing the subject.

"He knows I am ready but not what I shall wear," Charis replied. "I think it will be fun to surprise him."

They all chuckled, then Isobel added, "And he will not be the only one who is surprised. Just think how that will dash the hopes of a certain lady."

"Do you think so? That *would* be lovely."

"It would seem our cousin is in for a number of surprises," Harriet said with glee.

Chapter Sixteen

At last it was the day of the ball. All was in readiness—at least as much as balls are on that day. The elder Lady Huntingdon was in a dither because some dainty biscuits from Gunter's had not arrived as promised.

Seymour assured her he would personally see to it the biscuits were there at the proper time.

Harriet hovered around Charis like a mother hen over one surviving chick. "You are certain you want to attend? You truly ought not dance, and it may be excessively boring to sit on one of those gilt chairs merely to watch."

Charis bestowed a determined look on her much-loved authoress sister. "I will not give Lady Alicia the satisfaction of being right. Besides—my ankle feels quite good—almost normal. I will likely be able to dance once or twice." She glanced at the table before her window where bouquets sat. "Marcus brought me flowers, as did Lords Egerton and Pilkington. I will wear the ones Marcus gave me. I'd not want to tip my hand at this point."

"But I gather Lord Pilkington has your favor?"

"He was about to propose when Isobel and Barbara came to call. I'm sure of it. But until I actually hear the words, I cannot take a chance, can I?" She had but a tepid feeling for his lordship. However, it was necessary that she find a haven, and he seemed the most likely to provide it. She ignored her feelings for her cousin. It was pointless to cry for the moon you couldn't have.

A dubious Harriet agreed, exclaiming, "I think it is wrong to marry simply to get a roof over your head."

Charis didn't reply, for that roof would likely house
Harriet as well—at least until she married. And Charis
knew she could never remain under the same roof were
Marcus to wed—especially Lady Alicia.

Marcus glanced around at the glittering throng of people who graced his ballroom. Few houses could boast
one of this size, and he found it gratifying that all who
had been sent invitations accepted. It made for a crush,
but the elder Lady Huntingdon was in alt, for the ball
was bound to be acclaimed a success. Even the Archbishop of Canterbury had accepted his invitation, placing
a seal of approval that was next to royal favor. The
Prince Regent had sent word that he might arrive late.

Marcus made his way to where his cousin sat looking
neglected and just a little forlorn.

"How is the ankle?" he asked Charis. She was like a
golden angel, her dark red hair setting off a golden tiara
set atop her curls. Her dress had been altered so much
that other than the color and fabric, you would never
think it the same. Indeed, she ought to wear the color
more often, for it became her well. He would suggest it
when the chance occurred.

"It is amazing. I could think it had never been injured.
I highly recommend the potion Mama made for it." She
held out a dainty foot clad in a golden slipper for his
inspection.

He knelt to inspect it and ran his hand over the neatly
laced Roman sandal as well as the trim ankle above it.
"I admit it certainly looks normal. Well, see you don't
overdo."

She blushed a delightful rose at his familiarity. "Marcus, people will think I am fast, even if you are my
cousin!" she whispered. "Stop it at once. We may be
related but quite distantly. You'd not want to create
gossip!"

Marcus looked up at her and grinned. When he got
up, the crisp paper in his inner coat pocket crackled and
he hoped it would not be noticed by any of his partners.
"Shall you wish to open the ball with me as planned?"

Charis rose, smiling delightedly, and accepted his hand. Making a lovely curtsy, she walked with him to the center of the room. Marcus gave the signal to the musicians, and the music began. He'd requested a waltz, the intimate dance also one that would help Charis. He could support her in the event her ankle proved weaker than she claimed.

"This is unusual, cousin," she said. "I have never attended a ball that opened with a waltz." Her green eyes gazed up at him full of curiosity and perhaps something else. He wished he knew precisely how she felt.

"I rather like it, and what I say goes . . . here, at least."

"I am amazed, sir. I was under the impression you controlled the world!" Her eyes held a wicked gleam he longed to punish suitably. Her lips curved in an enchanting smile and looked eminently kissable.

"I confess it would be nice at times to have matters go as you desire." He waltzed around in a tighter circle, lifting her from the floor as they went.

"Marcus," she admonished, sounding breathless.

"Yes. I will always be your Marcus," he dared to say, and watched her face with care.

Charis caught her breath at the expression in her second cousin's eyes. What was he trying to convey to her? Or was he merely teasing? She wished she knew.

Once the dance ended, Marcus escorted her to the gilt chair with such care one would think she was fragile glass.

"Thank you, dear cousin," she dared to say, noting that he looked pleased at her words.

"Well, I must say I am surprised you are here this evening. I was certain you would still be abed." Lady Alicia sounded waspish. She glared at Charis as though she wished she might dump a bowl of punch over her head. While it was something Charis could see herself doing, she doubted Lady Alicia would actually commit such a solecism.

Charis barely prevented a grin. "Mama used a special potion for the compress. It was highly effective."

"So it seems." Lady Alicia turned to Marcus, placing

a slim hand on his arm. "I have saved this dance for you." She beamed a fatuous, complacent look at him. She curved her hand around his arm in a possessive grip.

"I wish I had known. I am promised to another." He politely removed her hand from his arm, bowed, then left.

Lady Alicia wore a furious, stunned expression. She glared at Charis. "I suppose you think you are so clever, having that first dance with your cousin."

"Actually, Marcus said he requested the waltz so it would be easier for me. I thought it extremely considerate of him." Charis smiled and fluttered her fan.

Lady Alicia appeared to recover some of her aplomb. "Well, you are his little cousin, after all. I expect he felt it an obligation. He is such a kind man, and I know he's worried about you. Although he did say you have disturbed his peace."

While Charis doubted Marcus had discussed her with Lady Alicia, she didn't doubt she had cut up his calm life. "I believe we all need to be nudged out of our path from time to time. Life can be so tedious otherwise."

Lord Egerton came up at that precise moment to beg a dance with Charis. She accepted his hand, thankful to leave the spiteful Lady Alicia. That lady turned to Lord Portchester, who appeared flattered at her attention.

"You looked as though you'd had enough of our blond, blue-eyed beauty. I don't think she has ever forgiven you for being lovelier, not to mention outranking her."

"I do seem to annoy her," Charis agreed. "Thank you for the flowers. They certainly gladden the heart of one who must remain quiet."

"Whose flowers found your favor, if I may ask? I see they are not mine."

"Since my cousin is giving this ball and we are related, I thought it polite to wear his offering."

Lord Egerton seemed satisfied with her words.

When he returned her to the gilt chair, he stood conversing with her throughout the next dance, allowing her to rest her ankle. Although she had to admit, she felt no pain . . . as yet.

Several dances later Lord Pilkington pushed his way through the throng of gentlemen clustered about Charis, telling jokes and vying for her favor. He bowed over her hand, sending her a meaningful look. "I trust the next dance is mine, dear lady?"

Over the protests of those around, Charis rose to accept his hand. "To be sure, I would be remiss if I failed to dance with you, sir. I have enjoyed your flowers very much."

Although the cotillion was rigorous, Charis felt no ill effects when they concluded. She agreed to walk about with him, thinking the room had become warm.

He echoed her thoughts. "You are warm—why do we not walk in the hall where it must be cooler?"

Her heart gave a little skip as she placed her hand on his proffered arm to walk at his side. She caught her cousin's gaze as they neared the door. He frowned, then pulled out his pocket watch as though to check the time. How odd.

"I was most disappointed that we were interrupted when I was last here," Lord Pilkington said as they strolled along the hall. He tucked her arm close to his side while gazing down at her. She could almost feel the warmth in his look. It made her uncomfortable but she dismissed it, thinking it was because she had never been alone with him before.

Charis paused to sniff the flowers in a vast arrangement on a hall table, thus freeing her hand. "You were? Why was that, sir?" She touched a rose while searching his face. He seemed kindly and gentle.

"You must know that I hold you in high esteem. Dare I speak further?" At her hesitant nod, he continued. "I seek your hand in marriage, fair lady."

This was it, then. He proposed. She did not love him. She freely admitted that to herself, if no one else. Could she consent to what he offered?

"Will you accept my proposal?" He turned to face her, looking tense, nervous.

Taking pity on him, Charis swallowed with care, then nodded. "I do accept you." What had she done? Was it right to marry this kind man she did not love, could likely never love? But then, the one she loved appeared to care for another. He certainly confused her.

Lord Pilkington smiled at her. "I planned everything in the event you said yes. We shall steal away this very night. Come." He grabbed her hand and whisked her along to the stairs.

"What?" Charis gasped, wanting to tell him this was madness. She needed to concentrate, however. They were rushing down the stairs, and she didn't want another accident.

"I know, you think this all very romantic," he said with patent satisfaction.

Charis wondered where on earth he had received that impression of her nature. If she had romance, it was not to be tearing along at breakneck speed.

"The carriage awaits us."

"But my clothes . . ."

"I know. All is set for you. Do not worry your beautiful head about a thing." He tugged her along through the entry.

They flew past Seymour, and Charis gave him a bewildered look.

He was quick to tell his master of the getaway.

Marcus nodded, again checking the time on the longcase clock that stood near the door. He did nothing other than dance with Lady Harriet, then Miss Barbara.

In the traveling coach Charis found pillows and other comforts—like her cloak. "It would seem you thought ahead."

He looked quite pleased with himself.

"If we are to be gone long, I should have liked to take my little dog, sir. Could we not get him?"

His lordship frowned. "I thought you didn't like to travel with the pup."

"Ruff goes everywhere with me. I quite dote on him."

Silence reigned for a time, with Lord Pilkington obviously not thrilled at this state of affairs. After a time he brightened and said, "You will have it later, my dear."

Charis gave him a stubborn look. What a nodcock to deny her Ruff. Surely it would not have been asking much to have a servant fetch the little dog for her.

"We shall not travel far, for I have heard you dislike it above all things. I've made arrangements, you'll see. A quaint little inn was recommended to me."

If this was an elopement, there certainly was little romance to it. Charis bestowed a disgruntled look at her swain. He had that self-satisfied expression again, and she was beginning to wonder if she had made a huge mistake. Actually, she hadn't wanted an elopement. She had hoped for a lovely wedding at St. George's, Hanover Square, possibly an intimate chapel, or at least in the drawing room.

"Perhaps we could wait and have a proper ceremony? It would be lovely to have Harriet as my bridesmaid. Marcus could give me away."

At the mere thought of her cousin, Charis lapsed into a worried silence. What would he say to this harum-scarum elopement? Would he even care? One thing certain, *he* would have let her take Ruff with her. And she also thought he would have agreed to a pleasant wedding at St. George's or the intimate chapel.

It would be lovely to show her cousin that she need not depend on him anymore. True, he had kissed her senseless and seemed to enjoy her company—as much as he enjoyed anyone else as far as Charis could tell. She would wager he'd not kissed Lady Alicia as he had Charis. She didn't know how the Divine Delilah had fared.

"Do you know the Divine Delilah?" Charis inquired before she thought better of it.

Lord Pilkington looked horrified. "That is not a topic fit for discussion with a proper lady."

"I guess I am not as proper as you thought," Charis murmured. "I merely wondered if she had any conversation at all."

Lord Pilkington looked about to expire.

They were saved from total disaster when the coach drew up before a small but neat inn. Lord Pilkington looked vastly relieved and assisted Charis from the coach with a smile. Albeit it was a strained smile, but he looked pleasant nonetheless.

"Is this not rather soon to stop? But then, you have no fear of anyone following us, do you?" Charis said, feeling a trifle put out for some peculiar reason.

The moon had slipped behind clouds, and now a misty rain began to fall. Charis requested her cloak, and his lordship returned to fetch it, getting quite a wetting in the process as the mist turned to heavy rain.

"I'm sorry you got so wet," Charis said, thinking that there must be a fair amount of padding in that coat, the way it hung now. Marcus didn't require any padding at all. She recalled how he had looked that time when she had plunged into his room while chasing Ruff. No, he did not require padding, not with those splendid muscles!

Lord Pilkington demanded the private parlor he had reserved, staring with hauteur down his admittedly long nose at the innkeeper.

A maid was directed to show them to the room, which she did with a cheeky smirk.

"I have ordered your favorite dish. I am sure you will be pleased with it!" his lordship declared once they were established in the private parlor.

Charis looked about the room. There were crisp white curtains at the small window, a goodly fire burning in the fireplace, and a comfortable-seeming settee close to it. She elected to sit close to the fire. Lord Pilkington joined her, sitting a bit too close for her liking.

"Please, sir!" she exclaimed when he slipped his arm about her shoulders.

"Dash it all, we are going to marry! Do you think we shall remain as strangers?" He looked highly affronted.

Charis gave him a dismayed look. She had not considered this aspect. Lord Pilkington was nice enough, but she hadn't thought of the more intimate side of married life with him. Oh, gracious!

They were interrupted by the girl who entered bearing

a tray with a number of dishes on it. A steaming platter held pickled pig's feet and cooked cabbage. The maid set the tray on a small table that she placed before the settee. She dished up an ample portion, then set the plate before Charis along with the proper cutlery.

Charis gave the food a horrified look before assuming a bland countenance. "Is this your notion of an appropriate meal, my lord?" she inquired politely.

"A little bird told me that it is a favorite with you. Mind you, I'd not have thought so. I vow I thought you would want something dainty to suit your fine taste. Shows you that you can never tell." He assumed that pleased expression again.

Charis, who utterly loathed both dishes, didn't know what to say. Should she confess that he had been misinformed? Or ought she be polite and make an effort to swallow a mouthful or two? She opted to taste the cabbage. However, it was impossible to look as though she relished the food when she truly hated it.

"Are they not to your liking? Is the dish prepared wrong? I don't much care for them myself, so I'd not know."

"That is it, sir," Charis replied, thankful to find a way out of the dilemma. "Our cook has a different way of offering these foods. Besides, I truly am not very hungry. Perhaps a bit of bread and jam with a pot of tea?" She nudged the offending food away from her. She even hated the smell! She could not imagine any foods she detested more than these. Marcus had teased her about her aversion.

Lord Pilkington smiled. "That sounds more like my dainty vision of you." He chuckled at his wit, and it grated on her ears.

Charis longed to tell him that she could eat quite well when she wanted. She might be slim, but she could consume anything she pleased and not gain an ounce. What would he offer her if she had admitted she was starving? No, she'd not do that—not if it meant eating pickled pig's feet and cooked cabbage!

"Well, I fancy you will enjoy this," he said as he uncovered a bowl of luscious ripe strawberries with a flourish. They had been brought at some expense from his estate's succession houses.

"They look beautiful," Charis acknowledged with a sinking heart. Could she explain that while she adored the fruit, it caused her to break out in a horrible rash? Should she eat much at all, she would be one large and dreadful red blotch! How *did* one account for such a thing? She'd never met anyone who shared her problem.

Lord Pilkington looked so enormously pleased with himself, she found it exceedingly difficult to tell him that he had yet another disappointment in store for him.

"Thank you so much for the thoughtful gesture."

She opened her mouth to explain her problem, and he popped a huge, juicy berry inside while grinning from ear to ear. Charis was aghast. She could almost feel herself developing the dreaded blotches.

"Please . . ." she began, and he followed the first berry with another even larger. She shook her head, trying to spit out the berry before her blotching became worse. He insisted. "Now, no maidenly timidity. You may enjoy the entire bowl if you like."

She clamped her lips shut, then with her hand before her mouth to prevent another berry from being forced on her, she said in a very firm voice, "I cannot eat those berries."

"What! Egad, I cannot believe you are rejecting the berries. I was told they are a favorite of yours."

"I break out in a rash, a horrible, blotchy rash," she snapped, angry that she had to explain such a matter to him. She unconsciously began to scratch the first of the blotches that crept over her skin.

"I never heard of such a thing!" he shouted at her.

"Well, it is real enough." The itching became worse.

"I can see that," he said, laughing at the splashes of red popping out here and there on the skin that was visible.

"You laugh!" That was the last straw for Charis. Where was the sensitive and considerate man she thought she was to marry? This . . . clod? Never! She jumped up from the settee.

"You want to cart me across the country without any change of clothes instead of a proper wedding at St. George's. You offer me that dreadful food, and then force strawberries on me! I am leaving here at once! You, sir, are not the man I thought you were!"

"Here, now, I thought you had formed a *tendre* for me!" His anger looked to match hers.

Charis wondered how she might extricate herself from this appalling situation. She feared he might retaliate in a frightful manner if she remained. "I shall leave here at once, sirrah. Do not follow me!"

"Ha! If you think I'd bother, think again." He turned his back on her, and Charis slipped from the room, wrapping her cloak closely about her as she went.

When she marched past the curious maid and frankly amused innkeeper, Charis opened the outer door to see it poured rain. It was though some mad fiend dumped buckets of the stuff just to make her life miserable.

"Oh, blast!" she yelled, stamping her good foot in utter frustration.

"Is there a problem, dear cousin mine?" said a soothing and familiar voice that brought her about.

"Marcus!" she whimpered, throwing herself into his open arms with a thankful sigh. She clung to him, relishing the familiar scent, the feel of her dearest relative.

"What happened?"

"That dreadful man, that is what happened. He had the temerity to take me away from your beautiful ball— the finest in the entire Season, I am sure. He brought me to this little inn and tried to feed me pickled pig's feet and cabbage and strawberries!"

"So I see." Marcus traced a red blotch, then kissed one that had erupted on her hand. "You poor darling," he said, holding her tightly in his arms. Then he scooped her into his arms, and after making certain she was well covered, swept her out to his carriage, ignoring the downpour.

"Marcus," she cried when he joined her, "I was never

so glad to see anyone in all my life. You always did rescue me as I recall." She turned her face up to his to plant a thankful kiss on his cheek.

Only it didn't work quite as she had planned. It so happened that he turned his head, and the thankful little kiss became a heated embrace that would have scandalized Lord Pilkington had he observed it. Like many men, he had the notion that a lady did not have such brazen emotions. Marcus knew otherwise.

Charis wasn't aware that the carriage had begun to move. She was totally wrapped up in her precious Marcus, the total sum of her existence at that moment.

"Ruff!" came the little bark her dog gave when he desired to be noticed.

Charis reluctantly pulled away from Marcus. "My dog?"

"Of course. I know full well that you never travel without him. I also have a trunk containing your favorite gowns. I promise you shall never for the rest of your life be offered pickled pig's feet or cooked cabbage, and we won't even grow strawberries. Charis, my love, will you consent to marry me?"

"I will!" she cried joyously. "I have loved you forever. I thought you did not even like me—you scolded me so often. You did not wish to marry that dreadful Lady Alicia?" she asked hesitantly, wanting to make certain her fears were for nothing.

"Never. Lord Portchester was at her side when I left."

"Your ball!" Charis gasped. "You cannot leave your own ball!"

"I can," he calmly asserted. "Of course, should you not desire to dash away with me, we could return to the ball. It so happens that I invited the Archbishop of Canterbury, and if you do not mind missing St. George's, we could be wed tonight."

"Even though I went to the Thatched House Tavern to hear you sing and to see the Divine Delilah? I meant to take care of you, you know," she explained with wary caution.

"Ah, yes. How comforting to know you have cared so

very much for me. I shall make certain it is never necessary again." He clasped her hand in his warm grasp. "So what shall it be, love? Our ballroom tonight before all the cream of Society, or the church when we can arrange it?" He punctuated his question with a heart-stopping kiss, nearly dissolving Charis into a puddle of desire.

"I had no idea you were such a romantic." She entwined her arms about him. "Oh, Marcus, I do love you so. And I do not believe I could wait, not if you promise more of those kisses."

Marcus grinned with the satisfaction of one whose plans have finally materialized into reality. "We shall be there in moments."

"My rash!" she cried as she remembered the awful red blotches. "I cannot have people see me with these spots!"

"Would a pretty white veil be acceptable, my little love?" He touched her chin lightly. "The rash is not objectionable to me, but a veil would hide the rash."

Charis thought a moment, then nodded. "That is a splendid notion. Marcus, you always did have an answer for everything." Again she paused before asking, "How did you know where I was?"

"Pilkington let it slip," he admitted cautiously.

"Oh." Charis thought a few more moments. "You never intended me to marry him, did you. I am beginning to see how your mind works."

"Not if I could help it. You see, my love, I have wanted you forever, but that dratted will complicated everything for me. I did not wish you to marry me because you wanted to retain your home and money. Foolishly, I also wanted your love. I hoped all would go as I planned, and that you would realize you love me. I did not want you to someday wish you had married Perry!"

"How clever of you. Noble, as well as devious. I suppose I ought to be furious, but I cannot. I believe that if you offer me another kiss, I just might forgive you."

Marcus obliged with a fervor that made Charis forget all about any thought of St. George's. Indeed, she could scarce wait to greet the Archbishop of Canterbury and have him marry her to the man she loved with all her heart.

"Ruff." The dog evidently decided he'd best accept being ignored. He settled on the cushioned seat, head on his paws. Who knew how long his mistress would be entangled with his favorite gentleman?

Author's Note

The rules set forth by the lady patronesses of Almack's Assembly rooms were listed in the novel titled ALMACK's, which was published in 1826. It is assumed that they were the accepted rules for that time.

Almack's Rules

No lady Patroness can give a subscription, or a ticket, to a lady she does not visit, or to a gentleman who is not introduced to her by a lady who is on her visiting list.

No more than two ladies of a family are to be upon the ladies' lists.

No lady's or gentleman's name can continue on the list of the same lady patroness for more than two sets of balls; but the ladies are not to consider themselves entitled to the second set of balls, unless it is stipulated on their subscribing to the first, and no lady or gentleman can have more than six tickets from the same lady during the season.

No application from ladies to procure tickets for other ladies, or from Gentlemen, for ladies' or gentlemen's tickets, can be attended to.

No gentleman's tickets can be transferred. Ladies' tickets are only to be transferred from mother to daughter, or between unmarried sisters.

Subscribers who are prevented from coming are requested to give notice to the ladies patronesses, the day of the ball, by two o'clock, directed to Willis' Rooms, that the ladies may fill up the vacancies.

The ladies patronesses request that applications for subscriptions and tickets be sent to Willis' Rooms, and not to their houses, in the consequences of the confusion that arises from notes being lost or mislaid.

In consequence of the numerous applications from families whom the ladies patronesses cannot accommodate with tickets, they are obliged to make a positive rule that not more than three ladies in a family can be admitted to any ball.

The subscribers are most respectfully informed, that the rooms will be lighted up by _____ o'clock, and, by orders from the ladies patronesses, no person can possibly be admitted after half past eleven o'clock; except Members of both Houses of Parliament, who may be detained AT THE HOUSE on business.

Applications for new subscribers must be submitted for the concurrence of all the lady patronesses.

King Street, April 6, 182 . . .